To Wed an Heiress

A Pevensey Mystery

Rosanne E. Lortz

MADISON STREET PUBLISHING

Madison Street Publishing

Prologue

Mr. Godwin peered out the window, anxiously anticipating the arrival of his next appointment. As senior solicitor at the firm Witansby and Sons, he had a difficult task before him this morning. Just last month, Dr. Stigand had performed the unpleasant duty of informing the Countess of Anglesford that the only thing likely to wake her husband again was the sounding of the last trumpet. Mr. Godwin must now inform her that the late earl's finances were in as nearly lifeless a condition as the earl himself.

For the sake of domestic harmony, most women turn a blind eye to their husband's foibles. Edith Emison was no exception. For thirty years and more, she had not only closed her eyes to her husband's financial imprudence but had genuinely considered him to be a model of fiscal propriety. Unbeknownst to Lady Anglesford, the old man had amassed tens of thousands of pounds in gambling debts and—had the Almighty not mercifully cut short his days—was well on the way to beggaring his wife and children.

The coach bedecked in black crepe arrived, and Mr. Godwin, who considered himself a friend as well as the family solicitor, came to the door to meet its occupant. Lady Anglesford was a petite, fine-featured woman, whose bright blond hair had only just begun to lose its luster. She gave Mr. Godwin her hand, covered with a dark mourning glove, and accepted his offer of tea before she sat down.

"I received your message and came as soon as I could." Her hands clasped and unclasped themselves repeatedly in her lap. "What is this news that could not wait?"

The solicitor cleared his throat. He had rehearsed many euphemisms to describe the egregious state of the late Edward Emison's affairs, but in the end, it seemed best just to state the simple truth and let tears fall where they must.

Mr. Godwin began a story nearly twenty years in the making of visits to gambling hells, of higher and higher wagers, of handing out vowels indiscriminately. "I am truly sorry, Lady Anglesford, but even your dower portion has been squandered. There is more than one moneylender clamoring to be paid, and I fear once you settle with all of them, there will be little left."

Lady Anglesford, who had listened to Mr. Godwin's news with growing horror, proved that she had not been a countess for thirty years without acquiring some degree of social aplomb. "I am sorry too, Mr. Godwin. And I daresay Edward was sorrier than either of us, and sadder too since he spent so many years keeping all this secret from me."

She swallowed bravely. "It is a blow; I do not deny it. But we must make the best of things, mustn't we? We shall give up the stables and the house in town and retire to the country." A wan smile played over her lips. "A little country air does wonders for the health, so I hear, and as long as my sons are with me, I will not mind rusticating a while out at Woldwick. Edward was the one who spent his childhood there, but I have always felt a special kinship with the place. I am never more at peace than when I'm walking in the gardens there."

Mr. Godwin clucked sympathetically and laid a fatherly hand on the widow's shoulder. "If only it were possible for you to remain there, but I fear that Woldwick is in just as much peril as your house in Mayfair. To repay the amount these moneylenders are dunning you for, both the country manor and all your lands must be changed into silver. Whatever is left—and it will be a modest sum—could be used to rent a small residence in Russell Square...."

Lady Anglesford gripped the handles of her chair. A residence in Russell Square! The situation was becoming positively nightmarish. Her fortitude and her forced smile were both beginning to desert her. Her mind flitted frantically to her eldest son. "And what about Haro? Is there any inheritance left for him?"

The solicitor sighed. "There is the title, of course. But any financial legacy is likely to disappear with the settling of debts and the disposal of the estate."

Lady Anglesford's face paled. Mr. Godwin asked if she would like something stronger to drink than tea. "No, thank you." Stumbling to her feet, she gave him her hand and looked up into his eyes through a faint mist of tears. The solicitor was not a tall man, but the top of her head barely came to his shoulder. "I think I had better return home while I am still able. There are others, besides me, who should hear this news as soon as possible."

Part I

1

Lord Harold Emison, or Haro as he was known by his family, had never expected his father's mantle to fall upon him so suddenly. At his death, the Earl of Anglesford had not yet attained sixty years of age. His health had been as good as that of most men. He could still jump a horse over a tollgate fence, still argue his way out of a visit to Almack's, and still drink lesser men under the table with a bottle of Madeira—up until the stroke that incapacitated him in early January and proved fatal a few days later.

Of his father's gambling, Haro had slightly more cognizance than his mother. After all, one could not reach the ripe old age of three and twenty without knowing that one's father was a devil's hand with the cards. But the staggering amount of his father's gambling debts still came as a shock to the young man.

"By Jove!" Haro whistled loudly and thrust his thumbs into the pockets of his waistcoat. "Are you certain that Godwin has a good grasp of the situation?"

Lady Anglesford assured him that she had never found their solicitor to be mistaken in matters of financial advice. If anything, the picture was probably far bleaker than he had painted it. She buried her face in her hands.

"By Jove!" Haro repeated, evidently too overcome by the moment to think of a more original exclamation. When his mother took the opportunity to retire to her boudoir, however, he took the opportunity to pour himself some brandy, and the exclamations came thick and fast.

"What are you damning so vigorously in here?" demanded Torin, entering the drawing room. The second son in the Emison family, Torin was seven years Haro's junior. Haro was blond like their mother and tall like their father, but

Torin's features had a darker, more diminutive cast to them. While Haro was enjoying his life as a young buck about town, Torin was still finishing his studies at home.

Briefly, Haro relayed the news of their imminent impoverishment, and despite Torin's younger years, the gravity of the situation was not lost upon him. "By Jove!" he echoed, pouring himself his own glass of stimulants. "And Woldwick must be sold too?" He tried to keep the tremble out of his voice, but the sloshing of the liquid in his glass betrayed him. Lady Anglesford was not the only person who felt a kinship with the hallowed hearth of the Emison home.

"That's what mother says Godwin says." Haro sprawled dismally on the sofa with the loose limbs of a large feline. His hand clawed at his exquisitely arranged cravat until the folds were mussed beyond recovery. He had entirely forgotten about his plans to take his pair of blacks out for an afternoon drive in Hyde Park. He had entirely forgotten that a certain young lady was expecting to ride with him in his phaeton.

"What are you going to do?" asked his brother's voice, breaking in on his reverie of self-pity.

"Do?"

Torin stamped his foot defiantly. "Well, for heaven's sake, Haro! You are the new Earl of Anglesford! You must do something to salvage the family fortune."

"How the deuce am I supposed to scratch up a load of blunt that Papa spent twenty years throwing away?"

Torin paced the room, throwing out suggestions. "Borrow."

"I daresay our family credit is rather low with London's moneylenders right now."

"Sell the family jewels."

"Godwin says they're already pledged as surety for some of Papa's debts."

Torin hesitated then forged ahead. "Well, then, there's no help for it—you'll have to marry an heiress, and a wealthy one at that."

Haro frowned and sat up straight on the sofa. "Impossible! And you know it!"

"Is it? And do I?" questioned Torin. "You're not currently betrothed."

"No," blustered Haro, "but—"

"And—much as I hate to admit it—you've got the looks, and the title, and the ton to attract some Croesus for a father-in-law."

"Yes, but—"

"So really," said Torin slowly, "there's nothing standing in the way of this plan except—"

"Except for the fact that Eda and I have an understanding!" Haro raked a large hand through his blond hair. "I don't consider that nothing."

Torin smiled wryly. "Eda's a sensible girl, Haro. However serious your understanding, I'm sure she would quite readily understand that a blow of this magnitude must set everything on its head." He ignored his older brother's glare. "And perhaps she won't care twopence for you any longer once she hears what a poor devil you've become."

He took half a dozen quick steps to the door of the drawing room. "In fact, I've half a mind to break the news to her myself. Eda! Eda!" He darted out into the hallway where a young lady in a black walking dress was impatiently awaiting her escort for a promised drive in Hyde Park.

"How much longer does your brother mean to keep me waiting?" asked Eda with good-natured rebuke as Torin came darting into the hallway. Her dark pelisse was trimmed with sable, instead of its usual ermine, a reminder that although the Emisons might drive out to take the air, the house was still in mourning for the late earl. Putting up a white hand, she touched her freshly-coifed black curls to ensure that they were all pinned securely beneath her hat. "Does he mean to beg off?" she demanded.

"Why, yes," said Torin pertly, "I think he may very well wish to beg off." He cast a glance over his shoulder to where his brother Haro was emerging from the drawing room with a thunderous look in his eye. "But I daresay he will want to tell you the news himself. I'll away to the butler's closet and see how much silver we have to sell. Might as well make myself useful before the auctioneers arrive."

As the sarcastic schoolboy made his exit, Eda's dark blue eyes flitted over Haro's face. His cheeks had lines of worry that she had never seen before, and it was obvious that some great blow had fallen upon him.

She knew that his father's death last month had shaken him, altering his existence as a young buck about town to that of a titled landowner. Where before he had social engagements and amusements to contend with, now he had duties to his family, his tenants, and the realm.

And though she had only just launched into society, Eda still knew enough about death to commiserate. She could remember when her own father had expired from a French musket ball and her mother from a malarial fever just a few months later.

But those memories were distant, a misty vapor from her early youth. There had been tears, yes, but there had also been consolation close on the heels of that disaster, when her mother's cousin, Edith Emison, had taken her into their family. No longer the penniless daughter of an Irish army captain, she had become the ward of one of the highest-ranking men in England, and Lady Anglesford had treated her in all things like the daughter she had never had. She had shared the same nursery with Haro and Torin, tortured the same governess, and tiptoed up to the same attic to hear crazy old Uncle Harold's stories of adventures in days gone by.

She looked at Haro now with sisterly concern, striving to keep the apprehension out of her voice. "What on earth is Torin babbling on about?"

Haro gestured to a cushioned bench, and they sat down together. "We've had some shocking news from Mr. Godwin today about Papa's financial affairs."

"Yes?"

"He's been dreadfully imprudent with his gambling stakes, making higher and higher wagers, especially in the last few years. The moneylenders are gathering like vultures, the estate is totally bankrupt, and, in short, everything must be sold to pay his debts."

"I see." Eda felt her stomach constrict with concern. It was even worse than his worried face had intimated. She had already relegated herself to the fact that, with her uncle's death, her first experience of the London season must be cut woefully short. But now it sounded like its discontinuance was permanent. She felt guilty even thinking about her lost season when she recollected about how much Lady Anglesford and her sons stood to lose.

She put her white hand on top of Haro's and squeezed it with sympathetic pressure. "How is your mother handling the news?"

"As well as can be expected. But the greatest blow of all is Woldwick—it breaks her heart to think of selling it, and yet there is no other honorable option to raise the sum we need."

"And are there dishonorable ones?"

He cast a sideways glance at her. "Yes, I suppose there are. But Eda...." He looked away from her, and she noticed that his foot had begun to tap on the floor.

She pulled her hand away from his, noticing that he had made no movement to reach for her in return. Then, rising to her feet, she walked over to the leaded glass window next to the front door.

Haro had never made a formal declaration to her—only oblique references to how much he admired her and enjoyed her company. The whole family, however, had accepted their eventual nuptials as a matter of course. Lady Anglesford had declared that their betrothal must not be solemnized until Eda had the chance to finish her first season. But it was Haro who had led Eda out for the first dance at her coming-out ball, and Haro who had escorted her to her first card party, and Haro who had kept her from yawning at her first assembly at Almack's. Though he had never said it aloud, there had always been the security of knowing that she would one day assume the title of Lady Anglesford.

And now? What had he meant when he said that there were dishonorable options?

Outside, it had begun to rain a little, and the clouds hinted ominously that the rain might soon change into sleet. "I suppose that's what Torin meant—that you might wish to beg off?"

Rising to his feet, Haro opened his mouth in protest, but she cut in before he could speak. "And I don't blame you in the least. It's stormy outside, and likely to grow worse." They were familiar enough with each other to understand that she was not speaking about the weather anymore.

Eda picked up the sable muff that would have kept away the chill on the drive through Hyde Park. "I daresay, that even together, we would neither of us be warm enough in the phaeton."

Her voice was firm but inside her bosom the tremors were strong enough to shake a building. She owed this to him, the opportunity to *choose* in this desperate circumstance where his father's behavior had taken almost all the choices off the table. And to be honest, she owed it to herself—the opportunity to know that she had been *chosen*. To know that Haro had weighed the options and committed to her despite the circumstances. To know that, come what may, she was first in his heart.

She waited.

He stared.

Silence lay like a pall on the cold marble of the entry hall.

It was only a moment, but it was as fateful and final as the last knell of midnight before the new year. If he would not speak, then she knew his answer.

She walked over to the stairs then looked back over her shoulder. "Good day, Lord Anglesford." The title rang coldly between them like a coin dropped on the marble floor.

"Good day, Miss Swanycke," he returned in a stiff voice, and she could not tell from her vantage point on the stairs whether the expression on his face was angry or pained.

2

When Haro stepped out to his club that afternoon, he discovered that rumors had already flown abroad about his father's imprudence and his family's misfortunes. Adopting a stern expression to deflect all questions, he retreated rapidly to the library, a room not much frequented by White's members.

But even this sanctuary was bound to be violated by some well-meaning associates. Guy Pontipale, a foppish young man who had known Haro since Eton, spotted his friend through the open door and popped inside to give his condolences. "I say!" said Guy, his Adam's apple bobbing up and down vigorously. "Wretched luck, that!" He settled himself delicately into a chair, careful not to crumple the tails of his exquisitely tailored coat.

Haro, who had been staring morosely into the fireplace, looked up briefly to grunt his thanks.

"If there's anything I can do, don't hesitate to ask." Guy paused and glanced around furtively. "Although, I'm awfully short of money myself right now, so I don't think I can forward you any blunt."

Haro smiled wryly. "I hardly think your quarterly allowance would do me any good at this point. What I need now is a miracle or a wealthy heiress, whichever is easier to obtain."

"Should think it would be the heiress," replied Guy, never one to put his trust in the supernatural. "I know several, and the ones whose fathers are in trade are angling like fishermen on the Thames to get a peer for a son-in-law."

"Oh, really?" said Haro slowly, Torin's mercenary advice beating a drum in the back of his mind. He was still furious with Eda for forcing him into a confrontation this morning. If she had only reminded him of their understanding, he would not have been able to even consider the option of playing her false. But she had pulled back from him at the critical moment, driven a wedge into the fissure and waited to see how he would react. He could not help but wonder whether Torin's comment about her own regard for him was true—did she *want* him to beg off now that he was no more than a penniless pedigree? Had he meant no more to her than a means of financial security?

Swallowing down the hurt, he focused his attention on Guy. "Do you think you could provide me with introductions to some of the more desperate candidates?"

"Don't see why not. But say! Ain't you already...?" Guy gurgled to a stop. It was common knowledge that the end of this season would see young Harold Emison leg-shackled to his distant cousin, La Swanycke. Guy had just remembered that fact, and suddenly, the situation had become as awkward as meeting a vicar in Covent Garden.

"Engaged?" asked Haro with a raised eyebrow. If he had been asked that question yesterday, he would have answered, "Any day now!" But after Eda's strange eagerness to allow him to beg off, his wounded pride wanted to minimize whatever understanding there had once been between them. "No, no, that's all finished," he replied breezily. "A season's flirtation that ended of its own accord, and no harm done to either party. I'm free as a swallow in flight, and I'd happily land my feet on some rich tradesman's doorstep, if you can point out one who has a pretty daughter on parade."

Guy scratched his head, trying to come up with the list of wealthy husband-and-title-seekers he had promised. But in the end, he could only think of one family that fit the description. "Have you met Miss Arabella Hastings?" he asked. "Brunette, tallish, just out this season."

Haro racked his brain for any remembrance of the young lady in question. There was a time when he could recognize the name and face of every eligible young lady out in society, but ever since Eda's debut this season, he had paid scant attention to the new arrivals in the marriage mart. "I don't think I've met her—should I?"

"Certainly suggest so if you're meaning to wed an heiress. Her father, William Hastings, made a fortune in the cotton industry. Has mills all over the country.

"And now he wants to spin himself a spot in good society?" asked Haro, smiling at his own pun.

"Imagine so," said Guy, who had no aptitude for or interest in wordplay. "He's paid a pretty sum to launch his daughter into the ton this season, and even the grumpiest dowagers have been won over by his liberality. She's enjoying a fair bit of popularity. Leading several suitors around by the nose already."

"Is she up to snuff?" asked Haro with a tinge of concern. One could trust that a lady born to privilege would act the lady, but who knew what reprehensible manners might lurk in a family tainted by trade.

"Seems to be. Mother met her. Said she was unexceptionable and possessed pleasant conversation."

"And why not," said Haro, speaking almost more to reassure himself than to respond to Guy, "when she's doubtless had the best governesses, and tutors, and drawing teachers, and dancing instructors that her father's money can buy? When can you introduce me?"

Guy cocked his head. "Ball at the Duke of Doyle's tonight. Girl's bound to be there. If you're coming, I could present you properly."

Haro shuddered inwardly. Upon receiving the invitation to the Duke's ball, Lady Anglesford had, of course, declined it since the Emison household was but newly in mourning. And now, with the news of their latest tragedy seeping through the streets like sewer water, Haro hardly wanted to show his face at such a large assembly.

But, on the other hand, if he wished to pursue this harebrained scheme of Torin's, time was of the essence. If he wished to keep Woldwick off the auction block, it was imperative that he meet a rich tradesman's daughter right away. His innate breeding hoped that the Duchess of Doyle would overlook the solecism of attending her gathering after the invitation had already been refused.

"I'll be there with my heart—and my title—in hand." Haro stood up to leave, then remembered one thing Guy had mentioned that could turn out to be a fly in the ointment. "You said Miss Hastings already had a line of suitors on a string?"

"Yes," replied Guy, crossing his legs with care. "But ain't none of them above the rank of baronet."

The new Earl of Anglesford smiled grimly. His father may have run through the betting money, but the high card was still his to play.

Back at the Emison townhouse, Lady Anglesford expressed some surprise when her oldest son told her that he meant to pull the black crepe out of his hat and spend the evening at the Duke's festive assembly. "I should have thought the appalling news we received today—if not the recentness of your father's departure—would give you a distaste for dancing and such conviviality." She had wrapped herself in a warm shawl and, despite the bright blaze of the parlor fire, declared herself unable to shake off the frigid chill penetrating to her very bones.

Haro shrugged with unusual reticence. He knew his actions appeared crass and uncaring, but he did not want to explain himself. Indeed, if his mother knew the whole of his plan, she would think it reprehensible in the utmost. He swallowed. The plan was reprehensible. But...what else was he to do? It was *his* responsibility to provide for her, for Torin, and for Eda.

"I suppose Eda means to go as well?" Lady Anglesford cast a glance over to the other side of the room where her cousin's daughter sat sketching in the window seat. A few tresses of her dark black hair hung down over her paper, and the flickering firelight did not allow anyone to see the object of her portrait.

"Oh no," said Eda, setting down her pencil to reply. Her dark blue eyes flashed with intensity beneath her fringe of dark eyelashes. "I have no wish to be merry tonight, and I am sure that I should only get in Lord Anglesford's way." She spoke that last remark sweetly enough to avoid a rebuke from Lady Anglesford, but the words were still pointed enough to rub salt in an open wound. Haro winced at the implications, and Eda smiled as if she enjoyed inflicting that pain. Then, dropping her eyes to her paper, she continued to sketch in a detached manner as if what Haro proposed to do with his evening was of no interest to her.

Haro's teeth clenched. It was unfair of her to treat him thus. His father's imprudence had brought him to *point non plus.* The only path forward was a dismal one, but if he was to do his duty as head of the family, he could not refuse to take it. He tried to catch her eye, but she did not—would not—return his gaze.

Lady Anglesford's small face grew worried, and she shivered uncontrollably. She sensed that her son and her ward had had a falling out. And this, on top of everything else she had to bear, was enough to overset her nerves.

The double doors opened. The absent member of the family circle entered the room rife with tension. "Ah, there you are, Torin." Lady Anglesford beckoned to her second son. "Your brother means to desert us all tonight and go to the Duke of Doyle's, but at least I have you to depend on to keep me company in this vale of tears."

Torin walked forward like a good son and hugged his mother perfunctorily, but all his attention was taken up by what Haro planned to do. "So, you're off to the ball after all?" His thin black eyebrows arched with interest.

"Yes, in accordance with your suggestion," said Haro, and the two brothers exchanged a cryptic look. He glanced over to the window seat and raised his voice to make sure he would be heard. "Although I'm beginning to think that it will be as much pleasure as duty."

The only response that came was a ripping sound. Whatever—or whomever—Miss Swanycke had been sketching was now being torn in two. Haro left the room abruptly and went to his room to dress for the evening's entertainment.

The new Earl of Anglesford arrived at the ball at a late hour, hoping to avoid too many questions from inquisitive acquaintances. A servant took his coat, and he stepped inside the room, feeling for one of the first times in his life a little lost amidst the swirling world of the ton.

But though his insides were shrinking with dismay, none of that showed to the rest of the guests. His flawless evening dress marked him as one of the most smartly dressed men in the room. His cuffs fell perfectly over his capable hands, and his cravat—the careful product of his valet Garth—cascaded over his shirt in crisp, clean folds.

If he had not been the eldest son of a titled family, he would have made an admirable officer. He was an excellent horseman, a commendable shot, and had shoulders broad enough to fill out a red coat. Perhaps he would have been too easygoing to command the instant obedience of the men, but he had a pleasant manner that made people like him wherever he went. With the family fortunes in tatters, perhaps he ought to consider the military in earnest—although if Godwin's gloomy predictions proved correct, there would not even be enough money to purchase himself a commission.

The whispers that followed Haro around the room were politely fenced in by the fans of the lace-capped matriarchs, and Haro was able to navigate the assembly without too much embarrassment. He discovered that Guy Pontipale had already cornered the damsel in question and was leading her out for a quadrille. Ignoring all the sympathetic glances, Haro settled himself against a pillar and began to observe Miss Hastings.

Guy had done her no injustice when he described her as brunette and tallish, but he had left out the finer details that would recommend the lady to a more discerning eye. She had regular features, a slim but attractive figure, glossy curls, and an air of elegance that can only be hereditary or purchased at a very high price.

Haro noted that she kept time in the dance very well and conversed with her neighbors effortlessly. He watched Guy lean in on one of the turns to utter some trite compliment. Miss Hastings responded very aptly with a smile and nod of acknowledgement. All in all, she was prettily adorned and perfectly mannered.

Haro felt a twinge of anxiety as the string players brought the dance to its final cadence. Soon, very soon, Guy would lead her to the side of the room and perform the necessary introductions. And while he was examining Guy's partner, Haro had not failed to notice another man also keeping a close eye on Miss Hastings from across the room. He had gray hair, a portly figure, expensive but gaudy clothing—and the way that he was sizing up Guy Pontipale, like a butcher weighing out meat, convinced Haro that he had sighted none other than William Hastings, the tradesman on the hunt for a title.

Catching Haro's eye as the dance finished, Guy Pontipale led his fair partner off the ballroom floor and in the earl's direction. When they were nearly close enough to shake hands, Guy uttered a wooden exclamation of surprise. "Egads! It's my old friend Haro. Haven't seen you in ages!" His left eyelid dropped slyly in a far too obvious wink. "Have you met Miss Hastings?"

"I have not had that pleasure." Haro did his best to exude charm. He was a little out of practice in that regard, he reflected ruefully, especially since his comfortable and familial relationship with Eda had required little effort to maintain. Eda did not expect gallantry, but an heiress certainly would.

"This is Harold Emison, the Earl of Anglesford," said Guy, laying particular emphasis on the exalted title. "We were at Eton together. A fine chap, a real Trojan." Guy's dogged determination to do his duty by his friend was a little too conspicuous for Haro's comfort.

"Enchanted to make your acquaintance," said Haro, and when Arabella offered him her hand, he pressed it gently to his lips and held onto it for half a second longer than necessary. "You must be thirsty after all those turns around the floor. May I procure you some punch?"

"Oh, allow me!" interrupted Guy, eager to disembarrass them of his company. He left his erstwhile partner at the side of the young earl and took himself off to the punch table where a long line had already formed.

"Are you well acquainted with Mr. Pontipale?" asked Haro politely.

"I've met him in company two or three times," replied Arabella. She met his eyes frankly. "He's a bit of a rattle, I fear."

"More than a bit!" rejoined Haro with a laugh that was not entirely natural. He steeled himself inwardly to continue this bout of repartee. "How is it that I have not had the privilege of meeting you in company this season?"

"I cannot say, my lord, although I'm sure the fault is none of my making. I've been everywhere anyone fashionable goes. We've taken a box at the opera and made calls all over Grosvenor Square." She pressed her painted fan to the lower half of her face. Haro suspected that it was a calculated move to make her eyes stand out to greater effect. "I'm afraid that you must have been playing the hermit this season, my lord, or else avoiding me on purpose."

"Avoiding you? How foolish of me!" exclaimed Haro, leaning in a little closer to the lady's fine eyes. He suspected that Miss Hastings had taken lessons on how to flirt, but even with that suspicion in the back of his mind, it was in his best interest to be susceptible to her lures.

"And if I wished to continue avoiding you tomorrow, what part of town should I keep clear of?"

"I should most definitely stay away from the Vauxhall Gardens," replied the girl without even a trace of a blush, "for I mean to be there all afternoon."

"Ah!" said Haro, attempting to inflect his voice with an air of mystery. Before he had exhausted his own stock of flirtation, a few bars of music wafted their way, the orchestra's signal that the dancing was about to resume. Guy had still failed to return with the promised cup of punch, and Haro assumed that his friend had slipped away to leave him to his own devices.

"Are you engaged for the next dance?"

"Only if you ask me to dance it."

Haro extended his arm with a courtly gesture. "It would be my delight, Miss Hastings." They stepped out onto the floor to perform the quick steps and the lively turns of a pair of country dances. The figures of the dance gave them little opportunity to talk, but as Haro had already observed, Miss Hastings was quite eloquent with both her smile and her eyes, and his injured *amour propre* could not help noticing how much sweeter Miss Hastings' blandishments were than Miss Swanycke's brusqueness.

By the end of the first dance, he began to feel as if he had drunk several tumblers of punch and not the sweet lemonade reserved for women and children. He was not so intoxicated, however, that he failed to feel the shrewd eyes observing him from the pillar across the room where William Hastings smirked visibly at the sight of his daughter's latest conquest.

3

THE WEATHER WAS UNUSUALLY fine the following afternoon, and Haro made a point of appearing at the Vauxhall Gardens shortly after the noon hour, wearing a modish pair of pantaloons with top boots. He walked from one end of the Gardens to the other, but Miss Hastings was nowhere to be found. The afternoon passed wearily. Haro had been to Vauxhall dozens of times, and neither the tightrope walkers nor the balloon ascension impressed him as they would a newcomer.

Eventually, when he had almost given up on the project—and was cursing himself for a fool—he caught sight of a familiar gray-haired, portly gentleman with a slender brunette in tow. The mill owner was clad in a overly tight suit of blue with puce colored lace, a garment made even more garish by the contrast with his daughter's elegant muslin gown.

"At least one member of this family has a modicum of taste," muttered Haro to himself. He tossed aside the meat pastie that he was munching to while away the time and began to meander toward the mismatched pair. "Why, Miss Hastings!" he called out in feigned surprise. "How fortuitous to run into you here! And this gentleman"—the word grated as it slid over his tongue—"must be your father?"

Arabella's brown eyes batted attractively. "Fortuitous indeed, my lord! Father, allow me to present the Earl of Anglesford. I made his acquaintance last night at the Duke of Doyle's."

"Yes, your daughter was kind enough to honor me with two dances," said Haro, swallowing back his growing distaste as William Hastings' thick fingers eagerly pumped his hand in greeting.

"And a very kind-hearted lass she is!" replied Hastings proudly. "The jewel of my life. Shall we walk?" He seemed to take it as a matter of course that the earl would be joining their party. Haro fell in step with the mill owner and his daughter, groaning inwardly at the thought of traipsing around the whole circuit of Vauxhall once again.

"Have we missed the balloon ascension?" asked Arabella, striding comfortably between the tall earl and her short-legged father.

"I'm afraid that you have," said Haro. "The balloon went up and the balloon came down, two hours ago and more."

"What a pity!" said Arabella, casting him a sideways glance from behind her eyelashes. "But at least you were here to enjoy it!"

Haro fumed inwardly, realizing that he had revealed just how long he had been waiting for the Hastings to appear. But on further reflection, he relaxed his annoyance. It did no harm to let the girl think he was besotted with her. After all, if he was to get a hold of her fortune, her goodwill was paramount.

"I would have enjoyed it far more had I experienced it in better company."

They paused to watch a troop of fire-eaters exhibit their skills, and Mr. Hastings—as if by prior arrangement—switched places with Arabella to become the center of the trio. "My condolences on your late father," he said insinuatingly. "I did not know him personally, but I understand that he was a fine man."

Of course you did not know him! raged Haro inwardly. It upset him to think that, except for his father's financial imprudence, none of the Emisons would ever have been required to know a man that smelt so strongly of trade and pretension.

"A father's death works great changes in a young man's life," pontificated Hastings. "Now that you've come into the title, you must be thinking about settling down, and setting up a household of your own."

"Quite so," said Haro, in as polite a tone as he could manage. His natural instinct was to swim away from the fisherman's hook, and he had to remind himself that this time it was in his best interest to be caught. "My mother has been urging such a step for some time."

"Trust a mother to know what's best for her son—and a father for his daughter." Hastings threw a thick arm around Arabella's slim shoulders. They moved on to view some of the other sights that Vauxhall had to offer. And somewhere in between seeing the dog that could walk on its hind legs and getting their fortunes told by an old Gypsy woman, William Hastings found time to drop another hook. "I've taken a liking to you, Lord Anglesford. Perhaps you'll join us for dinner tomorrow." He gave Haro the address, a rented house in Russell Square, the very place where his father's imprudence might soon condemn the Emisons to dwell.

"Most readily," replied Haro. His friend Guy had been right—these tradesmen were as desperate as a poor fellow in dun territory to throw their daughters into the arms of an earl. But since he *was* the poor fellow in dun territory, such desperation was all to his benefit.

Mr. Godwin paid a visit to the house on the following day to discuss with Lady Anglesford and the new earl what steps should be taken to pay the creditors. They retreated to the library, the dark wood of the bookshelves towering all around them like the walls of a fortress.

"Please be seated, Mr. Godwin," said Lady Anglesford, determined to endure the ensuing conversation bravely.

"Thank you," said the solicitor, settling down into an overstuffed armchair. His light gray morning suit stood out sharply against the purple and green stripes of the upholstery. "It is good to see you again, Haro." He smiled cordially at the younger man. "And may I say that your new title becomes you well. Let me express how pleased Witansby and Sons has been to hold the privileged position of solicitors for the Emison family. We hope to continue serving the new Earl of Anglesford as we did the old, if it is agreeable to you, my lord."

"Most agreeable. And from the sound of things, we have a great deal of business to be transacted. My mother tells me you are here today to discuss how we must retrench in order to settle my father's debts."

Mr. Godwin clucked sympathetically. "*Retrench* is perhaps too mild of a word, my lord. I have taken the liberty of drawing up some figures." He handed a ledger sheet to Haro, complete with columns of numbers and annotations on the side.

Peering over her son's shoulder, Lady Anglesford attempted to make out the meaning of the numbers. But a headache soon overpowered her, and she sank back into the cushions of the sofa.

After a moment's perusal, Haro looked up to meet Mr. Godwin's eye. "This is very grim."

"Yes, my lord. Even with the liquidation of all the Emison assets, only the most modest of sums will remain once the debts have been fulfilled. If we can find you a reasonably-priced residence in Russell Square, the remainder can be used to support Lady Anglesford with an annuity comparable to the income of a country parson."

The widow blanched visibly. Her own father had been a country parson, and she was aware of the thrift and deprivation that would be occasioned by such straitened circumstances. When one was used to the spacious halls of Woldwick with its silver chandeliers, velvet curtains, and large staff of servants, the idea of a cramped cottage or a townhouse with hardly enough bedrooms to house them all was grim indeed.

Haro continued to dissect the grisly anatomy of the Emison bankruptcy. "When do you anticipate beginning to 'liquidate assets,' as you call it?"

"Your house in London can be sold immediately, along with the horses and carriages. In the interim, the family can retire to Woldwick and pack your personal possessions. For an estate of that magnitude, it will take more time to find a buyer, and it may be several weeks into the summer before you must vacate it."

Lady Anglesford, who had hoped against all reason that Mr. Godwin's assessment of affairs would have altered in the interim since she had visited his office, crumpled wearily in her seat. "The townhouse and the stables I understand. I will not weep to part with them. But Woldwick? It is too great a blow to bear!"

"But Lady Anglesford, I'm afraid there is no alternative—"

"How if some of the money could be raised?" interrupted Haro. He looked at his mother with concern. To lose everything she was accustomed to, and so soon after the death of her husband—it was a blow from which he would spare her if he could.

"Well, yes, if the debts could be defrayed in some other way, then perhaps the estate could be kept." Mr. Godwin looked at the young earl with raised eyebrows, waiting for him to elaborate.

"I have a dinner engagement tonight," said Haro, with a little bit of embarrassment, "with a tradesman—a cotton mill owner—who might be willing to make up some of these deficits."

"A tradesman?" repeated his mother incredulously. She was not aware that her son fraternized with men of business in the middle class.

Mr. Godwin leaned forward in his armchair with interest. "And what reason would this fellow have for coming to the aid of the Emison estate?" The solicitor was not immune to the feeling of skepticism. What could the young Earl of Anglesford possibly offer to the mill owner for collateral?

Haro took a long breath and then came out with the dreadful admission. "He has a daughter just out in society." They stared at him in confusion, and Haro realized that he would be forced to spell out his plan with humiliating clarity. "An alliance with an earl is no mean thing."

Lady Anglesford gasped audibly. "A mill owner's daughter?"

"An heiress, Mama."

"But, but what about Eda!" she gasped. Then, remembering that they were not alone, she glanced anxiously at the solicitor. Mr. Godwin registered no surprise. He was deep enough in the family secrets to know that there had been an understanding between the earl and Miss Swanycke. But he was also pragmatic enough to realize that a connection with the impoverished Miss Swanycke could in no way aid his client amid these difficult circumstances.

"So," said the solicitor slowly, "you are proposing to salvage the family finances through a matrimonial alliance. That is very farsighted of you, Lord Anglesford—a selfless act, if I've ever seen one. Tell me, who is the tradesman, and what is his daughter's name?"

And while his mother stared and Mr. Godwin nodded encouragingly, Haro gave a thorough description of his advantageously affluent new acquaintances.

4

IF HARO HAD BEEN expecting a large dinner party at the Hastings' home that evening, he was sorely mistaken. When he arrived, he found that he made up the fourth in an intimate gathering. Mr. Hastings and his daughter glittered in fancy evening attire while a large and darkly clad duenna—introduced as Mrs. Rollo—lurked demurely in the background. It seemed that Mr. Hastings, despite all his desire for ostentation, recognized the necessity of small numbers when there was something important to discuss.

"You haven't told us anything about your family," said Arabella archly as the first course was laid on the table.

Haro blinked at the number of dishes laid out for such a small party—roast beef, roast fowl, fish with oyster sauce, game, macaroni, soup, cauliflower, and a plethora of creams and sauces that he could not even identify.

"There's not much to tell," said Haro, trying not to appear to be concealing some dreadful secret. "My father passed away just recently leaving my mother in poor spirits. I've one brother, Torin, seven years younger than me."

"No sisters?"

"No sisters by birth, although we've a distant relation named Edith Swanycke who has lived with the family for years and is as close to a sister as anyone can be. And then there's my mother's uncle, Harold, a kind old fellow, but a bit of an eccentric. He lives out at Woldwick, our country estate—positively refuses to come to town even when the rest of the family does."

"They sound perfectly delightful," said Arabella, tilting her chin to show off her pretty face to its best advantage. "I always wanted a brother or a sister as a companion, but Father never managed to provide one."

"I provided you with Mrs. Rollo, didn't I?" said Hastings with a guffaw. "The most accomplished companion money could buy!"

Haro gnawed his lip uncomfortably while the gray-haired woman stared self-deprecatingly down at her plate.

The cotton magnate turned to his dinner guest. "But it's true what my daughter says, my lord. She's my only child, my only heir." He took a liberal swallow of the red wine in his glass. "When I die, everything comes to her, and she'll be sitting pretty in cloth of gold."

Haro hardly knew how to respond to Mr. Hastings' undisguised boasts, but thankfully, Arabella was familiar with rescuing conversation from her father's faux pas.

"Speaking of cloth of gold," she said winsomely, "I hear the Prince Regent is planning to curtain his whole dining room with it at Brighton Pavilion."

The earl shuddered. "Is not the place gaudy enough as it is?"

"Do you think so? We visited it last summer, and I was rather impressed by the Indian style of the building and the Chinese murals in the banqueting room. The Saracen influence on the domes—"

"My daughter is a little too fond of architecture for her own good," interrupted Mr. Hastings. Haro sensed a coarse note of savagery in his voice, perhaps a hint for Arabella to abandon the subject and pursue some topic more frivolous.

Strange, Haro thought. He would have assumed that the old braggart would take delight in his daughter's architectural knowledge, another one of her accomplishments to showcase for prospective suitors.

The conversation continued in a lighter vein until the final course had been removed. "I think Mrs. Rollo and I must excuse ourselves now," said Arabella, playing the part of a proper hostess, "and let you gentlemen enjoy your port in peace."

"Yes, yes, run along," said her father with a wink, "but don't run too far, for I may have things to talk over with you later." The ladies floated out of the room, the younger with a small smile playing over her face, the elder with the same downtrodden expression she had borne all evening. Haro wondered if this Mrs. Rollo had always been so dour or if she had acquired her grim expression from constant association with Mr. Hastings.

William Hastings went over to the sideboard to retrieve the decanter, pouring both himself and the earl a generous helping of the after-dinner beverage. He eased himself back into his chair with a wolfish smile. "Well, here we are, my lord, alone at last and able to talk like men. I've had my ear to the ground ever since seeing you at the Duke of Doyle's. You need my help, I think. Come, admit as much, and then we can begin to talk...."

Pride is an unappetizing dish to swallow, and later on, Haro could barely believe how much of it he swallowed that night when he confessed the extent of the Emison family debts to the vulgar Mr. Hastings. It helped that the mill owner—having researched the earl's family most thoroughly—already knew the majority of the story. But it was still bitterly galling for Haro to be forced to air his family's dirty linen with this inquisitive stranger.

Fortunately, however, William Hastings did not seem to be at all put out or put off by the tale of the late earl's egregious spending at cards. "That's how these aristocrats are," he said with a familiar wink, "all flash and no fold, and not a one of them with any money sense." He rubbed his hands over the gold lace of his costume, obviously preening himself on the fact that he did have money sense, and it was that money sense that had led the new earl straight into his pocket.

"So if I understand correctly, you need"—and he rattled off an outrageous sum of tens of thousands of pounds—"to save your precious country estate and keep up the style of living to which your family is accustomed." Hastings sipped his port with an excitement he did not bother to conceal. "I happen to have that sum. I won't say it would be easy for me to come by it, and I don't say that it's ready to hand. But I have it, and could give it to you, should you engage to make it worth my while."

Haro put down his glass hesitantly. Now was the time for him to introduce Miss Arabella Hastings into the conversation, but such candor—or crassness—was far more difficult for him than it was for his host. "Obviously, I cannot offer you any collateral for such a sum, or indeed, have any hope of ever repaying you. There is one thing my father did leave me intact, however." He set his jaw and looked at the mill owner proudly. "The title of Earl of Anglesford."

"Yes, that is so!" said William Hastings, pounding a fat-fingered fist upon the table. "And for all my prosperity, a title like that is something I can never hope to have." He gave his guest a sly look. "And yet it is something that my grandchildren might aspire to."

By dint of sheer willpower, Haro managed to preserve an expression of equanimity. "Now that my father is gone, I have thought long and hard about abandoning the bachelor life and setting up my own establishment and household. You have a beautiful and intelligent daughter, Mr. Hastings—"

"So gratified that my lord should have noticed!"

"At first glance, it seems that she and I might suit each other quite well. I would like to request permission to call upon your daughter and become further acquainted with her."

"Ha!" shouted Hastings, reaching for the decanter to refill his glass. "Is there time to come calling when the wolf is at the door? The horse is already out of the gate, Anglesford! Either you place your bet now or not at all. Come, what is it to be?"

The young earl had been overcome with amazement at his host's gaucherie more than once this evening, but this last suggestion surpassed any other words that had been uttered at the table. Was Mr. Hastings actually suggesting he should propose marriage to his daughter that very night?

"You are very welcoming, and for that I thank you. But you know next to nothing about me. I would expect that you would wish to sound out my character a little before giving me permission to address your daughter."

"What is there to sound out?" replied Mr. Hastings dismissively. "You're not engaged already, I take it?"

Haro blushed. If circumstances had not intervened, he had intended to be so by the end of the season. "No, I am not."

"That's all right then," said his host. "Prior engagements can be shuffled under the table, but they do have the ability to make a nuisance of themselves sometimes. It may not surprise you to learn that I've already made inquiries about you, my lord. And everything I've learned has proved satisfactory. I think you're just the man for me—or for my daughter, I mean to say."

"I appreciate your goodwill in the matter, but I'm sure it will take me some time to get the lady's goodwill."

"Stuff and nonsense! I daresay she's expecting your declaration in the drawing room right now, twiddling her thumbs on the sofa while we keep her waiting."

Hastings pushed back his chair and rose from the table. Haro followed suit and followed his host to the door of the dining room. In that awful moment his fate had been decided for him. He was about to propose marriage to Miss Arabella Hastings. The tradesman angling for an earl had caught one at last.

The full gravity of the situation descended on Haro's shoulders like a cloak of lead as his host ushered him down the hallway and through the French doors of the decorated drawing room. Once a gentleman contracted an engagement and the banns were published, it was extremely uncouth of him to beg off. In fact, if he dared to do so, the young lady's family could sue him for breach of promise—and probably win. But William Hastings had made it impossible for him to involve his family, impossible for him to consult his solicitor, and impossible for him to delay.

As her father had prophesied, Miss Hastings was seated demurely on the sofa, stitching a sampler with her chin elevated becomingly. Haro wondered if needlework was one of the young lady's favorite pastimes, or if it was all for show—another ruse to convince the earl of Arabella's superior qualities.

William Hastings waved conspiratorially to his daughter then made a great show of shutting the drawing room doors, leaving the couple alone in awkward silence.

"I've just had a very remarkable conversation with your father," began Haro, trying to keep the tone of misery out of his voice.

"Oh, yes?" said Arabella, opening her eyes widely with an air of innocence. She begged the earl to sit down. Complying, he took the chair farthest from her, directly across the diameter of the spacious drawing room. It was a feeble, last attempt at independence.

"Yes, very remarkable," repeated Haro. He took a deep breath. "I asked him for permission to call upon you to improve our acquaintance. However, he assured me that our acquaintance is sufficiently advanced for me to presume to put a certain question to you."

Miss Hastings dropped her sampler on the cushion beside her and folded her hands in her lap. She was waiting for the question as expectantly as a cat sitting before a saucer of cream. Haro rose to his feet, crossed the floral rug in a few rapid strides, and lowered himself onto one knee. He already had the words down pat on his tongue—although he had always assumed he would be directing them to a different young lady.

"Miss Hastings, you would make me very happy if you would do me the honor of becoming my wife."

Her first words almost made him feel the complete fool. "This is very sudden, my lord!"

But the next syllables she uttered revealed that she had no thought of toying with him. "But though we've only known each other a short while, I must confess that I have felt an irresistible attraction to you. I would be honored to accept your proposal."

She gave him her hand—ungloved—and he kissed it. Then, because she seemed to expect something more, he rose from the carpet, seated himself on the sofa beside her, and kissed her lightly on the cheek. She smiled at him and took his hand in hers. It was not an unpleasant sensation, and Haro began to wonder if something slightly more than a kiss on the cheek might be expected.

He was soon overwhelmed with thankfulness, however, that no further display of affection had surfaced between them, for Mr. Hastings—who had made such a show of leaving them alone together—had retreated no farther than behind the drawing room doors. Throwing them open, he burst in to offer the engaged couple his felicitations. "Well done, my boy!" he said, clapping Haro heavily on the back. "And well done, Lady Anglesford!" he said, bestowing a hearty kiss upon his daughter and usurping a title that Haro had never heard used except in reference to his mother.

"When shall I enter it in the banns? Tomorrow morning, I think!"

"No, that is too soon," said Haro, panic constricting his throat like the coils of a snake. "You must give me some time to convey the happy news to my family before the ton is ringing with the surprise."

"The day after tomorrow then," said Mr. Hastings firmly. He was too shrewd a businessman to let a long period of reflection and remorse eat away at his customer. "And you must bring Arabella to meet your family tomorrow! I'm sure your mother will be overwhelmed with joy to welcome her new daughter."

"Overwhelmed indeed," said Haro, although he did not think that joy would be his mother's primary emotion. "'Til tomorrow then," he said, kissing his betrothed's hand formally.

"Adieu, mon cher!" replied Arabella, holding onto his hand until he pulled it gently from her grasp. Her brown eyes, he noticed, were shining like stars, but whether from the pleasure of this new romance or the pleasure of becoming Lady Anglesford it was impossible to tell.

5

MORNING LIGHT IS THE best time for revelations of a dubious nature, and so Haro brooded on his secret alone until he met his family members, one by one, at the leisurely atmosphere of the breakfast table.

"I've taken your advice, Torin," he said brusquely, as his younger brother helped himself to a plate of sausage and eggs from the sideboard.

"Unusual," replied the lad, "but somewhat gratifying." He sat down at the table and tucked a large white napkin into his collar. "Which advice of mine are you referring to?"

"I've engaged myself to marry Miss Arabella Hastings, the daughter of one of the wealthiest tradesmen in London."

Not many things could come between young master Torin and his food, but this revelation caused him to pause mid-mouthful. "Haro, I'm astounded! I know I suggested such a thing in fun—or perhaps in desperation—but I never truly expected you to do anything of the kind. And if you remember rightly, I suggested an heiress, not a tradesman's daughter. What sort of trade?"

"An heiress is an heiress no matter her parentage," replied Haro firmly. It was an axiom of whose truth he was still trying to convince himself. "And what does it matter to you where the money comes from, as long as it pays for your precious Woldwick? He's in textiles, if you must know. A mill owner, who has made his millions in cotton. He's offered to defray some of father's debts so that the estate can be kept intact."

Torin chewed thoughtfully. "I suppose I ought to congratulate you then, old man, in raising the needed blunt...although, it is a bit of a blow to poor Eda."

Haro glared ferociously. That wound was still too raw to be touched. "She's a sensible girl—you said so yourself. She understands perfectly well that circumstances and duty must make my decisions for me."

"And what decisions are those?" asked a cool, crisp voice floating into the breakfast room. It was Eda, in a dark mourning dress, her black hair pulled back loosely in a low knot at the nape of her neck. The scent of roses and lavender accompanied her, and to Haro—his mind full of last night's remarkable events—her natural ease of motion contrasted sharply with Arabella's studied graces.

The earl sent a silent plea for help to his brother, and Torin magnanimously offered the necessary explanation. "Haro's decided to marry a tradesman's daughter—the child of a cotton manufacturer, no less. It's all for the sake of the family, you understand, since none of us wants to let a house in Russell Square as Mr. Godwin says we must."

"Oh, I quite understand," said Eda, barely bothering to disguise her disgust. Her glance raked over Haro's fitted jacket and cut like daggers. She was not schooled in dissimulation. She was not at all like Arabella. "Russell Square would hardly agree with my refined tastes either. But thanks to your brother, I'll be able to batten off his betrothed, or at least off her father…as long as he agrees to keep your pauper relations housed under his roof." A cloud of bitterness came over her face. "I must congratulate you on your good sense, Lord Anglesford, and on your engagement."

"Thank you," said Haro stiffly. He could tell he had hurt her, and the unfairness of it all cut him to the quick. What would she have him do? Continue with their understanding and relegate his mother and brother to a life of poverty? Somehow, in the last couple days, the comfortable familiarity he had always enjoyed with Eda had completely disappeared. The girl he had known since his days in the nursery had put on the mask of a stranger and the tongue of a cockatrice. And bewildered, Haro felt he knew her little better than the tall, slim brunette whose name would be linked with his in the banns tomorrow.

Miss Hastings, along with her dour-faced duenna, Mrs. Rollo, did not waste any time before calling on Lady Anglesford. A card arrived shortly after breakfast with notice that Haro's betrothed would be calling that very afternoon.

Eda heard the news of the impending visit with outward equanimity, but inside she was seething. How dare he bring her here! She had always implicitly assumed that one day *she* would preside over the tea table in this house, but apparently Haro had other plans.

As she came downstairs to take her place in the drawing room, she saw Haro pacing in the entrance hall. It looked as if he was as apprehensive as she was! A brief pang of pity overtook her, but it was easily dismissed when she considered how utterly asinine the man was determined to be.

"Oh, it's you Eda!" he said, hearing her footsteps. His eyes narrowed as he took in her appearance. Following the announcement at breakfast, she had coifed her hair in a much more elaborate style and put on her most elegant pearl necklace. She would not be recognized as the "pauper cousin" at first glance! "I was thinking that perhaps you might have plans of your own to go out walking or riding—"

"I was thinking you might have plans of your own," retorted Eda, "to put on your beaver and bolt to the safety of your club."

Haro gritted his teeth.

"No," said Eda, slightly lifting the skirt of her dress to facilitate her descent down the staircase. "I shall be here all afternoon. And how delightful it will be to meet your betrothed!" She heaped such a copious amount of sugar onto her tone that he could not help but doubt her sincerity. "I know your mother is looking forward to it as well."

Inside the drawing room, Lady Anglesford had been combating her own attack of nerves. She sat down when Eda and Haro entered only to clutch at the embroidered cushions of the sofa and send to the kitchen for teacakes four or five times. "Your poor father would turn over in his grave if he knew I was welcoming a mill owner's offspring as his future daughter-in-law."

"I daresay Father would not be so squeamish," retorted Haro, "since the situation is entirely owing to his profligacy."

It was an insightful comeback—Eda was forced to acknowledge as much—and Lady Anglesford fell silent, no doubt wondering how she could have been so blind to her husband's behavior for so many years.

At the hour of two o'clock, the sound of the door knocker echoed through the hallway. The footman announced their guest, and Miss Hastings stepped into a room overflowing with curiosity, contempt, and agitation.

She was accompanied by a drab companion who was silent as a specter, retreating into the background and offering nothing to the conversation. Eda conjectured that Miss Hastings had doubtless chosen her companion for the sake of contrast—even an unremarkable pearl can seem brilliant when surrounded by the dingy shell of an oyster. And if truth be told, Eda found this Arabella Hastings quite unremarkable.

She was pretty, if one liked regular features of that kind, but with the same sort of prettiness that characterized half the young women in London. Her dress was apricot-colored with much more frill to it than the elegant lines that Eda favored. The sleeves and low-cut neckline were set with silver lace, and her trim little hat appeared to be the exact same color as the gown.

Haro introduced his fiancée to his mother, and both women greeted each other with proper etiquette.

"I am so pleased to hear that you have honored my son by accepting his proposal."

"Your son is everything I could have hoped for in a husband."

Eda, who was sitting in the window seat observing this pretty scene, let out a little yawn that could not help but attract attention. Haro ignored her out of annoyance, and the lot fell to Lady Anglesford to introduce her cousin's daughter. "Miss Hastings—"

"Oh, do call me Arabella!"

"Very well, then—Arabella, allow me to introduce Miss Edith Swanycke, a close relative of mine who resides with the family."

The two young women exchanged formal how-do-you-dos. Eda saw Haro breathe a sigh of relief that she had not given Arabella the cut direct right there in their own drawing room. She forced a smile onto her face. She was angry, yes, but she was not an unmannerly hoyden. As long as this decorated apricot pretended civility, she would too.

"Haro has told me so much about you," said Arabella.

Eda's eyebrows lifted, and she shot a venomous look in Haro's direction. Just what had he mentioned to this saucy minx? That he had thrown over Eda for her and trampled the established expectations of the entire Emison family?

"He cherishes you quite dearly, like a younger sister in fact. I have no sisters of my own, and how pleased I am now to have you in place of one."

Eda willed her face to remain calm. If Arabella knew anything about their family arrangements, her comment could only be seen as a calculated attempt to show Eda exactly what her new role was to be.

But Eda had never been one to let others dictate her place. She looked up at Arabella, who was several inches taller than her, and smiled silkily. "Yes, how pleasant it will be for all of us. I can see it now, the three of us walking in Hyde Park, with dear Haro in the middle and one of us on either arm. Although I fear that the two of us are so different in looks that people will forever be drawing comparisons—your brown eyes against my blue, your brown hair against my black, your slim figure against my full one."

Haro stepped toward the dueling pair, and Eda saw the thunder gathering on his brow. But Eda also knew that the best way to gain the last word was to leave after having said it. "I am so sorry to miss out on the rest of your visit, Arabella, but I have a prior engagement to go riding with a friend. Felicitations, my dear sister! And to you too, my fortunate older brother." She squeezed Haro's hand and planted a kiss—a little warmer than sisterly—on the earl's cheek. Then, turning in triumph, she slipped away to her fictitious appointment.

Silence rippled through the room. Haro glowered in embarrassment while Lady Anglesford tried to smooth over Eda's insulting behavior with comments about the weather. Haro had been certain that Eda would do something to upset the conversation, but he had not expected that something to be quite so...so...provocative. His cheek still felt warm from her much too friendly kiss. He raised his hand to wipe off the feeling but lowered it again, afraid that someone would see the gesture.

"Lady Anglesford," said Arabella. Haro could see that she intended to regain command of the situation. "My father and I were hoping to invite you to a soirée later this week so that we could further our acquaintance."

"You are kindness itself," said the countess, burying her hands in the folds of her black dress, "but we are not able to attend any gatherings at present...and I fear we will not be long in town."

Haro remembered Godwin's dispiriting recommendation that the town house be sold immediately.

"Eda, Torin, and I will be retiring to the country. Haro, of course, may stay in London if he chooses."

"Are you going to Woldwick then?"

Haro started. It seemed that Arabella had taken pains to memorize all the place names associated with the Emison family. Her father must have researched him thoroughly before adding him to his portfolio.

"How I should love to see the home where Haro grew up!" She clapped her hands together in excitement.

It was cleverly done. After such a pointed exclamation, Lady Anglesford could do nothing else but issue an invitation for Arabella to accompany the family to the countryside. "And perhaps you will wish to bring your chaperone," she said, looking hesitantly at Mrs. Rollo who had sat as silently as a deaf and dumb servant throughout the course of the visit.

"Oh, yes! And Father too," said Arabella quickly. "I know he would love to see the seat of an earl and the future home of his daughter."

And wallow in the triumph of his aristocratic conquest, thought Haro. "We would be delighted to have you both at Woldwick," he said aloud. "Nothing could give me more pleasure."

Haro sat up late in the library that evening, sipping one glass of brandy and then another, thinking over all the changes the last two months had brought. His father's death had been a blow, and an unexpected one to say the least. Haro had barely come into his majority, and he had not anticipated holding the title of earl at the age of three and twenty. There was so much more of the world to see, so many more larks to be had, but now, he must settle down as the sober, staid head of the family.

Not that his father had been exactly staid and sober. Haro remembered stumbling in, on more than one occasion, at three o'clock in the morning, his head a little befuddled by drink, and running into his father on the stairs in a similar state of befuddlement.

"Not a word to your mother!" was his father's standard greeting.

"Silent as the grave!" was Haro's standard response.

Once, he had met his father by chance at an upscale gaming establishment in St. James' Street. He had gone there with Guy Pontipale and two other friends, in search of some livelier sport than might be had at White's. The old earl had given him a nod of recognition and plucked his coat sleeve to pull him aside. "What are you doing here? Your quarterly allowance wouldn't even cover the stakes for one game."

"I should ask you the same," he had replied, a little put out to be taken to task in full sight of his friends.

"Something you should know, my boy—a man's purse is his own. If you have the blunt, you have the right to risk it. You, I know for a fact, do not have the blunt."

"Someday I will."

"Yes, someday," his father had said, his lips twisting upward into a curious smile. "And to that end, I'd best get back to my game of faro. Get yourself home, young man, and if you think of it, you could say a little prayer for my luck to rise. Oh, and Haro, don't tell your m—"

"I know, I know." And so Haro had gone home and held his peace—although, in retrospect, life might be running a little more smoothly now if he had mentioned something about his father's expensive habits to his more responsible parent.

Haro sighed and set down his empty glass. Yawning a little, he climbed the stairs and went down the corridor to his bedroom. Garth, his valet, was waiting up for him—a practice that Haro frequently insisted was unnecessary, but one that Garth considered essential to his vocation.

"You look a little blue-deviled, m'lord," said the valet. He was a slight, spry man in the prime of life, his brown hair flecked with gray. He helped Haro out of his tight-fitting jacket and began dusting it off in preparation for hanging it in the wardrobe.

"I suppose that's because I am," said Haro with a sigh. "You heard that we're bound for Woldwick tomorrow?"

"Yes, m'lord. And I also heard there might be some congratulations in order?"

"Thank you, Garth. Yes, it will be in the papers in another day or two."

"Her ladyship's maid gave me the news, and I caught a glimpse of the young lady as she was on her way out today." The walls had ears in this house, and the servants were well acquainted with the disastrous news that Mr. Godwin had imparted to Lady Anglesford. A penniless earl would have to turn them all out to find other positions, and the family's plight was just as concerning to them as it was to Haro.

Garth cleared his throat. "She looked very elegant."

"Very elegant, and very rich."

"Nothing the matter with that, m'lord," said Garth reassuringly.

"No," said Haro thoughtfully, as he unfastened his shirt cuffs. "I suppose not."

And as he turned down the coverlet to climb into bed, he reflected that there were a great many more people depending on him than just his mother, his brother, and Eda. There was the whole staff of servants in town and an even larger staff at Woldwick whose livelihood was bound up in his ability to carry through with the bargain he had made.

6

"EGAD! THE FIANCÉE AND her father!" said Torin when he heard the news about who would be accompanying them to Woldwick. "Don't you think that is a bit much?"

"Mind your tongue, Torin," said Haro. It was bad enough to have to deal with Eda's pique, but combating two detractors was the outside of enough.

"I'm sure this Mr. Hastings wishes to examine his investment," said Eda, as she directed the footman to bring her brass-bound trunk downstairs and outside to the coach. Dozens of hatboxes soon followed the trunk, carried down the stairs by in a parade of bright colors.

"You certainly didn't exercise economy in your packing," observed Torin, and Haro raised an eyebrow as well.

"Best not to leave anything behind since we don't know that we'll ever be coming back to this house. I certainly don't want any of my hats or gowns put up for auction!"

"By Jove! You're right!" exclaimed the young man, and he rushed off to his own bedchamber to ensure that his prize books were added to the packing pile.

"Since when did you care so much about frills and finery?" demanded Haro. The Edith Swanycke he knew was tasteful and restrained in her dress and could wear the same bonnet every day of the week and still look crisp and fresh.

"Since I found out they were what mattered most," replied Eda, her lips setting into a straight line. She pushed past him without another word and let him stew on the meaning of her words by himself.

The weather that day was warmer than it had been in months, although Haro had a premonition that winter was far from over. Mr. Hastings insisted on traveling down to the countryside in a procession with the Emisons. Haro was invited to ride with the mill owner, his daughter, and Mrs. Rollo in the Hastings' smart barouche. He surprised himself by accepting the invitation with enthusiasm, preferring the vulgar remarks of his future father-in-law to the needling remarks of Eda or the reproachful gaze of Lady Anglesford.

A coach followed them containing Miss Hastings' French lady's maid, Mr. Hastings' valet, and all the luggage that would not fit in the barouche. Arabella seemed to have exercised as little economy as Eda in her packing, and Haro wondered just how long she thought this visit was going to last.

"Nice country this," William Hastings said approvingly as they tooled through the hillsides and the winter-worn copses. He squinted hard at every barn and pasture they passed, figuring up in his head and sharing with the others what each of these farmers must be worth.

Arabella proved a more entertaining travel companion, quizzing Haro on various landmarks and drawing out stories from his childhood. "There is the tollgate I took at a jump when I was but sixteen." He rubbed his knee ruefully. "My horse was not as keen as I, and I still have the scar to prove it."

"You must tell us when we come close enough to see the manor house from afar," said Arabella, her shoulder snugged up against his as they shared one side of the barouche.

"But of course," said Haro with a smile, pleased to see her interest in his family home. He was making a devil's bargain in order to keep it in the family, but somehow, as he basked in Arabella's smiles, that bargain did not seem quite as burdensome as it had initially. He wondered what Eda and Torin were talking about in the other carriage and reminded himself that he was glad he did not have to endure Eda's chilly icicles all the way to Woldwick.

After a few hours of traveling and a long stop to rest the horses, the top of Woldwick's towers came into view at last. "There she is," said Haro proudly. The great house was a model of Elizabethan and Jacobean architecture. It was surrounded on all sides by a gigantic garden laid out symmetrically with intricate paths threading their way through the manicured plants. Outside the garden lay the country woods, leafless now in the wintry weather but still stately with their long limbs of white, gray, and brown.

"Who is that old man?" asked Arabella, her bright brown eyes catching sight of a pedestrian on one of the footpaths.

Haro leaned out the side of the barouche to get a better look. "Why, that's old Uncle Harold, my grandfather's brother, and my namesake. He lives up at Woldwick year-round and haunts these woods like a friendly ghost."

There was no room to take him up in the barouche, so Haro refrained from hailing him. "I daresay we'll make his acquaintance at dinner tonight," said William Hastings. Haro could see that he was looking forward to his next meal after spending so many hours traveling.

"Perhaps, although I should warn you that he takes most of his meals in his room and is quite shy of strangers. A bit of an eccentric, but a wonderful old gentleman through and through."

"Hmm," replied the mill owner, his tone laying bare his thoughts. While the up-and-coming middle class strove to meet every expectation society laid upon them, it was the prerogative of the aristocracy that they could afford to be peculiar. And it seemed that these blueblood families always had one crazy bat roosting in the eaves.

Woldwick was a large house with room enough to house a hunting party or host a ball. But somehow, William Hastings' personality was large enough to fill the whole residence and to make it seem cramped and insupportable for the rest of its inhabitants.

"A bit too English, your cook," Hastings remarked at dinner, disappointed by the style of cuisine and the paucity of dishes in each course. "Not exactly done up in the latest mode," he pronounced upon seeing the décor in the great room and various salons about the house. "Quite inconvenient," he groaned, upon learning how distantly the stables were located from the residence. It was the complaint of new money against titled tradition.

Arabella, although still doing her best to ingratiate herself with the family, was not without her share of Mr. Hastings' censorious spirit. "I declare, this drawing room is as dark and drab as a tomb! There will be some changes made when I am mistress of the place."

Lady Anglesford, adopting the role of martyr, endured the Hastings' criticisms with unflagging patience. If she ever gave vent to her feelings, the ears of her lady's maid were the only ones to hear it. The younger members of the household, however, were less guarded and more articulate in their annoyance. "If he makes one more remark about our 'inefficient chimneys' or 'tarnished candlesticks,'" snarled Torin, "I'll tell him where to take himself."

Eda patted his arm in commiseration. "It is strange to think that to save Woldwick we must endure these indignities to Woldwick. But much as it galls me to say it, I think you must tolerate Mr. Hastings as long as he holds the purse strings. Haro would hardly thank you if you told his fine father-in-law to go to the devil, or some such nonsense."

Torin pouted. "At first I thought Haro was much to be pitied, but now it appears he is the only one of the family quite pleased with the arrangement. He actually seems to *enjoy* Miss Hastings' simpers. One wonders if he would hang on her leading strings even if her father were not the wealthiest mill owner in England."

Eda's fair hands clenched into fists until the knuckles were bone-white, but Torin, schoolboy that he was, had not the presence of mind to notice.

"I don't know if I could bear it," continued the lad, "staying on at Woldwick with Hastings ruling the roost. I *hope* he will take his leave once the wedding has taken place—or perhaps he will presume upon his position of power and wear out the welcome we never gave him. Arabella I might be able to tolerate, although she is a bit imperious." Torin gave a weary sigh. "If the house grows too hot to hold me, I suppose I can always off to Oxford. That's been my intent for a while now. And even the demands of the strictest teachers might seem like manna after the unsavory dish of William Hastings."

Eda's dark blue eyes closed momentarily as she heard of Torin's escape plan. As a son of the house, he could come and go as he chose, and Oxford was an excellent steppingstone into a profession that would suit one of Torin's temperament. Eda had no such options of her own. Like Torin, she recognized that the new Lady Anglesford—and her father—might soon make life at Woldwick unbearable. But unlike Torin, Eda had nowhere else to go.

She thought back to the morning that Haro had surprised her with Mr. Godwin's dismal news. It had seemed so desperately important to her in that moment that she allow him the space to choose. And, merciful heavens, he had done it! He had chosen someone other than her.

As much as she wished that she could shake hands and wish him well, her wounded spirit was too raw. Her bruised pride was too fresh. If Haro was to make the rest of them unhappy, then it was not fair that he should find happiness in the act. She had too much Irish blood in her to take a slight with complacency. Whatever sound advice she might give to Torin about tolerating his prospective relations, she found herself unable to take such sound advice herself.

She would help Haro Emison realize just how poorly he had chosen when left to his own devices. She could sense that Arabella Hastings was a shrew, through and through, and it only needed a little clever management to display as much to Haro. And if that made her a vengeful harpy or a dog in the manger, so be it. She could live with that reputation as long as she exposed Arabella for who she truly was.

"Do you ride?" Haro asked his intended, the day after their arrival. Town had its own set of amusements, but one of the things he missed most while being in London was the opportunity to choose his own paces as he rode his favorite gelding through the forests around Woldwick. The temperature had plummeted after their arrival yesterday, but there was no sign of rain, and Haro always considered the cold air refreshing.

Lady Anglesford had retired to her room soon after breakfast. Mr. Hastings had retired to the library to read his newspaper and attend to his business correspondence. Mrs. Rollo had struck up a quiet conversation with the housekeeper and gone to tour the kitchen and pantry. And since Haro was left with only the young people to entertain, riding was the entertainment he selected.

"But, of course, I ride!" replied Arabella, a little too quickly. "I should have had Father bring along my chestnut mare. She's new, for this season, but I know her paces well, and she looks ever so smart with my red riding habit."

"Perhaps we can match you with one of the mounts in our stable."

"We certainly can," burst in Eda. Her dark blue eyes sparkled with enthusiasm. "I would be happy to loan you my mare Jenny."

Haro wrinkled his nose. "Jenny? I don't think th—"

"Oh, well, perhaps not, if you're not good with the reins." Eda sent an arch glance in Arabella's direction.

"I am quite an accomplished horsewoman." Arabella took up the challenge without knowing the whole of what it entailed.

Haro frowned. He disliked the way that the two women had taken the situation out of his hands. "I am sure of it. It's just that riding in the country is different than promenading a horse through Town, and Jenny is—"

"A little skittish at times," said Eda with a dismissive wave. "But I manage her well enough."

"But if she's to ride Jenny," interjected Torin, "then who will you ride?" The thought of playing chaperone, all alone, to his brother and his brother's intended was destroying all his interest in the projected outing. He had no definable grudge against Arabella, but her conversation was wearing on him and her very presence there a constant reminder of how low the family fortunes had sunk.

"Oh, I daresay I shall stay inside and keep your mother company, and maybe practice my embroidery."

"Ha!" Both Torin and Haro were well aware that embroidery was not a favorite pastime of Eda's. In fact, there was nothing she liked more than a brisk ride in the cold weather—red nose, wind-chapped cheeks, and all.

Obstinately, Eda gathered up some stray needlework from the workbasket, paraded over to the sofa by the fireplace, and sat down cozily in the corner. Haro snorted as she began to sort out the threads. He doubted she had even caught sight of this particular embroidery until now—it was probably one of his mother's works in progress. But he had no intention of pleading with her to change her mind.

"Well, come along then, Torin."

He took Arabella's hand and kissed it ostentatiously. "We'll have the horses saddled and to the door by the time you've changed into your riding habit."

"Don't forget to bring an apple for Jenny!" Eda called after them.

"It would take more than an apple to sweeten that nag," retorted Torin. But Arabella had already gone upstairs and thus missed the hint of warning veiled in the young man's comment.

It did not take Arabella long to realize how much less appealing of a mount Jenny was than the chestnut mare she was used to riding. Jenny's appearance was the first mark against her. When Arabella came out the door smartly clad in her riding habit, she saw Haro standing by the head of an oddly colored nag, with splotches of gray on dirty white. The side saddle on the ugly beast's back indicated that this was, in fact, her mount.

Haro could see that Arabella was having difficulty reining in her own annoyance, but at last, she forced a smile onto her face and came forward for Haro to lift her into the saddle. Putting his hands around her waist, Haro hoisted her into place. The girl's frame was slight and it only took a second, but she gave him a lingering look as if that touch had meant something. "Thank you," she said with a purr.

"Erm...you're welcome," said Haro, a little louder than he needed to. He had lifted Eda into the saddle dozens of times, and she had never made a fuss about such a thing.

He could see now why Jenny's appearance was so off-putting to his intended. The skirt of Arabella's red riding habit draped attractively over the side of the horse and her tight-fitting boots displayed trim ankles peeking at below. A long-legged chestnut would have been the perfect canvas for this equestrian elegance, but Jenny's patchwork coat and stocky build almost spoiled the effect entirely.

"Easy on the bit," said Haro as he handed Arabella the reins.

"Here we go then!" shouted Torin, swinging himself into the saddle. "To the village and back?" Without waiting for an answer, he flicked the reins on his own dark gray hunter, trotting away from the house and up the lane.

Arabella, determined not to be the dawdler of the party, followed his lead, urging Jenny onward with a less than gentle hand. The horse started moving but none too happily. Haro, mounting quickly, brought his own black horse beside hers in time to see that all-too-familiar glint in Jenny's eye. She had her hackles up now, and it was only a matter of time before she showed her displeasure.

They rounded the bend in the lane, hooves alternately thudding and squelching on the half-frozen mud. On every side they were surrounded by leafless branches and the warm mist of their own breath in the cold air.

Jenny began to pull a little to one side. Arabella shortened up the reins to guide her back into the center of the lane. And then, the thing that Haro had feared happened in all its horrible splendor.

Jenny balked.

If there had been a rabbit or a pheasant in the path, she might have had some excuse. But, no, Jenny balked because she was as ill-tempered a horse as ever lived. Jenny balked because she hated being ridden by strangers. Jenny balked because, somehow, she knew that Eda wanted her to.

Torin was far ahead on the road, almost out of sight, but, hearing Arabella's high-pitched squeal, he slowed his horse to a halt. He turned around halfway in the saddle. There was his brother, helping the visibly shaken mill-owner's daughter out of the muck she had fallen into. And there was Jenny, wandering riderless into the roadside hedge, pretending that she had no idea what all the fuss was about.

Haro, Torin noted, looked seriously concerned over the incident, and for a moment, the younger brother was afraid that the earl was going to clasp the distressed damsel to his manly bosom. But Arabella, it seemed, was more incensed than injured. "Wretched beast!" was only one of the phrases ricocheting off the bare branches. Neither her diction nor her riding habit were quite as elegant as when they had left the house a bare ten minutes ago. Haro was nodding, as if in agreement, and then, he put her up on his horse, sideways, in front of the pommel of his saddle, taking care to hold her steady as he climbed on behind her.

Once he saw that Arabella was unharmed, Torin began to laugh—a loud, lively, boyish laugh that resonated through the four corners of the Woldwick woods. Seated snugly in front of Haro on his black, Arabella could not help but hear it. If anybody could have seen the expression on her face, they would have known that Torin's laugh—and the knowledge that Edith Swanycke, snug by the fire in the sitting room, would soon be laughing too—was not something the daughter of William Hastings would easily forget or forgive.

7

"GOODNESS!" EXCLAIMED EDA. "WHATEVER can have happened to you, my dear girl?" She had risen at the sound of the returning hoof beats and come quickly to the front hall to see the ignominious entrance of Haro's fiancée.

Spangled with dirt and badly crumpled, Arabella's riding outfit had lost all its allure. The heightened color in Arabella's cheeks was the brightest thing about her.

"I'm sure you can guess very well what happened to me."

"But, no, I cannot! Please tell me."

Arabella set her teeth with a growl and, grabbing the folds of her riding skirt with her right hand, ascended the stairs with as much dignity as she could muster.

Torin, who was seeing to the horses, had not come in yet, and so Eda and Haro were left alone in the marble-floored hall.

"Temper, temper," tsked Eda with raised eyebrows.

"I've seen you lose yours on much less provocation." There was an edge of steel in Haro's voice that few people had ever heard.

"I'm flattered that you still find the need to compare her to me."

"Don't be. You do not come off the better for it."

"Pish! Simply because I can ride and she cannot?"

"Simply because you are a vindictive beast and she is an innocent victim."

Eda's eyes glowed like the coals in a recently raked hearth. "So now we are down to slinging insults, are we?"

"No insult—just the truth. Arabella Hastings has done nothing to harm you in any way. You maliciously goaded her into riding that monstrous mare of yours, knowing full well that it would do her some injury. She never had a thought in her head that you would play her such a vicious trick."

"You speak as if you had known her all of your life instead of me."

"Perhaps I wish I had."

The door flung open between them. "Upon my word, it's chilly out there!" Torin rubbed his gloved hands together and stamped his feet. "I say, Haro, I've put away your black and my gray, but—"

"You left Jenny out in the cold?" The question should have been directed at Torin, but Eda's eyes were focused accusingly on the face of the tall, blond earl.

"I left her right where she threw her rider in the mud, and I'll be damned if I go back and fetch her now."

Eda's eyes sparked fire. "I see your Arabella is not the only one to lose her temper. Very well, I'll fetch Jenny myself." And without a further word, Eda opened the door and stepped outside into the wintry landscape surrounding Woldwick.

"Eda! Eda!" She hoped that it was Haro, coming to apologize. But no, it was Torin running after her into the circular driveway. "I'll get her! Go back inside."

"No." Eda's arms were already so cold she wondered if they would fall off from frostbite.

An older man would have known how to take charge of the situation and head off a lady from such a foolish endeavor, but Torin was only sixteen and used to giving in to Eda's whims. "Well, then, at least you'll take my coat."

"No, thank you. I'm quite well without it." That settled the matter, and a worried Torin retreated into the house.

Eda gasped. The air was so cold that it hurt to breathe, but what did it matter? Jenny would be put in her stable and Haro would be sorry for what he said—those were the only two things that were worth thinking about.

Haro ascended the stairs in a towering rage, prepared to be angry with Eda indefinitely. But it did not take more than a couple glances from the upstairs window—at a black-haired girl braving the winter wind in a thin dress—to make him question his harshness. He started for the stairs more than once to go outside and bring her back, but the tendrils of pride held him back like ivy creepers until it was too late to redeem the situation.

When his mother—who had heard the story from Torin as well as from her shocked lady's maid—took him to task a few hours later, it was not long until he felt completely miserable over the whole affair. He needed to say something to Eda. He needed to make things right.

Unfortunately, when Eda returned with a blue nose and the smell of the stables on her, she retired to her room immediately. Haro saw several ewers of water being transported upstairs for a hot bath and knew that an opportunity for reconciliation would have to wait. Arabella, the other object of his concern, stayed closeted in her apartments as well. And so Haro found that all his sympathy and regrets must be expended on Mr. Hastings.

"What on earth do you mean, Anglesford, giving my daughter a mount like that to ride?"

Haro flushed red and mumbled an apology.

"I hope I'll see you taking better care of her safety in the future. You wouldn't want me to revoke my decision of allowing you her hand...."

"Oh, wouldn't he?" said Torin under his breath. Arabella's reaction to the accident had only served to deepen his dislike of her.

Haro continued to placate Mr. Hastings by uttering all the right sentiments. The only good thing seemed to be that Mr. Hastings had—as yet—no idea of Eda's involvement in the debacle. Haro could stand being taken to task himself, but he reflected that he might bear things very poorly should the mill owner set into Eda this way.

Not that she didn't deserve it. But, well, it was natural for the girl to be jealous since he had thrown her over rather suddenly. Her actions were childish, but they were understandable. If only he could make her understand *why* it was necessary and *why* it was the only way.

As the long afternoon drew to a close, Lady Anglesford entered the drawing room, bringing a welcome intermission to Mr. Hastings' scolding, but also an unwelcome reminder that dinner was about to be served. The probable reappearance of the two ladies in question gave Haro something else to ponder. How could he mend matters with Eda without seeming like a co-conspirator in the plot against Arabella? He sighed.

Arabella came downstairs first. She was in full dress fit for the finest ball—not quite the expected attire for an informal family dinner at Woldwick. Her high-waisted gown was made of pale blue silk, the neck swooping down low enough to expose the upper portion of her small bosom. She wore a few jewels on a gold chain, their fire flickering over her smooth skin. Three sleek feathers nestled against her brown curls, and dark blue satin slippers peeked out beneath the hem of her dress.

It was very apparent that she meant to dazzle, and Haro understood that he must respond with the right coin. "Enchanted," he murmured, taking her hand. It was warm to the touch. Haro raised it to his lips, trying to strike the pose of adoring fiancé.

Eda entered at just that moment, and the enchantment fizzled away like a fire doused with a bucket of cold water.

"Are we ready to go into dinner?" Her own dress—a simple black gown noting the fact that the family was still in mourning—stood in harsh relief to Arabella's expensive elegance.

"No, we are still waiting on Torin."

The clock struck five, drawing a disapproving glance from Mr. Hastings. Haro suspected that he ran his household with the precision of a factory foreman. Going in late to dinner was as unacceptable as leaving early from a shift in the weaving room.

Arabella released Haro's arm and made an exaggerated show of sitting down in one of the armchairs.

"Are you feeling all right?" Haro's solicitude stemmed both from a genuine concern and from an eagerness to mollify Mr. Hastings.

"I confess I am feeling a little weak. It may be from the fall I took earlier, or perhaps because no one remembered to send tea up to my room." She gave a wan smile to her betrothed.

Lady Anglesford started, her duties as a hostess having been called into question. "I am so sorry, my dear. I should have thought to have tea brought up."

"Oh, it is of no consequence," said Arabella, in a forlorn manner that belied the meaning of her words. "I am sure you have many things on your mind, Lady Anglesford, and I am glad that I will soon be able to spare you the running of the household after a certain happy event has been celebrated."

It was Lady Anglesford's turn to smile wanly. Up until a few days ago, she had not anticipated that her duties as Countess of Anglesford—duties which she usually enjoyed—would be terminated so abruptly.

"This is ridiculous!" said Mr. Hastings, as the clock hand winged its way to ten past the hour. He checked the accuracy of the house clock against the timepiece which he kept in his own waistcoat. "My daughter is famished, and this young dawdler will keep us waiting all night. Let us go into dinner without him—it will serve him right."

As might have been expected, Torin's slim figure appeared as soon as the gentlemen had seated the ladies at table.

"I say! You could have waited a moment." His voice sounded hurt.

"You could have looked at your pocket watch," said Mr. Hastings, his mouth full of ham, in a tone that was both jovial and unfeeling. Now that he had fork and knife in either hand, his mood had begun to improve.

"You'll have to learn to keep better track of the time," remarked Arabella primly, "if you're going to be punctual to all your classes up at Oxford."

"Who says I'm going up to Oxford?" Torin was instantly suspicious.

"Oh, your mother mentioned at breakfast that there was some thought of it." Arabella dabbed her lips delicately with a napkin. "I think it an excellent notion, and so does Haro."

Haro could not recall ever having spoken to his fiancée on this subject. He swallowed uncomfortably and forced a smile and a nod. He knew his brother's contrary nature, however. The fact that Arabella considered Oxford an "excellent notion" would immediately tarnish the idea in Torin's mind.

As Haro expected, Torin balked. "Hmm, well, I've done just fine on my own so far with my books and with a tutor—"

"Oh, if it's some question of the fee, I'm sure my father could sort that out for you. Right away, I imagine."

Mr. Hastings grunted affably, his mouth still absorbed with chewing.

Torin glanced from Eda, to Lady Anglesford, to Haro, his brown eyes expressive with concern. Was this chit trying to get rid of him?

Eda set her fork down. "I'm sure Torin is quite old enough to make up his own mind about it. He may not wish to attend Oxford at present."

"But he must do something! It's not as if he has a title like Haro. Younger sons must make themselves useful as they can." Arabella looked the young man up and down. "I hardly think you're suited for the army." It was a direct cut at his lack of physique. "Perhaps law then, or the church?"

Torin's face grew red, and his lips hardened into a thin line. He opened his mouth to say something, but Haro, certain that politeness would have no part in it, forestalled him by jumping into the conversation.

"'Pon rep! The house has been dull this afternoon. All of the ladies disappeared and we gentlemen were left to our own devices. It's remarkable how necessary the fair sex is to the enjoyment of daily life."

Mr. Hastings laughed. "My afternoon was hardly dull, but to each his own, Lord Anglesford. To each his own!"

"I am sorry you were so deprived of entertainment," said Eda, "but I should think each of us ladies had quite a good reason for disappearing." She straightened her shoulders in her simple black gown.

"Ah, yes," said Haro, having tiptoed around the sticky subject of Oxford only to step into a far muddier patch of conversation.

He looked down at Arabella sitting near him. "Despite all the unpleasantness, you still look marvelous—a rare beauty in that blue dress."

He continued his delicate balancing act by addressing the woman across the table. "And you look well, too, Eda. I...hope you found Jenny easily enough."

"No thanks to you." Her tone was still as chilly and pointed as the icicles on the eaves.

Haro knew he had made a mull of it as soon as the words came out. What kind of fool tries to compliment two ladies—rivals!—at the same time?

Arabella stiffened at the mention of the wretched beast. Her hand found Haro's underneath the table and held it tightly, as if she were in need of protection and aid all over again. Startled, Haro barely knew what to do. He rubbed his thumb tentatively over the edge of her palm and felt her relax.

"Your nag," said Arabella, "is not exactly a horse that I would be proud to keep in my stables."

"Then"—Eda set down her wine glass with a flourish—"it is just as well that these stables don't belong to you."

The rest of the dinner and the evening passed in like manner—William Hastings growing somnolent from a full stomach, Lady Anglesford becoming more agitated by the constant friction, Torin becoming more petulant as Arabella needled him, and Eda fencing every thrust with her own sharp tongue. Haro played the part of peacemaker as best he could, but over and over again, one question was running through his head: "Is Woldwick worth this?"

And there were more than a few times that night that he was tempted to answer no.

8

ON THE FOLLOWING DAY, Great-Uncle Harold finally made an appearance. He had come in from an early morning walk in the woods, dressed in an impossibly long greatcoat with a towering hat pulled down tightly over his ears. Like the young earl, Uncle Harold was impressively tall, and although age had stooped his shoulders a little, he still claimed that the top of his head was the highest in all the county.

The family and their guests meandered through the breakfast room, each at his own pace. Lady Anglesford had disappeared to speak to the housekeeper about the daily tasks. William Hastings had driven his barouche into the nearby village, both to take the air and to post some letters of business. The younger set was loitering outside the drawing room discussing their plans for the day when Uncle Harold materialized.

The Emison brood greeted him fondly. Both young men shook his hand with delight, and Eda—standing on tiptoe—planted a kiss on his wrinkled old cheek. Arabella hung back a little, her posture stiff and unwelcoming. Haro had mentioned his uncle to her, and indeed, they had caught brief sight of him when first entering Woldwick's grounds, but his odd appearance, his reputed eccentricity, and his failure to introduce himself to the Hastings upon arrival had done nothing to endear him.

Shy as he was of strangers, Uncle Harold was still a model of politeness when they were forced upon him. "Haro, my boy," said the old man, fixing his eye on Arabella. "Aren't you going to introduce me to this young lady?"

"But of course!" said Haro, taking Arabella's hand and presenting his fiancée to the elderly gentleman.

"Delighted to make your acquaintance," said Uncle Harold. "You put me quite in mind of the Countess of St. Petersburg when she was young."

Eda and Torin both began to giggle. One of Uncle Harold's favorite stories was how he had almost convinced the aforementioned countess to run away with him in the long-ago days of youth.

Assuming they were having a laugh at her expense, Arabella stiffened.

"And how do you like our winter woodlands?" asked the elderly gentleman, his skin still pink from an exhilarating walk through the landscape.

"To be honest, I find the woods a little too close," said Arabella. "I hope to have them cut back a few furlongs in the spring to allow more sunshine in the house and on the gardens."

Great-Uncle Harold stared at her as if she had just indicated a wish to chop off the Archbishop of Canterbury's head. "Ah, I see," he murmured after a moment. "An ambitious project, indeed, but ill-advised, most ill-advised. The trees are the soul of the place, you know, and poor old Woldwick would be quite dispirited to be shorn of her sylvan glory."

Arabella smiled condescendingly. "Yes, but I think the feelings of the inmates of the house are of rather more importance than the feelings of the house itself. And I find it quite dispiriting to have all the rooms so much in shadow. It will be a vast improvement, I promise you."

And as Uncle Harold continued to stare openmouthed, Arabella came closer to Haro and curled one hand possessively around his arm.

Haro swallowed, painfully. He had not realized that Arabella's plans for the place were fully settled, at least in her mind. It would be a bitter pill for many to swallow when she made good on her ideas for improvement. And however aghast Uncle Harold might be at her pruning back the woods, an eccentric recluse like him could have little power to combat the wishes of the new Lady Anglesford.

If Uncle Harold's appearance came as a shock to Arabella, the appearance of a mysterious stranger later that afternoon proved just as disconcerting to her fiancé, the earl. The betrothed pair had just finished a chilly promenade through the gardens when an unknown rider approached on the road.

The Emisons were expecting no guests, and so naturally, Haro squinted hard to see who the visitor could be. "That's not a county man," he said, judging by the great number of capes that decorated the rider's shoulders. "Come," he said to his fiancée. "Shall we see who it is?"

Arabella, who had also been straining her eyes to discover the visitor's identity, agreed—although when they came within shouting distance of the rider, she stumbled on the slick cobblestones of the driveway and almost turned immediately to go back inside the house.

"Miss Hastings!" said the rider, dismounting with alacrity. His face was all aglow from the brisk ride in the wintry air. "I was told that I could find you here and...that you were engaged to be married." He cast a questioning glance at the tall, blond man beside her.

Arabella held tightly to Haro's arm, perhaps to forestall another fall on the frosty cobblestones. "Ah, Monsieur Bayeux," she said formally, and then, in explanation to Haro, she added, "This is Philippe Bayeux, an architect that my father has employed more than once."

Haro noted that he was a handsome young man of middling height, whose nose as well as his name bespoke his French ancestry. "Pleased to make your acquaintance," said Haro, politeness keeping him from inquiring what the deuce the fellow was doing at Woldwick which was a good half hour's ride from the village.

Arabella trained her clear brown eyes on the unexpected guest. "I have invited him here to draw up some plans for renovations to the western wing of the house."

Monsieur Bayeux opened his mouth to say something then shut it again as if he had thought better of it.

"Renovations to the west wing?" asked Haro in surprise. He swallowed uncomfortably, unsure whether to address this issue with a stranger present. "You've mentioned nothing to me on the subject—"

"Oh, yes," said Arabella quickly. "I did not wish to ask your opinion until I had some concrete plans to show you. It is so hard to speak in vague generalities regarding architecture. But I do think that the west wing will need some updating in the Palladian style. It looks positively pre-Conquest as it is. Once Monsieur Bayeux has made some drawings, we can make a decision, yes?" She smiled encouragingly at Haro and at Bayeux as well.

Haro almost thundered out a "No!" But he remembered, before it was too late, that if it were not for the mill owner's money, he would soon have no control over Woldwick at all. It was best to be conciliatory, and perhaps, with a little time, he could dispel this notion of remodeling that had come upon Arabella so suddenly.

"I suppose the housekeeper can prepare a room for our guest," said Haro in slow, measured tones.

"*Certainement*, I can begin the drawings," said the visitor just as slowly. His dark, handsome face was clouded with some emotion which Haro could not decipher, and his eyes held a disconcerting intensity.

"Excellent," said Arabella with a briskness that matched the outside air. "Let's come inside then, shall we?" And leading Haro by the arm, she entered the main door of the house as if she were already mistress there.

William Hastings, it turned out, was just as surprised to see Philippe Bayeux as the young earl had been. As he returned from his day trip to the village, it had begun to sleet, and he found the others watching the dreary day out of the windows of the great room. With a quick hello to Haro, Mr. Hastings stomped over to the fire in the hearth to warm himself, rubbing his hands before the lively flames. When he turned around to warm his ample backside, he caught sight of the new visitor on the sofa and started visibly.

Monsieur Bayeux's eyes dropped, and no word of greeting passed between the two men. "Arabella," said the mill owner, clearing his throat ominously. "Come here." Retiring into a small alcove just off the drawing room, the father and daughter conducted a private conversation, although Mr. Hastings' gruff whisper was loud enough to be heard by those nearest to that side of the room.

"What is he doing here?"

Arabella's soft voice gave a lengthy and inaudible explanation.

"I will not abide it!"

Her hand plucked at his sleeve. She seemed to be entreating him not to make a scene.

The scene had already been made, however, and it was only the good breeding of the Emison family that made them feign ignorance to it. "And where did you receive your training in the field of architecture?" asked the Countess of Anglesford, trying to divert embarrassment from her new guest. No matter how unexpected or unwelcome he might be, a true hostess must disguise those facts.

"In France, my lady," said Monsieur Bayeux. The hint of Gallic accent in his voice indicated that he had probably been born there as well.

"Such a lovely country," said Eda, more for the sake of entering the conversation than from any sincere sentiment. Her blue eyes glinted devilishly, and Haro could see that she was up to no good. "And was it in France that you first met Miss Hastings?" Whatever embarrassment the Countess of Anglesford was trying to cover up, Eda was determined to bring out into the open.

Bayeux colored a little and gave a cautious answer. "No, I first met Mr. Hastings and his daughter in London, after I had come across the Channel to practice my craft."

"Miss Hastings is no doubt a great admirer of yours—of your work, I mean," continued Eda archly. Her eyes flicked over the Frenchman's dark, handsome face.

Haro stood up sharply and, casting Eda a look of menace, began to pace in front of the fire that Mr. Hastings had abandoned so abruptly. It was vexing enough to think that Arabella had made clandestine plans to renovate his boyhood home without Eda insinuating that there was some other motive in the architect's visit.

But despite Eda's leading statements, Bayeux would not be herded into saying anything untoward. "Yes, Miss Hastings has kindly expressed interest in many of my models and completed projects."

By this time, the whispered conference in the alcove had come to an end, and the Hastings—having come to an accord—rejoined the others.

"Well, Bayeux," said the portly mill owner, imbuing his voice with a joviality that his earlier reaction belied, "Arabella tells me you'll get started right away with plans for the new wing here at Woldwick."

"That is my intention," replied Bayeux, bowing his head courteously, "although I seem to have left some of my drafting materials behind, so I shall have to go into the village tomorrow to procure some. The horse I have is hired, so perhaps I might return him and borrow one from the stables?"

"Very good, very good," said Mr. Hastings, lending out one of the Emisons' mounts without so much as a by your leave. He turned to Haro with a coarse little laugh. "I suppose you did not expect me to make improvements on my investment so rapidly. Well, neither did I, my lord! Neither did I!"

9

HARO HAD BARELY RETIRED for the night before he heard a gentle tap at his bedroom door. Pulling on his Chinese-patterned dressing gown, he turned the door handle and found himself face to face with his great-uncle. "Haro, my boy," said Uncle Harold, walking in and making himself at home. "Do you have time for a small drink and perhaps a smattering of conversation?"

"Of course," said Haro, casually filling two glasses from the decanter on the bedside table. He gave his great-uncle the single armchair and flung himself onto the Roman couch at the foot of the bed.

"I've had a bit of a shock today," said Uncle Harold, hunching forward in his chair and rolling his glass back and forth between his hands. "A bit of a shock, I must say."

"Oh, yes?" Haro had an inkling of what—or who—had delivered that shock to his aged relative. He could see that Uncle Harold was struggling with how to phrase his complaint, perhaps from an inbred delicacy toward the weaker sex or perhaps from a sensitivity toward the young earl's feelings.

Haro generously flushed the subject out into the open. "Is it something to do with Miss Hastings, my fiancée whom you met this morning?"

"Yes, that's it! The tall, brown-eyed miss," said Uncle Harold, wagging a finger with excitement. He took a quick swig from the tumbler of brandy. "She's your bride-to-be, you say?"

Haro nodded. "We were betrothed just last weekend."

Uncle Harold raised a gnarled hand to his head and pulled at his gray hair with concern. "I don't mean to meddle—the last thing a young man wants is an old fool meddling in his affairs—but this Miss Hastings seems a very precipitate young woman. No sense of tradition, my boy. No sense of stability. You may not have heard her this morning, but I believe she actually stated that the woods at Woldwick were unsuitable and should be cleared!"

The old man's eyes opened wide with distress; Haro reflected that his distress would be considerably increased if he knew Miss Hastings' further plans to rebuild the west wing of the manor house.

"It is not at all the kind of attitude one might wish in the next Countess of Anglesford!" He paused and looked anxiously at his great-nephew, trying to see if he had gone too far and given offense. "Of course, I am sure that in other matters Miss Hastings is a very unexceptionable young lady, possessed of many good qualities. Although, I must confess, I had thought you quite taken with someone else. Someone else altogether."

"I may have had a modicum of affection for another young lady in the past,"—Haro shrank from mentioning Eda's name, especially to one who knew them both so well—"but circumstances have altered that."

The old man's eyebrows lifted and his face displayed his puzzlement. Haro smiled grimly. Apparently, none of the family had thought to inform Uncle Harold of the debacle that had overset the Emisons' fortunes.

Briefly, he outlined the tale of his late father's financial imprudence and, with as much tact as possible, explained the importance of his new connection with the Hastings. "Miss Hastings is a very amiable and attractive young lady, and though she is perhaps a little too forthright with her own tastes, I fear that her father's fortune more than makes up for the failing."

"So you've become a fortune hunter then, my boy," said Uncle Harold, and Haro heard—or perhaps merely imagined—a hint of disappointment in his voice. But before Haro could excuse his own conduct, the old man's voice broke into a cackle. "You silly gudgeon! Why did you not apply to me for the money? I'm rich enough, you know. I traveled the world in my day and brought back a chest of treasures from the East. Rubies, diamonds, gifts from Indian rajahs and the caliph of Baghdad. It's enough to pay for Woldwick and more, and I'd sooner give it away now than save it for my funeral pyre."

Haro shifted uncomfortably on the couch. Throughout his boyhood, he had heard his great-uncle's stories a hundred times, how he went to Russia and Cathay and back again, how he stole the Duke of Bavaria's horses from out of his stables, how he nearly inveigled the Countess of St. Petersburg into running away with him. But whenever he had asked his parents, "Is it true what Uncle Harold says?" they had shaken their heads somberly.

"He fought in the wars, you know," Haro's mother had said sympathetically, "and the poor man is a little touched in the head."

"He's never had any blunt that I've caught sight of," Haro's father had said dubiously, "and he's eaten at my expense ever since your grandfather died."

And so, thanks to his parents' common sense, Haro had grown up knowing that his Uncle Harold's stories were merely fairy tales and that the fabulous fortune he had amassed was the creation of a troubled mind. "You're most generous, Uncle," he said now, trying not to wound the old gentleman and exercising the same sensitivity that the other had shown earlier. "But I think your diamonds and rubies had better stay safe in your treasure chest. The betrothal to Miss Hastings is already settled. It's entered the banns, and I cannot beg off now."

He patted the old man kindly on the shoulder. "I'll speak to her, however, about the woods and their wonders. She's a stranger here, you know. Once she becomes more familiar with the place, I'm sure she'll come to love it as we all do."

After Uncle Harold had taken his leave and Haro was finally able to settle into his bed, he found that sleep did not come as easily as he would have wished. He had spent the last couple days reconciling himself to his lot as the husband of Miss Hastings. But now, at the advent of the architect, he felt all his original anxieties return. How much did he really know about this slim, brown-eyed girl and her title-seeking father? Was this highhanded decision to remodel Woldwick a harbinger of what was to come now that the Hastings pair held the purse strings?

All night, these concerns gnawed at him, forbidding him his rest, and in the morning he decided that—for his own sanity—he must have the matter out with Arabella. She might be the daughter of the wealthiest mill owner in England, but he was the Earl of Anglesford, and devil take him if he let some tradesman's chit walk all over him. If he did not establish who was to be master of the house now, he might never have a chance to regain his authority.

Yesterday's sleet had turned to snow overnight and then stopped, leaving a soft layer of white on the ground. After the family had partaken of a large breakfast, Haro invited Arabella to drive out with him in the curricle. Changing into a warm pelisse trimmed with fur, Miss Hastings was soon ready for their outing. She seemed determined to make herself agreeable, perhaps in penitence for yesterday's awkwardness. She complimented Haro on the ease with which he handled the reins and interested herself in every view of the countryside that he pointed out.

Flattered by her smiles and companionability, the Haro could feel his resolution slipping away. But if he did not address the subject now, when would he next have the opportunity?

They had come to a narrow stretch of road running through a stand of leafless, white birches. He slowly reined in the horses, and the curricle came to a halt. "Arabella...."

"What is it, my darling?" She pulled a warm hand out of her muff and placed it on his thigh. He could feel the heat of it through the fabric of his breeches.

He swallowed convulsively, completely taken off guard. He had never expected a well-bred young lady to be so free with her attentions.

"This plan of yours, with the architect, and the west wing, and...."

"Oh, it's just an idea is all," cooed Arabella in conciliatory tones. She lifted her hand and brought it slowly to his face. Haro froze as she began to trace his features, her fingertips feathering against his cheek, his nose, his lips. "If you don't like the plans Philippe draws up, we can call off the whole thing."

"Truly?" said Haro, curious and confused and uncomfortable all at the same time. Her nearness was so befuddling that he failed to notice her use of the architect's first name.

"Truly," she echoed, leaning her face forward and bringing her lips to where her fingers had been. "Now, where were we?"

"Oh, Arabella, I say—" But Haro's objections were overruled. The horses were forced to stamp irritably in the cold for a full quarter of an hour while the curricle's passengers tarried in the road. But the shivering horses were not the only thing the Earl of Anglesford and Miss Hastings ignored. Arabella was so intent on becoming better acquainted that they also failed to notice the moving shadow behind the shivering stand of birch trees.

Only later, as they turned the curricle around to return to the house did they sight the far-away figure of someone leading a horse that appeared to be lame in one foot.

From the window of the music room upstairs, Eda watched Haro and Arabella tumble out of the curricle and walk hand in hand into the house while Jimmy, the groom, stepped up into the curricle's seat and took it away to the stables. She walked to the staircase, looked down, and froze in place.

Haro was assisting Arabella in removing her furs. He teasingly placed his cold hands on her red cheeks. Arabella giggled. Then Eda heard Haro call for Cook to send tea into the morning room, and clinging to each other's arms, they went away to warm themselves by the fire.

Eda felt numb, and she had not even been the one to go out in the cold. But that feeling passed quickly and gave way to a rising tide of anger. Swallowing hard, she went into the music room and pulled out a particularly stormy piece by Beethoven. Her fingers thundered through the minor chords, unleashing the feelings inside of her on the keys of the pianoforte.

"I say, you're making it rather hard to read a book in peace!" said a friendly but irritated voice from the doorway.

Her hands dropped onto the keys with a discordant clang. "Sorry, Torin. You could always read downstairs?"

"I tried...and almost cast up my accounts seeing those two lovebirds in the morning room. If they were sitting any closer to each other, she would be on his lap. I thought this whole affair was going to be a marriage of convenience, but Haro looks as smitten as that daft chap Romeo."

Eda, whose romantic relationship with Haro had always been more amicable than amorous, gritted her teeth. "What a cake he's making of himself!" she muttered, and added a few other invectives, a credit to the Irish captain who had fathered her.

All those months in London, he had never spent an afternoon mooning over her like this. They had been too busy riding in Hyde Park, taking tea with one of the duchesses, or planning for some amusement at the opera to make calf's eyes at each other.

Had he ever really been in love with her? Or had their relationship just been a comfortable state of affairs that he had resolved to formalize into matrimony? If he ever had resolved that. Lady Anglesford had intimated as much, but Haro had never declared himself outright.

At first, when he had thrown her over, she had had the consolation that he had probably done so for the sake of familial duty, but it seemed now that duty was not the only deciding factor.

Eda stamped her foot. It was not to be borne. He must be punished for his desertion. She started down the stairs, only to see Lady Anglesford coming from the direction of the defiled morning room.

"Oh, my dear! Would you care to drive into the village with me?" Lady Anglesford's small hand clutched Eda's arm and tried to turn her the other way. "Mr. Hastings is reading his newspaper in there—let's not disturb him. Come back upstairs and we shall get our pelisses."

"No, thank you," said Eda firmly, grateful to her aunt for trying to spare her from witnessing the painful scene but also determined to stand her ground and execute some mischief.

She peered out the window in the entrance hall and saw their French visitor coming back to the house from the stables. "I mean to sketch all this afternoon, and now that Monsieur Bayeux has returned with his drafting materials, perhaps we can keep each other company with our pencils?"

Lady Anglesford sighed and slipped back into the morning room, doubtless out of concern to invest the situation with more propriety rather than any real pleasure in observing the burgeoning romance.

Eda kept her eyes at the window and assaulted the architect as soon as he entered with a demand for company.

"Oh, absolument!" said the Frenchman with a wan smile that belied his words. His chiseled face had dark circles under the eyes, signs that he also had not slept well, perhaps due to an unfamiliar bed. He had been to the village and back that morning and had procured a great stock of paper, a straight edge, a triangle, and the requisite writing utensils.

Judging from his reaction, Eda could tell that the man was not entirely keen on sharing a drawing table with her, but she refused to acknowledge the possibility of a rebuff. "The morning room has the best light," she said—a fact that was not entirely a fabrication. "Let's sit there and put our pencils to work."

As they entered the morning room, Eda had the satisfaction of seeing both Haro and Arabella startle in their seats. Haro made a sudden movement to pull his hand away from Arabella's, but her long fingers held on to his and would not be denied.

Eda took Bayeux's elbow and steered him over to the table by the window. "How I love to see a real architect draw! You've had the chance to survey the building and the grounds, and you must have such grand notions piling up in your head of how to renovate our dear old Woldwick."

"*Oui, très grandes*," echoed the architect unconvincingly. He reached into his bag of drafting materials and pulled out a square edge and a bit of India rubber and set it down tidily by the side of his paper. Eda smiled at him encouragingly. He picked up a piece of sharpened charcoal and began. Eda wrinkled her nose and set to work on a sketch of her own, glancing up every so often to consider the subject of her new portrait.

10

"I AM SORRY THINGS are so dull today," Lady Anglesford said to Mr. Hastings. The mill owner had taken up residence in a high-backed chair by the side of the great hearth, one that watched the door of the large morning room so that he could oversee the comings and goings of the rest while he perused his newspaper. "We have a few families nearby with whom we visit—Sir Robert Blount and his wife always dine with us at least once while we're in the country, and their son Stephen is a friend of Haro's—but with my husband's death so recent, we will not have visitors calling."

Mr. Hastings dismissed her apology with a wave of the hand. "No matter, no matter. I'm sure we'll have visitors enough once the nuptials are celebrated. The whole countryside will be coming around to gawk at the new Lady Anglesford. Won't they, my dear?" He smiled benevolently at his daughter and rubbed a gleeful thumb over the fob of his too-large pocket watch.

"Which reminds me, my boy,"—he turned to Haro—"we need to set a date for the happy day!"

The scratching of pencils ceased entirely at the table over by the window. Both Eda and Philippe Bayeux had been working busily on their drawings for the last hour, and now, it seemed, they had come to a stopping place. Arabella sat up a little straighter on the sofa and brushed the back of her hand against Haro's. Torin, who had wandered in to find his Vitruvius, stared open-mouthed.

"Oh, but it would be most improper to set a wedding date while we are still in blacks," said Lady Anglesford, her mouth quivering.

"Dashed right it would!" chimed in Torin, too annoyed to mind his language in mixed company.

Mother and son looked earnestly at the heir of the house, expecting him to lend them support.

Haro, who had spent the last twenty-four hours becoming further and further enmeshed in the net that Arabella had spread, tried to couch his words with care. "It's not unheard of for a wedding to be held while a house is in mourning."

"Yes, I'm sure such things happen all the time...in Australia," said Eda, "but things are a little different when one does not reside in a penal colony."

Haro glared at the window and found Eda returning his glare measure for measure while Bayeux leaned forward in his chair at the other side of the drawing table. The thought of a precipitate wedding was discomposing, but he had no wish for Eda to think that his resolve was weakening or that *she* had won.

"I happen to know," said Haro, "that the Marquis Vitalis was wed while his family was still in blacks, and I can't be positive, but I seem to remember that Sir Henry Huntingdon was as well. And in any case"—Haro rose from the sofa and drew himself up to his full height—"I believe the date is for me and my intended's family to settle." He threw a conciliatory bone to his mother. "Though I would, of course, like to consider your wishes, Mama."

"Thank you, my dear," said Lady Anglesford. "But perhaps it is best if you settle it with Arabella and her father and leave me out of it. I am feeling a little faint, and I think I will retire to my room."

The room quieted as they watched the small woman get to her feet and walk toward the French doors, placing a steadying hand on the patterned wallpaper as she made her way out.

"What say you then?" asked Mr. Hastings, clapping his hands together. "Next month?"

Mr. Bayeux, sitting at the table, was suddenly overtaken by a fit of coughing and Eda quietly summoned a footman to fetch him a glass of water.

Arabella looked up at Haro with calculating eyes and reached out her hand for his. Uncomfortable at this public display of affection, he forced himself to cradle her fingers in his palm. The room, already warm from the blazing fire, grew warmer all of a sudden with the stares and the sensations of Arabella's fingertips, and Haro had to resist the urge to loosen his cravat.

"Next month?" said Arabella, looking around the room and considering each of its occupants in turn, the expression in her eyes almost one of challenge. "Is that enough time for everything to be ready?"

"Ha!" laughed the mill owner. "You are a clever one, my girl. I imagine the earl is champing at the bit to have you, but *we* must have a little time to order the finest fabrics, send for exotic foods, commission the best entertainment. A cathedral wedding, I think. In London."

"What? London?" Torin folded his arms akimbo. "All of the earls of Anglesford have been married at Woldwick. It is tradition."

Hastings snorted. "No, no. It is too small, too dark, too dreary. We must have the wedding somewhere much larger, and much closer in—somewhere the rest of the ton can easily come to see my daughter wed an earl. What say you, Monsieur Bayeux? Is there a building in London grand enough to house the sight?"

The hawk-nosed Frenchman frowned and set down his glass of water. "I would not know, *monsieur*."

"You are an architect. You must know your buildings. Where?"

"I could not say." Bayeux slipped his paper and drawing materials into his satchel. "And now, if you will excuse me, I have an appointment in the village."

"An appointment?" Mr. Hastings' eyes narrowed suspiciously. "You just arrived in this county. Whom could you possibly know hereabouts?"

The architect rose to his feet. "When I went into the village earlier this morning to procure my drawing materials, I inquired after stone masons and found a man of good repute. I must confer with him about the materials available locally for use in this renovation."

"Ah, well." Mr. Hastings relaxed. "Very good, very good."

"Will you be returning in time to dine with us?" asked Eda, playing the gracious hostess now that Lady Anglesford had retired from the room.

"No." Bayeux sent a glance to the sofa where Arabella and Haro were seated cozily. "I think not."

By the time dinner came—unfashionably early as usual since Woldwick's cook was accustomed to keeping country hours—the wedding date had been fixed for three weeks from the following Saturday.

"That is such short notice," said Torin, seizing fork and knife in either hand, "that I may not be able to attend. I shall consult my calendar, but...." He shrugged and took a bite of jellied eel.

"What social engagement could you possibly have?" said Haro. He would have added the phrase, "you young twit!" if his betrothed had not been present. "You said it yourself—we're in mourning. I doubt you've accepted any invitations to join a shooting party or dance a reel that weekend."

Torin swallowed and laid his fork down with a clatter. "My old tutor Mr. Swaine has invited me to stay with him in Dorchester."

"I'm sure you can easily send him a note and change your visit to another date." Arabella raised her perfect eyebrows and gave Torin a chilly stare.

"I'm sure you can just as easily change your wedding to another date!"

"Torin!" Lady Anglesford, who had recovered her spirits enough to descend for dinner, looked in need of her hartshorn once more.

"Mind your words," said Haro, with a hint of menace in his voice. With his easygoing nature, it was easy for them to forget that he was half a head taller than everyone in the room, weighed fourteen stone or more, and could knock a man down—especially one as slight as Torin—without much exertion.

"No need to take offense on my account, darling." Arabella placed a hand gently on Haro's wrist, her supposedly conciliatory words causing the divide between the two brothers to grow even deeper. "If Torin cannot change his visit, then he cannot. I'm sure we will all be sad to have him absent, but then, his presence is hardly essential to the ceremony, is it?"

A piece of jellied eel fell from Torin's fork onto his plate.

"Hardly essential?" Eda's mouth dropped open in disbelief. "I'm sure Haro would wish Torin to stand up with him."

"There are certainly plenty of acceptable gentlemen who would be willing to fulfill that task." Arabella turned to Haro. "Isn't Guy Pontipale a particular friend of yours?"

Haro's nose wrinkled involuntarily. "A friend, perhaps. Though not exactly a particular one."

"That fellow who introduced you two?" Hastings nodded. "He'll do."

And so the question of Haro's best man was decided without reference to Haro's wishes in the matter.

Arabella, however, was not finished with the conversation. "And, of course, if you wish to go straight to Oxford from this Mr. Swaine's house, you'll be nearly there. Such a fortuitous proximity."

Torin was taken aback. "Must you keep harping on about that? What difference does it make to you whether I go to Oxford or not?"

"It would make things a little less crowded, don't you think? They say that newlyweds need a little space of their own, and there are"—she glanced around the table—"so many of you."

"Yes," snorted Eda. "It's a pity that Lady Anglesford decided to have as many brats as a fishwife from Billingsgate. Haro, Torin...." She counted on her fingers. "Why, I do believe that's all of them."

"Oh, but you must not forget to count yourself, dear Eda." Arabella smoothed a hand over her pale pink dress. "I daresay you take up as much room in the family as any daughter. Perhaps more."

"A pity you can't pack me off to Oxford along with Torin!"

"Pack you off to Oxford?" Arabella tittered. "Certainly not. I don't think it would suit you, nor you it. There are other places far more appropriate to house unmarried ladies with no prospects."

Haro's eyes darted quickly to Eda, on tenterhooks to see what response she would have to that jibe. To his surprise, however, no words issued from her mouth. Her face looked as motionless as an alabaster statue and her dark blue eyes as hard as glass. And despite the frustration she had created in him over the past week, he would not for all the world have her hurt.

A feeling of cold desperation welled up inside of him. He had thought that he was sacrificing his own happiness to secure the future for all of them but it now appeared that he was sacrificing others' happiness in the bargain and that he had grossly overestimated his own ability to manage the situation.

11

EDA HAD BARELY SHUT her bedroom door behind her before the tears came—thick, fast, angry, and heartbroken. Dinner tonight had been intolerable. To hold a wedding while the family was still in mourning for Uncle Edward? It was more than insensitive—it was inhuman. And for Haro to agree to it? Eda snatched up a pillow from the bed and began to beat it with her fists.

She had expected Arabella to turn on her when she stood up for Torin at the table, but she had not been prepared for the concentrated power of the venom that dripped from Arabella's fangs. If Arabella would turn Torin out of doors, she certainly would not stop from ousting Eda. It was a thought she could not even bear to dwell on.

After dinner, the ladies had retreated to the drawing room while the men sipped their port. Lady Anglesford had talked incessantly. Eda suspected her aunt was terrified of what her headstrong ward or her future daughter-in-law might say to each other and wanted to allow no opportunity for them to exchange words.

Arabella, however, seemed to prefer to save her cutting wit for Haro's presence. She spotted an old book on the table that Torin had left out and sat on the sofa intensely engrossed in its pages.

Eda casually glanced over to see the name on the cover of the volume—De Architectura, by Vitruvius. Just the title made her loathe Arabella even more. Previously, she had enjoyed imagining her as too vapid for anything more than a Mrs. Radcliffe novel, but now it seemed she had intelligence as well as money...as well as Haro.

There had been another scene when the gentlemen had rejoined them. Torin spotted his book immediately and saw that Arabella had dog-eared two or three of the pages. It was an action amounting to sacrilege in his code of ethics, and he had laid into her like a broadside from one of Admiral Nelson's frigates.

"Oh, fustian!" Haro had said, taking Arabella's part. "You obviously don't care enough about the book to put it away properly, so why should you care about a few bent corners?"

Torin had retired in a rage, and Eda had slipped away soon afterwards, taking out her spleen on the embroidered pillow instead of on Miss Hastings...or Haro.

Her aunt's lady's maid knocked on the door to help her dress for bed, and she tried to compose herself enough to keep from embarrassing a servant.

"I beg your pardon, Stamford," she said, wiping away a stream of tears that refused to stop running.

"Oh, don't be afraid of a few tears," clucked the plump, blond dresser. She unfastened Eda's black dress and took it over to the wardrobe. "Her ladyship did warn me that you might not be yourself."

At the beginning of the season, her aunt had asked if she would like her own lady's maid—a French one, perhaps, as was the fashion. But Eda, who preferred simplicity in her toilette, had declined, continuing to borrow the offices of Alice Stamford, her aunt's maid, as she had when she was not yet out of the schoolroom. Eda frequently dressed her own hair, but it was essential to have someone help her lace and unlace her dresses in the back—although if Arabella had her way and sent her to a ladies' seminary or a workhouse or Australia, she would need to contrive without a maid altogether.

Stamford did not linger, and Eda, now dressed in her nightgown, took down her hair herself, shaking out the black curls. Thankful that the scullery maid had built up a large fire in the grate, she slipped beneath the thick bedclothes and tried to sleep.

The events of the day kept arising in her mind, however—images of Arabella's hand tangled with Haro's on the sofa, the sound of Arabella's tittering laugh as she said the word "Oxford," the calculated gleam in Arabella's eye and she made Haro jump to the tune her father played.

She rolled over onto her back. What was it that people said? "He who marries in haste repents at leisure." Haro was making a mistake he'd soon regret. Someone needed to tell him, before it was too late. But who would do it? And would he listen?

She grimaced. No, Haro was in too deep. And the Hastings, having got their claws into him, would never let go without a fight. She could think of only one possibility that might send Arabella packing from Woldwick. But was she willing to risk that? Even for Haro, did she dare?

Haro was interrupted again that night after retiring to his bedchamber. It was beginning to become a pattern, and an annoying one at that. At the sound of the gentle tap, he swung his legs crossly over the side of the bed and—without even bothering to put on his dressing gown—threw open the door. "Now, see here, Uncle Harold! It's dashed late—"

The visitor in the hallway was most definitely not Uncle Harold, and before Haro could protest, his room had been invaded. He stared openmouthed. It was Eda, although a version of Eda that he had never seen before. Her long black tresses tumbled wildly about her shoulders, and she was not only missing her black dress but also her petticoat and her stays. The thin, white fabric of her nightdress was the only thing that kept her from being unclad entirely.

"Good Lord! It's cold in here!" she uttered matter-of-factly, setting her candle down on a small table near the door. "Why did you not have the servants add a log to the fire when you retired?"

"If you had troubled to put on some more clothes before visiting me, you might not have found things so chilly." He averted his eyes.

She looked down, as if she had at that moment realized that she was not, in fact, dressed. "If you were a gentleman, you would give me your dressing gown."

"If you were a lady, you would already be wearing one." He snatched up the article in question and tossed it to her and continued to look away as she belted it tightly around her small waist. "What do you want, Eda? You oughtn't be here, you know."

"Oughtn't I?" she asked, a devilish little smile playing over her red lips. She sat down defiantly in the armchair that Uncle Harold had occupied on the previous night. "I thought it would be as good a time as any other to have a little tête-à-tête." She took a deep breath. "I see you've been becoming better acquainted with your betrothed."

"Yes," said Haro, seating himself cautiously on the Roman couch across from her. "I hope that you will as well, and indeed, the whole family since she is to be one of us. If you could only feign a little pleasantness, we should all rub along together much more smoothly."

"Do you find *her* pleasant?"

Haro looked at her warily. "Of course." It was not strictly true, but there was nothing else to say.

"Hmm." Eda shivered in her chair.

Taking pity on her, Haro knelt down by the fire and spent a few moments resurrecting the banked coals into a blaze.

"Thank you," said Eda, her hard look softening a little. "I will admit that it has been decidedly *un*pleasant watching you disport yourself with her all day—although at least we were spared the sight of your courting in the curricle."

Haro flushed red to the roots of his hair. "Who told you about that?" Nothing too improper had happened among the trees, although Arabella had been extraordinarily affectionate and far more knowledgeable about kissing than any young lady had the right to be....

"Never you mind!" She leaned forward with a flash of intensity, and Haro's dressing gown, which was far too big for her, gaped open in the front revealing a flash of fair skin below her neck. "And it seems you've been bullied into setting a wedding date."

Haro wanted to object to that description of events, but if he was honest with himself, that was exactly what had happened. Dash it all—what a mull he'd made of things!

"Listen, Haro," said Eda frankly. "Perhaps it's time to start exerting yourself a little—let the new Lady Anglesford know who is lord and master here."

"What on earth do you mean?"

"What do I mean? If you weren't blind and besotted, you would know that she's vexing us all to no end. I'll say nothing about myself. But your mother's made herself ill worrying about the changes that chit will make to the house, and you saw what happened with Torin tonight. He's likely to do something rash if she doesn't stop ordering him about like a trained poodle."

"What are you suggesting that I do?"

"You must say something! You must make her mind you!"

Haro recalled how his resolve to do just that today had fizzled out like a torch in the rain. "I don't know how necessary that is—"

"Well, if you don't know, then you're a fool. You're handing your title to Hastings on a mother-of-pearl platter, and you're handing your manhood to his daughter with permission for her to trample it."

"Oh, come now!" Everything she had said he had already told himself in private. But she had set up his back now, and he could not admit his folly in front of her. "I will conduct myself with Arabella as I see fit."

"Very well then. Do as you like. Although you should know that a woman likes a man who has a little backbone underneath his coat from Weston's." Her eyes flicked disdainfully over the open front of his nightshirt. Haro suddenly felt self-conscious, realizing that he was as dishabille as she was.

"If matters continue in this way, then I warn you—I will no longer be able to continue using my best behavior towards her."

"Best behavior? Is that what you've been using up until now?"

"Yes." Her chin jutted out defiantly. She stood up, and he followed suit. The sitting area in Haro's room was small, and they were very nearly face to face in the dim room. "My father was an Irishman and a soldier, Haro. I'm not afraid of a brawl." She picked up her candle, casting a warm glow over her white face and fine collarbones.

Haro could not help admiring the flash in her eyes, while at the same time deploring the sentiments she had expressed. "Stop talking twaddle." She opened the door to the corridor, and he dropped his voice to a whisper to avoid waking the rest of the household. "I'll have no brawling at Woldwick."

"And, of course, your word is law, Lord Anglesford," she responded, stepping out into the hallway. Haro had the distinct impression that she was mocking him. "Good night," she said, peeking back over her shoulder, "and pleasant dreams."

He stood at the door and watched her go until her candle-lit silhouette disappeared at the end of the corridor.

12

HARO WOKE THE NEXT morning wondering whether Eda's nocturnal visit had merely been a mirage from an overtired mind.

Garth, his valet, was laying out a pair of black stockings clocked with gray on the bed when he cleared his throat ominously. "I don't know if I'm speaking out of place, m'lord, but there's a rumor going round the servants' hall that Miss Swanycke has a Chinese-patterned dressing gown that looks strikingly like yours draped across the chair in her boudoir."

"My dressing gown?" Haro's eyes opened as large as cannonballs. There was no point in denying the gown was his. His valet knew every stitch of his clothing by memory. Fiend seize it! Why had he let her slip out into the corridor with his dressing gown still on? Why had he ever let her into his room in the first place?

"Yes, m'lord. Jane the scullery maid saw it when she was lighting the bedroom fires. Normally, I would mind my own business, m'lord, but it seems with such important guests in the house, a rumor like this—"

"Yes, yes. You were quite right to say something. Who all knows?"

"By now, all of the staff, m'lord."

"Including Mr. Hastings' valet and Miss Hastings' lady's maid?"

Garth pursed his lips. "Perhaps not. They've held themselves aloof from the rest of us—a little too lofty for their own good. But Mrs. Rollo, the companion, spends considerable time with the housekeeper."

Haro groaned. "One can only hope she keeps as quiet with her employers as she has with us in the drawing room."

Garth grunted doubtfully but had no suggestions to offer. He had done his duty by his master, and now it was up to the earl to sort out the disaster in the making.

After he had shrugged into his tight-fitting jacket, Haro headed downstairs with a sinking feeling in the pit of his stomach. He sat down several times at his writing desk to answer a little correspondence but rose again just as quickly, unable to concentrate on anything but the nightmare at hand. Would Arabella assume he had visited Eda's room in the middle of the night? Would this mean the end of their betrothal? Would that mean the end of Woldwick?

He cast aside his quill pen and paced in tortured anxiety, trying to calm himself enough to go in and join the others at breakfast. Taking a deep breath, he entered the breakfast room, feeling momentary relief when no accusations came flying in his general direction. He seated himself beside Arabella who gave him good morning with a smile.

"Ugh," said Torin, propping up his eyelids with his fingers. "I should have crawled back under the covers and asked Cook to send up my breakfast."

His mother covered a small yawn with her hand and lifted a cup of chocolate to her lips.

There was one person, however, who seemed unaffected by the dreary atmosphere. Eda swept into the room, dressed in a dark green dress that followed her figure and framed her black hair nicely. Haro was so distracted by his worries that he did not even notice that she had discarded the obligatory black mourning dress in favor of something far more alluring.

"And how are you this morning, dear Arabella?"

"Quite well," said Arabella, with a smile that was obviously forced. She reached lovingly for her betrothed's hand and placed it against her own cheek—as if to remind this presumptuous relation that Haro was quite as much hers today as he had been yesterday. Her lips brushed his wrist in purposeful accident.

Haro's heart began to settle its erratic beat. She had not heard. She *must* not have heard.

He thought of yesterday's curricle ride with Arabella out in the bare birch wood and her boldness at proclaiming her affection. He had been equal parts intrigued and repulsed, and in the end, he could not decide whether he found such behavior attractive. But then, he had little experience with courtship—the only other girl he had ever had a serious *tendre* for was Eda. And—this next thought came as a bit of a surprise—he had never given her anything more than a brotherly kiss on the cheek. Indeed, up until this last week, she had never behaved in anything more than a sisterly manner.

Haro took a deep breath, stuffing down the recollection of Eda appearing at his door in her nightdress last night and raising his blood in a manner that was decidedly not brotherly. He was engaged to Arabella. He would not think those thoughts.

Maybe he simply needed to meditate more deeply on Arabella's good qualities and stir up *that* interest for her. Haro reached over and traced his finger across Arabella's forehead and down her temple, tucking a perfectly formed curl behind her ear. The sensation seemed to please her, but it filled him with an even greater sense of anxiety inside.

Torin nearly choked on a bite of sausage. Lady Anglesford looked down at her cup of chocolate with pinched lips. Mrs. Rollo, had she been a true lady's companion and not simply a hired drudge, might have nudged her charge in rebuke, but as it was, she simply continued spooning her plain porridge into her even plainer face. Mr. Hastings was too immersed in his newspaper—and too complacent about his new conquest—to feel the revulsion radiating from the earl's relatives.

"Wonderful to hear that you are doing well!" continued Eda. "I was afraid all the gloom of Woldwick—with its dark trees and horrid curtains—might have dispirited you. But I see you are coping as best you can."

"And coping quite well," added Haro, "considering that she has even more vexatious things to deal with." He glared at Eda, his mind willing her to vacate the breakfast room. He could only hope that she had discreetly hidden the dressing gown before leaving her bedroom that morning.

But Eda was irrepressible, and she had no intention of leaving just yet. "There is something I wanted to show you, dear sister."

Haro's heart nearly stopped. Even the incorrigible Eda would have qualms about discussing her nocturnal adventures in front of the family over the breakfast table, would she not? But as the sparkle in Eda's eye brightened, Haro began to fear the worst had come upon him.

Eda darted over to the door and retrieved the item in question from a console table in the hallway. "Here is a sketch I made of Monsieur Bayeux yesterday." She placed it enthusiastically in Arabella's hands.

It was well executed, a near-perfect likeness of the man. Eda had toiled long over some of the features—the chiseled cheekbones, the noble forehead, the wavy hair. She had also imbued his eyes with such a smoldering quality that Philippe Bayeux looked like he was ready to come off the page and into the viewer's arms with intent to ravish.

Arabella's eyes widened, and her mouth fell open a little before she recovered her aplomb. "Very well executed," she said primly and made to hand it back to her fiancé's jealous relation.

"Oh, I thought maybe you would want to keep it? A little something to hang in your home?"

"Why would I want it?" There was an edge of warning in Arabella's voice.

"You should know that better than I," said Eda carelessly.

Haro thanked his lucky stars that the architect was absent from the breakfast room, for he doubted that Eda would have withheld the portrait even if its subject had been present. He had been fearing the appearance of the dressing gown and the explanation that must accompany it, but this sketch that Eda had produced was almost as disconcerting.

Arabella's chin rose. "Very well, I shall keep it. I will need some new artwork to display once I get rid of some of these ghastly oils. That one, for example." She pointed at a gilt frame containing a young woman seated amidst a Grecian-inspired landscape. If her hair had been black and not brown, it could have been a portrait of Eda herself. It was Helen, Eda's late mother, in a painting commissioned by the young Lady Anglesford before the Irish captain had charmed her cousin away.

At this comment, Eda's mocking manner vanished. She gave Arabella a look calculated to turn her into stone. Haro blinked his eyes to confirm that his cousin's coils of black hair had not actually turned into venomous snakes.

"The day you get rid of that painting is a day you will regret for the rest of your life—however short that may be."

"What's all this?" demanded William Hastings, putting down his newspaper at last and trying to make sense of the conversation. He did not like to hear anything at the breakfast table louder than jaws chewing, and all this commotion was starting to irritate him.

"I believe dear Miss Swanycke is threatening me," said Arabella, eyebrows arched, "though I'm certain it's all in fun."

"Eh?" grunted her portly father. He glanced from Eda to his daughter with a furrowed brow that did not quite apprehend the situation.

Just then Bayeux made his appearance. Arabella casually turned the sketch over on the table to avoid further comment from either the artist or the subject.

"Speaking of fun," interjected Haro, determined to distract from any further revelations, "perhaps you'd like to go out and see the pond. The footman tells me it's completely iced over from the cold spell we had last night. I'd love to show it to you." A brisk walk—without use of the horses—would be safe enough, and there would be no tittle-tattling servants near the ice.

"Time to sharpen up the old skates?" said Torin.

"Not quite." Haro shook his head. "It'll be a week or more before the ice is thick enough to bear our weight. But it is beautiful to look at, all sparkling like cut crystal."

"What a splendid idea!" said Eda, including herself in the invitation that had been meant for Arabella. "And perhaps you'd like to make a fourth and join us on our expedition, Monsieur Bayeux?"

The architect hesitated. "I have a good deal of work to do on the plans—"

"Nothing that can't wait. And I'm sure Miss Hastings would join with me in entreating your presence."

Arabella laid down her napkin, and Haro rose to his feet to pull out the chair for her. "Come if you like," she said with a shrug of indifference. She took Haro's hand as she stood and held onto it for a second or two before sliding her fingers down to the crook of his arm.

Philippe Bayeux's eyes narrowed. "I think I will accept your invitation, Miss Swanycke. I never cease to be amazed by the new things I see out in the country."

"Marvelous. Perhaps you'll have time to eat a little breakfast while the future Lady Anglesford and I put on our furs. Haro will keep you company. I'm sure you have a shared interest or two you could discuss while we ladies look for our muffs."

After the young ladies excused themselves, an uncomfortable silence settled on the room. The current Lady Anglesford took herself upstairs to her own sitting room, too overcome with anxiety to face more conversation with the house's inmates. Mrs. Rollo ambled off to the sitting room on the other side of the house, perhaps to fall asleep in an armchair near the window. This left the room empty of all but the four gentlemen and the remnants of breakfast laid out on the sideboard.

"How are those plans coming?" asked Mr. Hastings abruptly, just after the architect had taken a bite of scrambled eggs.

Bayeux swallowed and then wiped his mouth delicately with a napkin. "They are nearing completion, *monsieur*. You should be able to start knocking down walls and putting up new ones in no time. Although I would suggest waiting until late spring before you commence the renovations."

"You seem a little confused," Torin blurted out, "about which one of the men in this room actually owns the place. He won't be deciding when and how to renovate. The last I knew, my brother Haro was still the Earl of Anglesford."

"Quiet down, Torin," said Haro, his face suffused with red.

"Now, now," said Mr. Hastings, digging into his waistcoat pocket for a cigar. "Let the boy have his say. Tell me—are you offended that I want to improve the place, young man?"

"If improvements are what is actually meant, then no, I take no offense. But if these renovations are simply to tear down what is old to put up what is new, then that is no improvement. On the contrary, it is a desecration."

"But, surely, you acknowledge the benefit of brighter windows, more efficient heating, and roomier chambers. There is an energy to the new that the old always lacks."

"And there is a stateliness to the old that the new can never achieve."

It occurred to Haro that his brother might not even be speaking about architecture anymore. It also occurred to him that his brother might be right.

Mr. Hastings lit his cigar, happy to have exercised his intellect in sparring with the earl's brother, but still convinced that the lad's opinion was of little importance. "You are a fine speaker, young man. You'll do well at Oxford."

"Why does everyone think that I'm dashed well going there?" Torin rose from the table.

Mr. Hastings laughed at the boy's outburst. "Because you are, young Torin, you are! I've written to my banker about the fees this morning."

Grinding his teeth, Torin thudded out of the room in search of Uncle Harold. He had need of a conference with someone who actually wanted him at Woldwick and appreciated the old house's charm as much as he did.

"Finished already?" asked Haro politely, seeing that Bayeux had cleaned his plate and laid his fork upon the side of it.

"But of course. It is not my habit to keep people waiting on my account."

"A fine sentiment," said William Hastings with a guffaw, "but unfortunately, not one my daughter shares. She could be upstairs for an hour, trying on this set of furs and that one before she settles on the one that fits her mood. I expect it will be easier for Miss Swanycke as she'll not have so many sets to choose from."

"Oh, undoubtedly," said Haro, by now so used to the mill owner flaunting his wealth that he barely even bristled. Eda would have an easier time of it—Haro recalled that she had only worn her dark sables and dark dresses since his father's death. Although, come to think of it, that was a green dress she had been wearing earlier. Had she decided to truncate the period of mourning that etiquette demanded? She always looked fetching in green. She needed emeralds to go with that dress and to set off her black hair and her white throat....

"Well,"—Mr. Hastings folded his paper noisily—"as long as there's no fear of my daughter incurring injury today, I suppose I can leave her in your hands, Lord Anglesford."

Haro stopped his daydreaming about Eda, chiding his foolish imagination in no uncertain terms. "Certainly, Mr. Hastings." He gave a wry grin. "A walk to the pond is hardly life-threatening, but I'll be sure to watch out for her safety nonetheless."

The mill owner grunted, and, looking down at his pocket watch, left the room to keep some scheduled appointments with his business accounts.

Haro rang for Garth and asked him to bring down his coat. "Shall he fetch yours as well?" he inquired cordially of Philippe Bayeux.

"*Oui*, merci. And my cane." The Frenchman seemed surprised that the earl thought him of enough consequence to be served by his valet.

"And then we just wait on the ladies," Haro said, trying to keep matters jovial. "It's a man's lot in life—always waiting on a woman."

"Bien sûr, Lord Anglesford," said Bayeux, his dark eyes opening wider and shining with a sort of luminescence. "But a man cannot wait forever, can he? Especially if the woman does not wish him to." His empty breakfast plate was still in front of him, and taking the fork in hand, he pressed it so hard against the table that the tines bent askew.

"I suppose not," said Haro, frowning for his mother's sake at the contorted flatware. He suspected that the architect was no longer talking about their walk. But what he was talking about, the earl had no idea.

He did not know which would be the more unpleasant ordeal—enduring a lengthy tête-à-tête with Monsieur Bayeux or escorting two ladies who would rather be at each other's throats than inmates in the same house.

13

At long last the ladies returned. Arabella was wrapped in a ruby red pelisse trimmed with ermine on every edge, and she carried a large ermine muff to boot. Her long, slim figure stepped sinuously down the stairs of the great staircase, with an eye to the gentlemen watching her descend.

Eda followed close behind. Her own pelisse was purple, a brilliant contrast with the green of her dress, and as Haro had conjectured, her furs were sable. She looked every inch an empress, except for the barely concealed smile that lingered on her lips and betokened she was hiding some secret amusement.

The front door opened, and the four walkers stepped out into the chill of the late morning. Arabella and Haro led the way, the mill owner's slender daughter leaning against the earl like a vine climbing an oak tree. The other two fell in step several paces behind them. Bayeux's face twisted into an unmistakable scowl. He kept his hands securely in the pockets of his many-caped greatcoat and, no matter how much Eda tried to draw him out, had little conversation to offer.

Arabella and Haro, on the other hand, had no lack of things to discuss. At Haro's instigation, they walked forward quickly until they were out of earshot of the others.

"I must apologize for Miss Swanycke's rudeness," said Haro, inclining his head a little toward his fiancée. It was best to acknowledge the annoyance of the inappropriate sketch and get it out of the way. "She is still grieving over my father's death, and I beg you to excuse any irregularities she displays."

Arabella looked up at him, her eyes quite serious. "Irregularities like having your dressing gown in her room?"

Haro blanched. Thunder and turf! She knew. He determined to brazen his way out of this mess.

"My dressing gown? What on earth do you mean?"

"After I went to my room to collect my furs, I knocked on your cousin's door to see if she was ready—and also to return that odious picture she foisted on me at breakfast. She bade me enter, and there, slung over the back of her zebrawood chair, was a Chinese dressing gown, much too large for her, and obviously designed for a man.

"She must have caught me looking at it, for she gave a little laugh and said, 'Oh, that! It's Haro's.' And catching it up from the chair, she tossed it upon her bed without any further explanation." Arabella sniffed. "And is that, pray tell, one of the irregularities I am supposed to excuse?"

"Of course not!" Haro cast about for some suitable explanation that did not involve Eda coming into his rooms in the dead of night clad only in her nightdress. "I can only assume the maids must have mixed up the laundry, and she decided to make a joke of it at my expense. Eda has always enjoyed her jokes...."

Arabella, it appeared, did not share this enjoyment, for she had not the slightest twinkle in her eye when she responded. "If there are so many inhabitants in the house that the maids cannot sort the wash correctly, then perhaps it is time to ease their labor. And I daresay your relative's grief would heal more swiftly were she to remove herself from an environment that holds such painful memories."

"You want Eda to leave Woldwick?" Haro could have foreseen this request, but it still felt like someone had planted him a facer. He stopped in the middle of the path.

"It is three weeks to our wedding, and I cannot share a house with her." The words came out shrill, and it seemed that Arabella knew almost immediately that she needed to soften them. Her warm hand came out of her ermine muff and found his cheek, now glowing from the exercise in the cold air. "You understand, my love?" Her thumb caressed his ear.

Her skin was soft, but it might have been dragon scales for all he cared. He could not deny that Eda was becoming more than a nuisance, both to the peace of the house and to the peace of his own heart. But to turn her out of doors? Impossible! Where would she go? Of her father's relatives in Ireland, there were none that lived in anything better than a hovel. Of her mother's relatives in England, only Lady Anglesford remained.

And yet, if Haro were fair, he must admit that it was unconscionable to expect a bride to live in such proximity to her husband's former intended. She must know that there had been an understanding between them. And she was within her rights to demand that her rival depart—more than within them if she had any inkling of last night's midnight encounter.

There was no help for it. For her own good, Eda must go. Haro resolved to ask his mother about it later that day. Perhaps Lady Anglesford would know a place where her foster daughter would be welcome and safe and treasured as she deserved. The only thing Haro knew for certain was that Woldwick was no longer that place.

"Come now, *monsieur*," said Eda as they picked their way along the path to the pond. "You must tell me something of interest about yourself, or I shall give you up as an altogether disobliging man."

"Very well," he said, bestowing on her the first small smile he had given throughout the whole of their walk. "My father died in the service of Louis XVI. My mother was the daughter of an aristocrat in the south of France, and she was forced to flee to England when I was just un enfant, leaving me behind."

"Oh goodness! How very exciting!"

"Not very." He stabbed his cane sharply into the earth with each step they took. "Although it ended up being the making of me. For had the Terror never happened, and had she stayed in France, I doubt not that I would have grown up idle and uneducated. But after she was gone, I grew up quickly, for I knew that I would have to earn my own bread. I applied myself to learning, and my studies acquainted me with architecture, the second great love of my life."

Eda had no qualms conjecturing which love he held higher than his chosen vocation. "And your studies of architecture led you to meet our dear friends, the Hastings."

"Yes." He proceeded more cautiously. "Mr. Hastings became a client of mine several years ago. I designed his house for him in the north of England, a grand mansion with over forty rooms in the Palladian style."

"It sounds very fine! And did Miss Hastings approve of it?"

"Yes, very much so." His voice warmed a little, though the air was still cold enough to see his breath. "She has a passion for architecture."

"I did not know that." Eda resolved to try a more direct approach in gleaning information. "I only knew that she had a passion for earls."

"*Non!*" His voice turned bitter. "That passion belongs entirely to her father."

Eda stayed silent, praying that he would continue.

"There was a time when a mill owner would find a man of his own station—worthy to pursue his daughter's hand. But now, all sense of order is overturned, and capitalists aspire to be kings on the backs of their children's marriages." He hit his cane against a nearby log with astonishing force.

"So, this Mr. Hastings has convinced his daughter, against her will, to accept our Haro's hand?"

"I am sure of it—or, at least, I was sure enough to come here."

"And now that you are here, what will you do?"

"Je ne sais pas. I've had no chance to speak with her alone, to reason with her, to understand her heart. And now they have set a date!"

"Three weeks." Eda pronounced the words like a verdict of doom.

"Three weeks! Mon dieu! Is there nothing I can do?"

"Nothing other than convince the lady to stand up to her father and throw Haro over. Are you that persuasive? Are you that charming?"

Bayeux shrugged. "Perhaps. But it is only possible if I can gain an audience with her. Alone."

Eda gave the man a sympathetic smile. "That is something that I might be able to help you with."

"Don't go too near the edge," warned Haro as he helped Arabella down to the shores of the forest's frosted pool. They called it a pond, but it was more of a lake, stretching out like a long finger toward the nearby village. A slow stream fed into it, bridged by a few weathered, wooden boards so that the path could continue unbroken around the water. At the end of the stream, just under the bridge, the ice began. White lines of frost zigzagged across the surface like intricate designs on a dish of white porcelain.

"It looks delicious," said Arabella, no doubt thinking of the ices she had ordered for one of her father's last parties in London. Haro suspected that she was making a deliberate attempt to humor him with her praise. From what he could tell, she had no innate appreciation for natural beauty but was simply trying to reward him for acquiescing to his mother's ward being thrown out of the house.

"A fine sight," Haro agreed. "I told Torin it wouldn't be ready for skating until next week, but I wonder...." He put a tentative boot upon the edge of the ice. He took another step and left the safety of the shore. Another step—he felt it creak beneath his weight. One more step and it would be sure to crack.

"Watch what you're doing, boy!" said a voice from the bridge. Startled, Haro shifted his weight, and the hard sole of his boot broke through the ice with a splash. He regained his balance ingloriously and recovered the safety of the shore by Arabella's side, thankful that his top boots had protected his breeches from a dousing.

"What are you doing out here, Uncle Harold?" he demanded. The old man was in little more than his shirtsleeves and trousers, and it was as cold outside as a Russian Christmas. Haro could see the gleam of frozen water on the boards of the bridge. "And you should watch what you're doing the same as I. There's ice on those steps!"

Uncle Harold came down from the bridge, his feet surprisingly sure for an octogenarian. As he came closer, they could see that he was holding a large loaf of bread in his hands. "Ice? Pshaw. This is nothing compared to the winter I was in St. Petersburg. There was ice on our eyebrows every time we walked outside."

"But I daresay the countess kept you warm enough!" called out a cheerful voice. Haro swung around to see that Eda and Bayeux had come around the bend and were closing the distance between themselves and the water.

Uncle Harold smiled. Eda always had been his favorite, or at least, so Haro suspected. He wondered how the old man would take the news of her imminent eviction from Woldwick.

"I see you've already managed to spoil the pristine beauty of the pond," said Eda, gesturing at the jagged hole Haro's boots had made near the shore.

Haro tensed. So, she meant to sink her claws into him as well as into Arabella this morning. Well, then, let her! It would make him feel like less of a blackguard when he was forced to turn her out of her adoptive home.

"He tried walking on it!" said the old man with a snort. "Walking on it, when it's hardly thick enough to hold a sparrow, let alone a great, galloping lad!"

"What does it matter?" said Arabella. "There's ice aplenty to look at, and once you've all looked your fill we can return to the house. Some of us"—she glanced at Uncle Harold—"may be warm enough in our shirtsleeves, but I, for one, am starting to feel the chill."

"By all means, then, let us return," said Eda, acting far more agreeable to the idea than anyone would have guessed. "We should switch walking partners for the journey back, for Monsieur Bayeux tells me he has several questions to put to you regarding the house plans."

Haro frowned at this, but the architect had already stepped up on Arabella's other side and was blathering on about beams, and gables, and cornices.

"Will you join our party?" Eda called out to Uncle Harold.

"No, thank you, my dear." The eccentric old man waved good-bye with one hand while his other hand clutched the loaf of bread. "I still have my birds to feed."

"There's a thick mist settling in through the trees," Haro called out to the figure receding into the bare branches. He knew the old man was familiar with the woods, but still, there was a chance that he could lose his way in all the fog.

"Just leave him be," said Eda, taking Haro's arm and giving it a pull. "He's too stubborn to listen, and we might as well get back to the house before your beloved's nose turns blue."

The path was not wide, but neither gentleman seemed willing to leave Arabella's side, so they pressed on four abreast, jostling elbows and nearly stepping on each other's feet. The fog was growing rapidly, and soon it was hard to see more than a dozen paces ahead of them.

"Oh dear," said Eda quietly, falling behind the rest and bending down on one knee. Haro, who had been walking beside her, was the only one to notice her disappearance—the other two were talking far too animatedly about friezes and fixtures. He bit his lip in frustration, but whatever his feelings, the idea of leaving a female behind in the fast-growing fog was too ungentlemanly to be thought of. He murmured something to Arabella about being "right back in half a second" and turned around to come to the aid of his confounded cousin.

"What are you doing?" Haro demanded. The fog had already swallowed up the other two, and he was alone with Eda's kneeling figure, surrounded by a thickening wall of white.

"I've broken my lace and need to fix it before I can go on."

"Wouldn't it be more effective to pretend that you've twisted your ankle?"

"Why, Haro! How clever of you! I do believe it would." She stood up with a show of anguish and hobbled over to the earl's arm. "Would it be too difficult for you to carry me? Yes? Perhaps if I lean very heavily on your arm, I will be able to make it back to the house without fainting from the pain."

Haro grimaced as she hung her full weight upon his forearm, and he began to drag her slowly down the path. It rankled him more than a little that this charade had forced him into the very proximity with her that he wished to avoid, but it also occurred to him that now would be an excellent time to broach some unpleasant news.

"I hear you've been flaunting my dressing gown in a most inappropriate manner."

"It's very comfortable," said Eda, forgetting to wince with each step now that Haro had addressed her in conversation. "I'm thinking of keeping it. Will your fiancée approve?"

Haro snorted. "I imagine any decent woman would approve if it kept you from wandering the halls in your nightdress."

"Oh," said Eda disappointedly. "So, she didn't take a pet about it and jilt you?"

"Devil take it, Eda, no! She doesn't think that I—that you—that we—" He looked at her sharply. "Is that what you wanted her to think?"

Eda shrugged. "I thought it might be useful."

"Useful?" echoed Haro with growing fury. "Useful!" He turned and took her by the shoulders, his eyes burning with intensity. "You thought it would be *useful* to ruin your reputation, and drive me mad, and fill both our lives with regrets?"

"Oh," said Eda, quailing beneath the onslaught. "I didn't think—"

"You didn't think at all!" said Haro, all his senses rioting uncontrollably. He began to breathe heavily, his arms still gripping her shoulders as if holding on to the lifeline on a ship. "I have made a choice, Eda. I have *engaged* myself to Arabella Hastings. And whatever my feelings are on the matter, this is what I have done and I must live with it."

"But why?" whispered Eda, her eyes sparkling with unshed tears. "Why must you live with it when it can still be changed?"

"You know why. I have a duty. To my mother. To my brother. To the servants, the tenants, and the Anglesford name." He wrenched away from her, her red lips a siren call that he was determined not to answer. "I know you think me weak, Eda," he said slowly. "But I'm not a coward, and I *will* see this thing out to the end." He stared at her, bracing himself for the horror of what he was about to say next. "And I think it would be better for all of us if you left until after the wedding."

Eda gasped. She reached out, her fingers tightening around his arm. "Haro, what on earth do you mean?"

She was trembling now, and he felt his defenses giving in. He would take her up in his arms right now if he did not stop himself.

He stepped back, steeling himself to the task and reminding himself that, sometimes, a gentleman must be cruel in order to be kind.

"I mean you've been the most horrible harridan this past week or more, vexing Arabella to no end with your taunts and your tittle-tattle. I've made up my mind that it would be better for all concerned if you left Woldwick."

"You've made up your mind, or she's made it up for you?"

"There you go again! I'll not have you sneering at her like that. Dash it all, Eda! She's going to be my wife."

Eda caught her breath. "I was going to be your wife."

"Maybe," he said coldly, reminding her that their understanding had never been official. "But things have changed. Perhaps for the better."

"No." Her face, already pale by nature, went a shade whiter at his words. "You have changed, and certainly not for the better. The Haro I knew would never put money before kindness."

"Now, see here, Eda—"

"There's no need to make excuses. Never fear—I shall pack my things. I will not stay where I'm not wanted."

She pulled her furs around herself more tightly and forged ahead through the fog. Haro felt a sickening feeling in the pit of his stomach. Should he hurry after her? No, let her walk back to the house alone. It was better for both of them to avoid further conversation that they would both rue and regret.

14

THE WALKERS—ALL FOUR OF them—straggled into the house at different times. Arabella came in first with a crinkle between her brows and slipped quietly up to her room. Bayeux opened the door a little later, very red in the face as if the winter wind had chapped his cheeks. Eda entered third and stormed up the stairs in high dudgeon to begin gutting her wardrobe of its contents. Haro came through the door last, his movements slow and pensive as the conversation with Eda replayed itself over and over in his mind.

Later that afternoon, Haro discovered that the unpleasant scene would need to be reenacted, this time with his mother in the opposing role.

"What is this Eda tells me?" asked Lady Anglesford, floating into the billiards room where Torin was performing the unusual feat of besting his elder brother.

"I don't know, Mama," said Haro, a bit untruthfully. "What is it?"

"That you are turning her out of doors into the cold?"

"What a lot of fustian! I simply said it would be best for her to leave Woldwick at present. I hoped that you could find her a suitable place."

"But why?" demanded Torin, putting down his billiard stick and staring openmouthed at his brother.

Haro gave him a sideways glance. "I should think it would be obvious."

"The only thing that's obvious to me is the fact that your Miss Hastings can't hold a candle to her. Is that why you're sending Eda away?"

"Don't talk rubbish!" Haro tried to brace himself with the remembrance of Arabella's most attractive qualities, but he had trouble remembering just exactly *what* those were.

"I'll tell you what's rub—"

"Hush, Torin," said Lady Anglesford, her lip quivering. Haro feared, with good reason, that she was about to cry. "I daresay I could find her a place, but for how long? Did Arabella ask you to send her away?"

"Yes." Haro walked over to the window and looked out to the bare birch trees surrounding the house. "And I don't know for how long. A lifetime, I presume. Arabella cannot stand to be in the same house as her for a moment longer—and in truth, Eda has been making things so difficult that I can hardly blame her."

"Does she know that you and Eda were enga—"

"That we had an understanding?" Haro corrected her preemptively. "Yes, I believe she does. And, naturally, that is another reason to want Eda away from Woldwick. I recognize that it is hard on Eda to be sent away from what has always been her home, but Arabella is my intended and has claims that cannot—and should not—be denied." The young earl stared fixedly at the misty landscape, his duty as shadowy as the trees in the distance.

"Oh, my dear boy," said Lady Anglesford, placing a hand on her heart. "This is a heavy burden that your father has laid upon you—that I have laid upon you. Perhaps we should reconsider this alliance, or rather, this mésalliance with the Hastings. Perhaps we should give up Woldwick, as Mr. Godwin suggested, and take our chances in Russell Square."

Torin groaned at the mention of that awful place.

"And break the betrothal? It's too late now, Mama. I've given my word."

"Just as I've given my word to shelter and provide for Eda."

It was Haro's turn to groan.

"Let us take a week or two to think on it," said Lady Anglesford, feeling a strong need to retire to her chamber and rest but resisting it until the matter could be settled. "Surely, the Hastings cannot wish us to turn Eda out at a moment's notice."

"I would not put it past them," muttered Torin.

"I must have some time to write letters to ladies of my acquaintance. Eda would make a fine companion for an elderly widow. Perhaps I can secure her a place."

Haro nodded. It was not exactly the happiest prospect for a girl who had, but two months ago, been enjoying her first London Season. But it was better than Ireland. It was better than nothing.

"Where have you been keeping yourself all afternoon?" Haro had finally found Arabella staring out the windows of the upstairs parlor. Her face held an expression of puzzlement—or was it worry?—that was papered over with a smile as soon as he spoke.

"I had some correspondence to write, so I took tea in my room." She left the window and walked over to take his hand. "I'm sorry to have deserted you, my darling." She laid her lips on Haro's cheek, and the kiss surprised him. It was warm, uncalculated, as if she actually desired his person and not just his pedigree. "Three weeks," she said, her eyes alight with anticipation.

"Three weeks," echoed Haro, trying to feign an excitement of his own.

Arabella had dressed for dinner, looking lavish in cloth of gold. She was as pretty a woman as a man could ask for, and prettier still when one knew the size of her father's pocketbook. She knew how to adapt herself to the circles she found herself in. Given the chance, she even had the possibility of transcending her lowbred parentage.

But, even with all that, there was something lacking. There were no shared loves and loyalties to bind them together. There was no fire blazing between them that would always warm him inside and out.

Three weeks.

"Would you like me to send out a boy to take your letters to the post?"

"Letters?"

"You said you spent the afternoon writing correspondence."

"Oh, yes...a letter, but it is not finished. I will send it into the village with my father tomorrow."

"Very well." Haro stood quietly beside her, both of them staring out the window and into the distance. She leaned against his shoulder, touching the drapes carelessly with her opposite hand. Haro reflected that by this time next year those drapes, this window, and maybe even this view would be changed for something different—something the fashionable new Lady Anglesford would find more appealing.

"Has that fellow Bayeux completed any plans yet?"

"No." Her head lifted abruptly from his shoulder, her neck tensing like a terrier backed into a corner. "Why?"

"I just wondered...since you two seemed to be discussing the finishing touches on our walk home this morning." Was that what they really had been discussing? Had their conversation continued in the same vein when he had hung back to assist Eda with her broken lace?

"Oh, yes, we were, weren't we?" Arabella's brow furrowed. "I believe he will need to return to London tomorrow for a meeting with another client. Perhaps he can finish up the plans and send them by courier from there."

It seemed that his departure was to be as sudden as his arrival. Curious, Haro decided to probe a little deeper. "Perhaps he can give them to us in person when we return to London for the wedding."

"No." It was a firm and definite refusal. "There is no need for us to see him again."

"As you wish," said Haro, just as the gong for dinner sounded. He gave her his arm, and they went down the staircase together, the earl more curious than ever just what had transpired between Arabella and the architect during their tête-à-tête in the forest.

Uncle Harold decided to join them for dinner that night, making the acquaintance of William Hastings for the first time.

"How do you do?" said Mr. Hastings, pumping the old man's hand vigorously just before they entered the dining room.

The family and guests took their seats around the table. Uncle Harold insisted upon seating Lady Anglesford while Torin pulled out a chair for Eda, glowering at Haro all the while. Monsieur Bayeux's eyes were unnaturally bright, his head bobbing a little, and Haro suspected he had been plying the bottle all afternoon.

"I daresay you'll have heard the name Hastings before," said the mill owner proudly, leaning back in his chair with his thumbs in his waistcoat pockets.

"What was your father's name?" asked Uncle Harold. He was trying to place the portly guest and failing miserably.

"Robert Hastings. He was in cotton too. The 'cotton king,' some called him. Which, I guess, makes me the 'cotton emperor'!" Mr. Hastings fell to laughing at his own joke.

"Dear me—an emperor! I knew several of those back in my day...although they went by other names like tsar. Have I told you that your daughter puts me in mind of the Countess of St. Petersburg?"

Haro rolled his eyes while Arabella sniffed.

"Does she?" Mr. Hastings' face suffused with pleasure. "I'm not surprised. A good girl, she is. Looks every inch a countess. She'll be one in name, too, in three weeks, don't you know?"

Uncle Harold did know, but he had already fallen into a reverie about his long-lost sweetheart. "Maria was her name. She would have run away with me, too, but her sister got wind of it and told the count. Jealous of Maria's good fortune, I heard some say later. The ship had almost set sail when her husband arrived."

William Hastings frowned, clearly disgusted with aristocratic views on morality and propriety. "'Pon rep! I hope this family doesn't hold with French notions like that."

"*Eh bien*, French notions like *love?*" slurred Philippe Bayeux.

"Goodness!" Eda broke in. This was a story she had never heard before. "And then what happened? Did you fight him?"

"How could I avoid it? It was pistols at twenty paces, on the docks, without even time to arrange a second."

"And you won?" demanded Torin, his moodiness having disappeared in the thrill of adventure.

"We fired almost simultaneously. He missed. I didn't."

"Did you kill him?" Torin was on the edge of his seat.

"Regrettably, no. Through the shoulder, but not the heart. He bled all over his white shirt and yellow waistcoat, and Maria was so affected by the sight that she could not go on. I fetched a doctor, and she decided to return with her husband. We said our farewells, and the ship weighed anchor."

"And you never saw her again?" Eda's blue eyes were wide, her spoon poised above her bowl of soup.

"Never. But I heard word of her—things I did not wish to hear. It was not two months later that she was killed."

"Oh my!" Lady Anglesford raised her napkin to her face.

"Killed? By whom, sir?" asked Mr. Hastings.

Uncle Harold cocked his head. "I don't remember what the verdict was. Perhaps her husband? Or her sister?"

"You don't remember? Upon my word, that is an important detail to be forgetting!"

Uncle Harold's shoulders stooped a little over his plate. "I've forgotten my manners to have even mentioned it at dinner. There, there, dear Edith,"—he patted Lady Anglesford's hand—"we will talk of happier things."

Dinner progressed quickly, and the ladies prepared to retire and leave the gentlemen to their port. Lady Anglesford exited first with Arabella close behind and Mrs. Rollo slipping out like a shadow that did not belong. Haro caught Eda's eye just before she stepped out the door. "Your ankle looks much improved."

"Yes, it's fortunate—since I'll soon be hobbling through Bath carrying some old dowager's smelling salts and reticule."

"Oh?" Haro was a little taken aback. There was a smile on her face, and she seemed to have recovered her temper from the last time he had seen her. "Did Mama find you a place so soon?"

"Of course not, you gudgeon. But I know how it will be when she does."

"Eda."

"Yes?"

He cleared his throat, trying to put into words exactly what he wanted to say. "Try not to judge me too harshly."

Thunder and turf! That was not what he had meant to say at all.

She looked at him curiously. "I don't, Haro. I never have." And without another word, she was gone.

15

FIVE GENTLEMEN WERE LEFT with glasses and the decanter, but that number swiftly dwindled to three when Uncle Harold wandered out a side door into the cold darkness and Torin decided to take to his heels before Oxford could be mentioned once again.

"Your uncle, he's not...dangerous, is he?" asked the mill owner. He undid a couple buttons on his waistcoat to ease his digestion.

"Dangerous?" Haro echoed. "How do you mean?"

Mr. Hastings snorted. "You know these old fellows with bats in the belfry—could snap at any moment and become violent. You heard him say that he almost killed that fellow in St. Petersburg, and he the one running off with another man's wife!"

Haro gave a dismissive wave. "Don't put too much stock in Uncle Harold's tales."

"So, it's not true? I'm glad of that. I was almost afraid the old dotard had killed that countess himself, the way he clammed up and said he could not remember who did it."

Haro bridled a little. "What are you insinuating?"

"There, there. No offense meant, Lord Anglesford. I suppose I can stand a few skeletons in the closet as long as the closet has a coat-of-arms painted on it, eh?" He tossed down his glass of port—much more quickly than that fine old vintage deserved—and announced that he had bookkeeping to look over. "The life of a businessman, eh? Never done, never done."

Haro bid him a cordial goodnight and found himself alone with Bayeux. "So, you're going up to London tomorrow?" he inquired politely.

"Is that what she told you?"

Yes, Haro decided, Bayeux had been drinking all afternoon. And now he was drinking again, already downing his third glass of spirits since dinner.

"Yes, she said you had another client to visit."

"Well, it's not so!" Bayeux's speech was a little slurred. "I'm staying here until matters are sorted to my liking." The corner of some paper—a letter?—had begun to peep out of his waistcoat pocket, and he tucked it back in violently.

As master of the house and fiancé to the lady in question, it behooved Haro to inquire further. "What matters are those?"

But the architect had ceased listening to him. His head was lolling back onto the side of the chair.

Haro pursed his lips and decided to ring the bell for the footman.

"Henry, will you see Monsieur Bayeux upstairs? He's had a bit too much of the bottle, I believe."

"Right, m'lord," said Henry, a young dark-haired fellow who looked quite dapper in the Anglesford livery.

Bayeux came to his senses a little bit, as Henry hoisted him upright and put an arm around his waist for support.

"Hold tight, Bayeux," said Haro, pronouncing his words clearly so even a muddled head could understand. "Henry will help you upstairs and get you to bed."

"Merci." Bayeux's eyes cleared for a moment. "You are un bon homme, Anglesford. If circumstances were different, I could even like you, I think."

"Very kind of you." Haro grinned wryly. "And don't forget your letter." He bent down to retrieve the folded paper that had fallen out of Bayeux's waistcoat.

"Mustn't forget that, must we?" Bayeux jammed it into a clenched fist, and Haro caught sight of a flowery script filling half a page. The Frenchman slipped from the footman's grasp, and Haro caught his sleeve to hold him up. "You are English—you are lucky. You do not have the French heart; you do not suffer love."

"I'm not so sure of that," said Haro wryly, righting the Frenchman and turning him back over to the footman. "But in any case, I think both the French and the English need their sleep. To bed, Monsieur Bayeux."

"*Oui!* Lead on, Henri!" And with that, the inebriated Frenchman was bundled off to bed to sleep off his spirits.

Haro was alone, his only occupation to sit beside the fire and wait for the ladies to have their time to converse. For the sake of tradition, it ought to have been the gentlemen carousing loudly while the women talked in animated voices about embroidery, children, and the domestic arts. But it seemed that neither group was inclined to conviviality tonight.

Indeed, melancholy was the name of the mood. What was it Bayeux had said? That Haro, as an Englishman, was lucky not to suffer love? Haro groaned.

Suffering was the right word. Two weeks ago, in London, he had no notion of just what it meant. He thought it meant retrenching. Losing his horses, his club, his allowance. Saying good-bye to his ancestral home.

He had no notion that it could mean even more than that. Losing a person who was as much a part of him as one of his limbs. Saying good-bye to a dream that he had never fully appreciated until it was dying.

He stared into the fire, meditating on the meaning of suffering, till the silence was abruptly broken by a high-pitched scream. In one swift motion, he dropped his glass on the table and bounded up from his chair.

Torin popped his head into the room. "What the deuce is all that noise?"

"I don't know, but I'm going to find out."

The two brothers crossed the hall together and shoved open the door of the drawing room. The diminutive Lady Anglesford was perched on the edge of her seat in shocked silence. Mrs. Rollo's grim mouth had fallen open in a way that made her plain face even more grotesque than usual. And standing in the center of the room, like two dueling gladiators, were Eda and Arabella.

No blood had been drawn, but the taller, slenderer woman had a bright red mark across her left cheek. By all appearances, she had just been slapped, and quite vigorously, by the sturdy, black-haired daughter of the Irish captain.

"What is happening here?" demanded Haro.

"What is happening?" repeated Arabella, her voice pitched unnaturally high. "This woman has just given me the greatest insult possible by striking me in the face!"

"Eda?" Haro's tone was as hard as ebony.

"The provocation justified the offense."

"What provocation?"

Eda's face was as white and gray as Jenny's coat. She declined to answer, and Arabella was not forthcoming with what had precipitated the violence. Haro cast a glance at his mother, but she only shrugged mutely. Perhaps she had not heard the argument that preceded the slap. Haro refrained from questioning Mrs. Rollo, assuming that she would have little to offer no matter what he asked.

Torin looked uneasily from one woman to the other. "Perhaps if you would both apologize—"

"I will not!" said Arabella before he could get any further. "Nor will I accept any apology from Miss Swanycke other than her immediate departure from this house."

"I say, that's rather harsh." Torin swallowed, looking glad that Haro—and not he—had the unenviable responsibility of sorting out this situation.

"It is not only harsh, but also unreasonable."

Arabella's eyes glittered dangerously as she heard her fiancé siding with his cousin. The color began to come back into Eda's face.

Haro took up a position between them. "Whatever trouble has arisen between you two ladies, I would be much obliged if you would—for my sake—forget it as best you can and shake hands as friends."

Slowly, Eda stretched out her right hand. Haro could admire the sheer exercise of will that kept her fingers from clenching tightly into a fist.

But Arabella would not reciprocate. Leaving Eda's hand hanging in midair, she slipped past Haro and Torin and paused with her fingers on the drawing room door. "I thought you would show better sense than this, Haro. You will not like what my father has to say once he hears about this."

Haro inclined his head a little sadly. "I'm sure I shall not, but if you knew me at all, Arabella, you would know that I cannot do otherwise than I have done. Good night, my dear."

He said the last phrase sweetly, a white flag run up in the thick of a melee. Arabella, however, ignored it as surely as she had Eda's hand and disappeared into the corridor without another word to be said.

"Who does she think she is?" exclaimed Torin, staring scornfully after Arabella. "The Prince Regent's daughter?"

"Enough!" Haro quelled him with a word.

The whole family felt the need to frankly discuss this turn of affairs, but the alien presence of Mrs. Rollo constricted their ability to converse. "Perhaps you should see to Miss Hastings," said Lady Anglesford, giving the dour-faced companion a gentle hint that her presence was no longer wanted. Mrs. Rollo complied with a grunt, and the room lightened like a spring landscape with a break in the rain clouds.

"I am sorry, Haro," said Eda. "Truly, I am." Her penitence was unfeigned. She was still angry enough to drag Arabella to the floor by the hair, but the full impact of what that slap had done to Haro had hit her across the face as soon as he entered. She had wanted, over the last few days, to cause a rift between Haro and Arabella, but now that she had done so, she feared the pain that it would cause him.

What had he said in the fog earlier? That he was honor-bound to see this engagement out to the end? She stared at him anxiously. Would he hate her for this?

"You are forgiven," said Haro, his eyes examining her face with care. His own face split into a weary grin. "I suppose I should congratulate you on your restraint. At least a slap doesn't leave any scars."

His own sideburns hid the evidence of the scratch marks she had given him years ago when he had teased her mercilessly in the nursery.

"No." Eda smiled wanly. "I think the scars from this encounter might be meted out elsewhere."

"William Hastings is going to ring you a fine peal!" Torin whistled. "By Jove, perhaps I should slip away to Oxford and take Eda with me."

"Eda's not going anywhere." Haro's feet were planted firmly on the ground, his hands clasped behind his back.

"I'm not?" Eda looked up at him with surprise. Her usual shell of cynicism cracked a little, letting her vulnerability show in her dark blue eyes.

"Certainly not. Woldwick is your home, the same as it is mine."

"But Arabel—"

"Is for me to worry about, not you."

"But earlier you said—"

"Forget what I said. Just sit down and do some embroidery, or whatever it is you do."

"Very well." Eda walked over to the window seat and retrieved her sketchbook. She pulled out the torn pieces of a sketch she had started—and destroyed—back when they were in London. Piecing them together, she smiled to see Haro's face staring back at her. Then, she pulled out her pencils and set to work on a new sketch. It was the earl again but this time with a firmness in his jaw and a command in his eye that she had never noticed before. It was true what she had said last night in his room—a woman did like a man with some backbone beneath his coat from Weston's.

"Good night, Mama," said Haro, bestowing a kiss on Lady Anglesford's cheek. "Good night, Torin." He gave his brother a nod. Then, he strode out of the drawing room with all the solemnity of ascending the Mount of Olives.

"What does he mean to do?" asked Torin, a little awestruck.

"That I can't tell you," said Lady Anglesford, "but I'm certain that, whatever it is, we shall all be immensely proud of him."

16

Haro sat quietly in the Chinese-patterned dressing gown that had been kindly returned to his room once its usefulness was over. He might only be imagining it, but he liked to think it smelled a little like roses and lavender—a little like Eda. Patiently, he waited until his valet had brushed off his coat, hung it in the wardrobe, and gathered up the crumpled pile of shirt, cravat, breeches, and stockings. "Can I ask a piece of advice, Garth?"

The valet's eyebrows shot up at this unusual question. "Certainly, m'lord."

Haro had had ample time to think out his phrasing. "Would you gamble on the probability of wealth and limited happiness, or hold out for the certainty of financial ruin and the possibility—however slim—of earthly bliss?"

Garth was taken aback. "I couldn't say, m'lord, although"—he hesitated—"it was your father that was the gambling man, not you."

"Yes, but I've found that we've all got to stake our wager on something in this life, and I'm wondering if, perhaps, I've staked mine on the wrong horse."

"Ah, I see. You refer to Miss Hastings and Miss Swanycke."

"Exactly. And tonight, the situation has been further complicated by Miss Swanycke—"

"Giving Miss Hastings a basting she's not likely to forget."

Haro looked at his valet in surprise.

"Sorry, m'lord, but the scullery maid was there tending to the fire when it happened, and they can't talk of anything else belowstairs."

"Hmm. What else are they saying belowstairs?"

"That Miss Hastings as good as had it coming, and there isn't one of them but wouldn't have liked to have done it himself." Garth pursed his lips. "But perhaps I oughtn't t'say anything, m'lord."

"No, no, go on." Haro leaned forward with interest. "I was not aware that my betrothed was so universally despised belowstairs."

Garth flushed. "Beg pardon, m'lord—"

"No apologies. Just tell me the truth, man. What do they say about her and why?"

"I'm not one to carry servants' tales, m'lord, but Mrs. Alfred's been keeping company with Mrs. Rollo, and she says her mistress is a proper devil to the hired staff. Her abigail's the only one she treats fair and fine. But when the mistress comes off cross, woe to groom, or cook, or scullery maid who ventures in her path."

"Has she abused any of the servants at Woldwick?"

"She's laid no hand on them, m'lord, though she gave Jane, the scullery maid, such a tongue lashing that the girl cried all through her pinafore."

"Did Jane do some wrong?"

"She dropped a log when she went to lay the morning fire and woke Miss Hastings from her sleep." Garth grimaced. "And Mr. Hastings ain't no better, m'lord. I've had him tell me a thing or two when I brushed up too close to him in the corridor after leaving your room."

Haro put the tips of his fingers together, tapping them thoughtfully. "So, to return to the subject of wagers, it seems you're agreeing with me that I might have staked the wrong horse."

"I wasn't of that mind at first, but 'pon reflection, it seems that way, m'lord."

"But, of course, once you've laid the bet, there's hell to pay if you don't come up to scratch. And besides the breach of promise, there's the original problem to consider. I'd have to sell Woldwick, you know. And would the staff really prefer being turned out of doors to enduring a hardnosed mistress?"

Garth finished folding Haro's cast off clothing and, seizing his boots to take them downstairs for a good polishing, paused a second at the door. "It's not my place, m'lord, but if it were, I would say worry less about the staff's likes, and more about what you would prefer. Good night, m'lord."

The following morning, Haro requested an audience with William Hastings. The portly mill owner, as it turned out, would have requested a meeting on his own if Haro had not broached the subject. "I can only assume this is about that black-haired hussy. God's blood! How dare she lift a finger to my Arabella! First that jade's trick with the horse, and now this. And what I want to know is what you intend to do about it!"

"Yes, that is the question, isn't it?" Haro had seated himself in one of the wing-backed chairs by the fire in the library while Mr. Hastings paced the room in a fury. "I strongly suspect Miss Swanycke was provoked in the matter."

"Provoked? You mean by Arabella?"

"Yes, although neither lady will admit what words passed between them."

"Thunder and turf, Anglesford! Do you actually mean to make excuses for that girl's vicious attack on my daughter?"

"No, simply to understand it."

"What is there to understand? The vixen is a menace and must go. Arabella told you as much last night."

Haro stood up. "Yes, but here's the rub, Hastings. I don't like being dictated to in my own house. And Eda, for all her faults, is my mother's ward." He crossed his arms. "She'll not be leaving."

William Hastings sputtered, astounded that the young earl was actually daring to stand up to him. "Well, if she won't be leaving, then we shall. And you know what that means, Anglesford—you can say farewell to your precious Woldwick. I won't be handing over my blunt to a bullheaded man who won't listen to the advice of his future father-in-law."

"And I won't be handing over my title to a woman who bullies my servants, distresses my mother, and orders me about like a schoolboy."

Hastings stopped pacing, his face nearly apoplectic with rage. "You mean to break off the engagement? I'm warning you, Anglesford, I'll take you to court over it. And whatever pittance you have left to your name after your father's foolishness will disappear into my pocket. You'll be ruined."

"Perhaps." Haro was inflexible. "But better an honorable poverty than a dishonorable alliance. Arabella is not—"

"Why? What have you heard?" Mr. Hastings' eyes were instantly wary.

"—the wife for me. She knows how to please a man well enough when she wants to, but all of her best qualities are on the surface, and underneath, there's more petulance and ill-temper than I'd care to wake up next to every morning."

Mr. Hastings lapsed into a volley of expletives that were doubtless common currency at his place of business.

"Enough, sir!" Haro put up a hand. "You bullied me into engaging myself to your daughter in the first place. You won't bully me into staying engaged when I've finally made up my mind to escape this entanglement."

Mr. Hastings let out an inarticulate roar. "You call yourself a gentleman? Faugh! You have no consideration for my daughter's feelings."

"I intend to do her the courtesy of telling her myself."

"A pretty piece of courtesy, Anglesford! I ought to bar you from seeing her ever again...." An idea flew into William Hastings' head that seemed to calm him a little. "Very well, then—tell her yourself!"

Haro nodded and left the library, while Hastings leaned on the chair a minute until his angry breathing had slowed. It was painfully apparent to the mill owner that he had lost his hold over the earl. But Arabella—cunning Arabella—might still be able to net him with her wiles.

After Haro had concluded his tumultuous conference with Mr. Hastings, he set off in search of his fiancée to break the unpleasant news. In the breakfast room, he discovered Torin and Lady Anglesford idling away the morning at the table.

"Where's Arabella?"

Torin shrugged. "Not awake yet, I suppose, or pouting in her room. Trying to devise some way to make good on her threat to throw Eda out of—"

"Yes, well, that's my worry, not yours." He paused. "Where is Eda then?"

"She ate an early breakfast," responded Lady Anglesford, "and went to look for Uncle Harold. Mr. Hastings hasn't been in for breakfast at all, which is strange since he is quite fond of his food. And Monsieur Bayeux ran out of doors an hour ago with scarcely a good morning, saying he had some business in the village."

"Give the poor fellow some grace," said Torin with a laugh. "He looked like he had ten-penny nails being driven into his skull. He must have drunk like a fish last night and awakened with the sunrise."

"He was rather foxed after dinner. But forget him—it's Arabella I'm looking for."

"I thought it was Eda," said Torin pertly.

"Yes, well, all in good order." Haro grinned with assumed confidence to disguise the nervousness building up in his insides. Bearding Mr. Hastings in his den had been easy. Facing Arabella would require far more courage.

An inquiry to Miss Hastings' abigail ascertained that the lady in question had dressed herself warmly for a walk out-of-doors. Haro's brow furrowed. He would not have expected Arabella to take a wintry walk through the hated woods unaccompanied.

He donned his own coat and gloves and peered behind the frozen hedges in the garden but without any success. She must have ventured farther afield. Striding briskly to the stables, he let his horse out of the stall and fastened the girth of his saddle. "Did Miss Hastings take a horse from here this morning?" he asked the groom.

"No, m'lord." The groom stamped his feet and blew on his fingers to keep the blood circulating in the cold air. "The only person who's been in here this morning is Monsieur Bayeux. Saddled up while it was still half-dark and set off for the village.

"Hmm." Haro stepped up into the saddle and urged his horse out the stable doors. A gnawing worry was beginning to plague him, but about what, he did not know.

He rode up and back the lane a quarter mile but saw no sign of a red pelisse or an ermine muff. The chill in the air came under his collar. Fiend take it!—where was she?

He turned off to take the path that led to the pond. The naked birch trees shot up on either side like white phantoms in the frosty mist. He rounded the bend and found the frozen lake glinting dully. The cold weather had done its work, and yard after yard of frosty ice stretched into the distance.

The bridge, with its dark, rough boards stood in stark relief. Haro dismounted. He would not risk his horse on the icy planks. Cautiously, he edged his way onto the middle of the bridge. There were footsteps in the frost, indicating that someone had trod these boards before him just that morning. Some of the footprints looked small, the size of a lady's foot. He scanned the perimeter of the lake—still no sign of Arabella, just ice, unbroken ice, as far as the water's expanse.

Perhaps it was skating weather already. He thought about how it would be to tie on his blades and sail out across the frozen lake with Eda at his side, holding onto his arm with a laugh and then sliding free across the glimmering surface. But before that could happen, he had an unpleasant duty to attend to, an unpleasant interview that he wished were over.

He looked down, and his eyes opened as wide as the portholes on a ship. Good God! Had someone tried skating already? Below the bridge, fissures shot through the ice, radiating like lightning from a jagged hole in the slick surface.

It was horrifyingly apparent that someone had fallen through the ice into the murky water below. And Haro was certain, beyond a shadow of a doubt, that that someone was Arabella Hastings.

Part II

17

THE HOURS FOLLOWING THE fateful epiphany at the pond passed by in a whirl of activity and horror. Haro nearly fell off the bridge himself while running back to his horse. Mr. Hastings' bellows filled the house as footmen, grooms, and even valets came running with poles and hooks and nets to break the ice and drag the pond.

Arabella was found after ten minutes' effort and pulled out of the water in her sodden red pelisse, cold and white and lifeless. Haro sent for Dr. Stigand, the same physician who had pronounced Edward Emison dead not two months before, and he arrived on the scene after an hour had passed.

Arabella's body lay motionless in the bedroom she had occupied. Haro had carried it back from the lake, ignoring all the offers of help from the servants, the heavy weight of the girl's wet dress making his arms as numb and frozen as his mind. Dr. Stigand made an examination of the body with Mrs. Rollo in attendance. The family and the aggrieved father gathered in the small, adjoining sitting room, Haro and Torin standing uncomfortably, the ladies sitting close together on the sofa, and Mr. Hastings monopolizing the only armchair.

"You are to blame for this! You are to blame!" William Hastings beat the arm of his chair furiously.

Haro, at whom these accusations were directed, said nothing. Perhaps he felt it better to ignore the mill owner's acrimonious grief. Perhaps he agreed with him that the guilt lay at his own door.

"Now, see here!" remonstrated Torin. Out of all of them, he displayed the fewest symptoms of shock at this turn of events. "Haro was the one who found her. He didn't push her in."

"Didn't he?" demanded Mr. Hastings. "Perhaps not literally, but it was him that did it—his faithlessness and ingratitude."

"What on earth do you mean?"

"He jilted her—this very morning! He took the poor girl's heart and crushed it under his foot."

"Haro?" Lady Anglesford took a deep breath and tried to quiet the nervous palpitations of her heart. "Is this true?"

Eda looked up at him with unwavering eyes, her expression inscrutable.

"Yes." Haro ran a hand through his blond hair. "I intended to call off the betrothal. But the thing is—I hadn't told her yet!"

"Then she must have heard it from someone else." Mr. Hastings growled and leaned forward in his chair. "Some servant who overheard us, or some other member of this filthy family." He put a pudgy hand on the armrest and pushed himself to his feet. "Why would she run into the woods by herself? Why would she climb up the bridge and fall off it? Because she was in distress! Because she knew! Yes, you, Lord Anglesford are certainly to blame for drowning my daughter."

Dr. Stigand came out of the room, wiping his fingers fastidiously on a white cloth. "Drowning your daughter, Mr. Hastings? I think not."

"You are defending him?" Mr. Hastings' rage turned ugly. "The country doctor who battens off the lord's estate—of course, you think he had nothing to do with drowning my daughter.

"Whether Lord Anglesford was involved is more than I can say." The white-haired old doctor picked up his instrument case with a little show of pique. "But I can tell you one thing—no one drowned Miss Hastings. She was dead before she struck the ice."

A barrage of questions flew at Dr. Stigand.

"How?"

"What do y—?"

"Egad!"

"My God! Are you say—?"

The country doctor shrugged his shoulders. "There are purple marks about her neck that indicate pressure was placed on the airway leading to asphyxiation."

"You mean—?"

"He means she was throttled!" Mrs. Rollo stood at the door to the bedchamber, her face as ominous as a hurricane sky. Haro could not recall hearing her speak a single word before this moment. It was a formidable first sentence to utter.

Mr. Hastings gave a loud roar and leaped at the young earl like a bloodhound. Taken completely by surprise, Haro barely put up his arms to defend himself before he found himself caught in a giant bear hug and hurled against the wall. He was younger, taller, and much leaner than the mill owner—he could have shoved the man off him if he had tried. But as it was, he let the grieving father pummel him, too stunned by the doctor's news to do more than block the flailing fists with his forearms.

Torin and Dr. Stigand came to Haro's rescue and using all their strength, pulled William Hastings back. Having his arms pinioned did not halt the expression of his anger, however, and Lady Anglesford put her hands over her ears as the mill owner began to hurl insults and unseemly epithets at her firstborn.

"Be quiet!" said Eda, interposing herself between Mr. Hastings and his quarry. "We all understand that this is an awful matter, but it won't help matters for you to go throttling someone yourself."

"He's murdered her!"

"You don't know that."

Haro did not understand how Eda could be so calm.

"Who else was outside? Who else went to provoke a quarrel with her?"

"I don't know, but until you have all the facts, it is unwise and unchristian to make such an accusation."

"And how would you suggest I gather those facts? No one saw him do it!"

"You could start in a gentlemanly fashion by asking him what happened." Eda looked up at Haro. Her dark blue eyes were uncompromising, demanding the truth no matter how painful it might be. "Harold Emison, did you murder Arabella Hastings?"

"Upon my soul, I did not!" Haro's breath came fast and short. He spoke the words to Eda alone, willing her with all of his might to believe he spoke the truth.

"Faugh!" shouted Mr. Hastings, desecrating the silence that hung between them. "Why should I take him at his word? He had already broken his word to marry my daughter. Forsworn twice, you villain!"

"No, you are right," Haro interjected. "You cannot trust me simply on my own assertion. We must find an independent party to investigate the case."

At these words, William Hastings calmed a little, causing Torin and Dr. Stigand to cautiously release their hold on his arms. Then, the mill owner surprised them all by agreeing. "Yes, an investigator must be had. But do not even suggest this fellow Stigand." He cast a snide look in the doctor's direction. "He's hand in glove with you already. I know just the man to investigate, a man from London whom I've had occasion to use before—a Bow Street Runner."

"What? A common thief-taker?" asked Lady Anglesford, dabbing at her cheeks with a handkerchief.

"There's nothing common about him!" retorted Mr. Hastings. It was an unusual statement for one so used to trampling the lower classes as he tried to pull himself upward into the ranks of the peerage. "He's one of the best at his profession, in serving writs, in apprehending criminals, and in sniffing out the true story—no matter how well a man tries to cover it up."

"Very well then." Haro straightened to his full height and squared his shoulders. "Send for your Runner. I've nothing to hide about your daughter's death, I want to find the one who did it, just as much as you do."

"Do you?" William Hastings' eyes roved around the room, from Torin, to Eda, to Lady Anglesford. "I rather think you might not, my lord. For it'll only come about that if you're innocent, then someone else in this house is not!"

It was mid-afternoon by the time the doctor departed. Lady Anglesford, as might be expected, had retired to her room to rest her nerves. Eda was downstairs, trying to pacify the terrified housemaids and convince Cook that even though there was a murderer on the loose, dinner must be served as usual. Torin was immersing himself in his books, hoping that Euclid and Aristotle could bring some order to a world turned upside down.

At first, William Hastings announced his intention of sticking closer than a brother to Lord Anglesford, lest the earl take to his heels and run for it before the law had a chance to arrive.

"Now, see here, Hastings," said Haro sternly. "I won't be running anywhere. And if I do, my face is known throughout this whole county and beyond. You'd lay me by the heels quick enough. And what's more, I won't have you dogging my steps or holding me on a leash like a deuced lapdog." Haro wished that he had had that much courage when conversing with William Hastings a week ago.

"I've dispatched a boy with your note. He has more than enough money for changing horses, and he'll be in London by nightfall, knocking on the door of your precious Bow Street Runners."

William Hastings grunted. "Good! My man'll be here in the morning then. He'll scent the truth of the matter, no matter how cold the trail."

"Then why don't you take yourself off and leave me to go about my business? I give you my word as a gentleman that I will not leave this house until the investigation is finished."

William Hastings harrumphed at this and made more slighting comments about the value of the Earl of Anglesford's word. But in the end, he stamped off to his room and left Haro to his own devices.

At first, Haro was elated to be rid of his ball and chain. But he soon found that although Mr. Hastings was not there to accuse him, his own thoughts were just as competent. Why had Arabella gone outside all alone? Had a servant told her of his argument with her father? Had she already known the news he was about to tell her? Was it his fault she had been attacked?

Haro paced the length of the upstairs parlor. And who had come upon her there by the lake? A stranger in the woods? Or—dare he think it?—another inmate of Woldwick? His mind began to plot a map of everyone's whereabouts that morning....

"Will you be dressing for dinner tonight, m'lord?" Garth intruded upon his thoughts with a much-needed return to the mundane.

"Dinner? I heard that Cook was in too much of an uproar to touch the stove."

"She was, m'lord. But Miss Swanycke's talked some sense into her, I believe, and there'll be roast and Yorkshire pudding at the usual time."

"Then, yes, I will dress for dinner. Isn't that what we English do? Carry on despite the storm?" Haro folded his hands behind his back and planted his feet with an assurance he did not feel.

"Very good, m'lord. I will lay out your coat."

But Haro's mind had begun turning again, and coats were the last thing in his thoughts. Torin and Lady Anglesford had been at the breakfast table. Mr. Hastings had been with him. That left Eda unaccounted for, and that Bayeux fellow, and—

"Wait a moment, Garth. Have you seen Uncle Harold?"

"Not recently, m'lord. He came in a little while ago from feeding his birds, but then he disappeared into the attics, as usual."

"And the architect?"

"Monsieur Bayeux's just back from the village. I told him the news, and he seemed quite distressed. He bade me tell you he'd keep to his rooms and be off as soon as possible in the morning. He doesn't want to occasion any further distress for the family by remaining here an unnecessary guest."

"No," said Haro, "tell him he must stay. Hastings is sending to London for a Bow Street Runner to investigate this whole affair. He'll need to interview everyone to try to find the guilty party."

Garth's graying eyebrows lifted skeptically. "And what if this Runner can't sort out who's guilty?"

"Then Hastings will find a way to pin the murder on the man with the most motive and opportunity. And in that case, you'll be needing to look for a new master, Garth, for I'm the one that will hang."

18

THE FAMILY WAITED FOR the Bow Street Runner to make an appearance all the next morning, like children with their noses pressed against the window in hopes of seeing a hobgoblin.

"I don't see why we need a Runner to tell us what happened," said Torin, trying to disguise his impatience with an air of false knowledge. "It's plain to see that it was Monsieur Bayeux. Did you never think how queer it was, him showing up so suddenly? And then the Hastings being so secretive about their acquaintance with him? Mark my words! There is some dark past there that needs to be brought to light."

"He certainly did have a *tendre* for Arabella," said Eda, "but why should that make him want to kill her? Haro, as you recall, was quite enamored with her as well."

"Thank you for reminding me of that," said Haro, who was standing not a shoulder's width away. It seemed strange now—the thought that he had even considered tendering his heart to Arabella Hastings earlier this week. There was only one lady now for whom the Earl of Anglesford had a *tendre*, and here she was shooting her barbs at him in a demure black dress from just a few feet away.

"I'm sure the Runner will consider that too," said Torin morosely. "But if the evidence must lead in one direction, I'd rather it led to Bayeux than to Haro. Wouldn't you?"

Haro snorted in exasperation. "Don't talk about me as if I'm not standing right here!" Eda and Torin did not even dignify his objection with a response.

"But maybe Haro and Bayeux aren't the only ones the Runner will consider." Eda traced her finger along the glass of the drawing room window. "They certainly weren't the only ones whom Arabella got her claws into."

"Well, he won't think it was me. I was with mother all morning. I have an incontrovertible alibi. And"—Torin cleared his throat—"I didn't go around slapping her in the face like certain other people did."

"Stop!" Haro's voice filled the room. It was bad enough to hear them dissecting the probability of him committing murder—he did not even want to venture into the possibility of Eda being accused. The purple finger marks on Arabella's neck...a woman, even a strong one, could never have done that, could she?

The cravat around his own neck felt far too tight, and he lifted a hand to loosen it.

"I'm certain it was some itinerant blackguard," said Haro, "perhaps a prisoner escaped from Newgate. The investigator will find out as much and be on his way."

Haro's brother and Eda stared at him dubiously.

A knock came on the drawing room door, and the entering footman announced a visitor.

He was as slender as a stick with red hair on his head, even brighter red hair in his sideburns, and a colony of freckles on his face. His dark clothing, though not expensively cut, was impeccably neat with barely a trace of mud from the road.

"Jacob Pevensey, at your service. Attached to the London magistrates' office, and here at Mr. William Hastings' request."

The two brothers and Eda gaped. "But...we've been watching out this window all morning," exclaimed Torin, "and we never saw you ride up!"

Jacob Pevensey smiled in a manner that could only be described as mysterious. "I availed myself of the servants' entrance on the side of the house."

"Ah," said Haro, not sure what else to say. The Runner must have skirted the main drive and ridden through the trees. But why? Simply to surprise them? "Have you been apprised of all the facts of the case?"

"Only what was in the letter I received. However, I did stop at the home of the local magistrate on my way here and learned a little more."

"Sir Robert Blount?"

"Yes—just to clarify jurisdiction, you understand."

William Hastings had been right—this man was skilled at his profession. It had not even occurred to Haro to send a servant round to Sir Robert to apprise him of the situation, but Pevensey—a stranger from London—had taken the correct step before even arriving at the house.

"Sir Robert is content to have me act as his deputy in this matter. He is...incapacitated at the moment and unable to pursue an inquiry in person."

"Ah," said Haro again.

"What is that supposed to mean?" asked Torin.

"His gout, you gudgeon," said Eda. "It's taken a turn for the worse."

"Yes," said Pevensey, flashing a debonair smile at Eda.

Haro could see that he was examining her intently, not in a lecherous way, but with the practiced eye of a student of human nature. He could also see that Eda did not like it—she was going to be recalcitrant during this investigation, he could already tell.

"I was fortunate enough to encounter Dr. Stigand there tending to Sir Robert's leg, and he familiarized me with the medical details of the case."

"Well, then, it seems you are already filled to the brim with facts," said Torin. "I doubt you'll even need to interview us at all!"

"Oh, I wouldn't say that," replied Pevensey. His quick eyes darted from person to person—probing, considering, evaluating. "But perhaps I shall save your interview for later, once I've established a timetable from the domestic staff."

"If you need any assistance, please let me know," said Haro, forcing himself to play the polite host. He planted his feet firmly on the floor and clasped his hands behind his back, trying to ward off the anxiety assailing him. He had nothing to do with the events at the pond! Why then did the appearance of the investigator affect him so? Was he afraid for himself, or for someone else?

"Thank you, my lord. I will let you know if anything is needed." Pevensey's close-cropped red head inclined briefly, but his eyes did not leave Haro's. "And now where is Mr. Hastings? He'll be wanting to see me first thing, and I know better than to keep that man waiting."

"So *that's* a Bow Street Runner!" said Torin, a little let down by the man's appearance. Although he had never taken the time to thoroughly imagine what a Runner would look like, he had some vague notion of a beefy, imposing man with a loud, barking voice and a brace of pistols prominently displayed.

"He looks...clever," said Eda. She also seemed a little let down by this assessment.

"Well, let's hope he's clever enough to find out what really happened," replied Haro, taking determined strides over to the fireplace as he tried to quell his own subconscious insistence on pacing the room.

"I'll warn Mama he's here," said Torin, exiting the room posthaste and leaving Haro and Eda alone together.

Haro leaned up against the mantelpiece. "Eda?"

"Yes?" She sat down carelessly in a nearby armchair, her satin slippers—and well-turned ankles—peeking out from beneath her black scalloped skirt. She had resumed wearing black since Arabella's death; he would have thought less of her if she had not.

Haro realized he had been holding his breath and took in a much-needed gulp of air. "Yesterday morning after you breakfasted...where were you? Who were you with?"

Eda's eyelids dropped slightly, building a roof of inscrutability over her dark blue eyes. "Here and there about the house."

"I remember Mama saying you went to look for Uncle Harold. Were you with him?"

She pursed her lips. "No."

"In the kitchen then, speaking to Cook?" He was grasping at straws now.

"No, alone. In no specific place. With no one to vouch for me."

Her perversity in answering his questions would have filled Haro with annoyance if the answers had not already filled him with concern. "Eda, you must have some sort of alibi—"

"Why? Because I slapped her face and—as Torin says—I'm sure to be suspected?"

"Exactly." Haro was too disquieted to be subtle.

She blinked her eyes at him. "I didn't think you'd mind that much since it will take some of the suspicion off of you."

Haro ground his teeth in frustration. How could he explain that he would rather swing by the neck until dead than have anyone accuse Eda Swanycke of murder? Why must she be so difficult?

Probably because he had jilted her.

Well, then, he would have to earn back her trust—something easier said than done. He took the fireplace poker and began thrusting it into the center of the half-burned logs in the fire. "I certainly would mind if the law apprehended the wrong person, whether that be me or you, since both of us are innocent."

"Kind of you to say so," said Eda, turning her beautiful white neck toward the window so that Haro could only see her profile.

Haro put down the fireplace poker. Kind? He wanted to be more than kind. "Eda, I—"

She rose to her feet quickly. Something in his tone must have frightened her—either that or repulsed her. "I need to look for Uncle Harold. Someone ought to warn him there's a man here who'll be asking him questions. It might upset him otherwise."

"Yes, well, very well," said Haro, no longer sure what he had been about to say. The moment had disappeared and Eda along with it, and the young earl was left alone in the drawing room, wondering how long before this Jacob Pevensey would return to interrogate him.

Eda hurried on the staircase, her small feet running up the steps like fingers over a pianoforte. Once she was certain that Haro had remained in the drawing room, her pace slowed a little, allowing her shaken thoughts time to settle.

That moment at the fireplace—what had he been meaning to say? An apology? An explanation? A declaration?

Whatever it was, she did not want to hear it. Not now. Not with this hanging over them.

Not that she had any doubts about Haro. She was certain he was innocent.

Or perhaps certain was too strong a word, since her certainty was somewhere in between a hope and an inalterable belief.

He had seemed concerned for her—but why? Did he really think that she had had anything to do with Arabella's demise? A worrying tendril of suspicion wound itself around her long white neck—suspicion about what the earl might suspect. Did he really doubt her integrity thus? Did he think her jealous, vengeful, and violent enough to strangle her rival and topple her into the ice?

She could see the accusation forming on his very lips as he stood there leaning against the fireplace mantel. Eda's heart began to flame with a burst of anger, but by a triumph of will, she managed to let her cooler head take command.

No, he had seemed concerned for her, and that concern was doubtless rooted in a certainty of her innocence—or if not certainty, then the same thing she felt about him, something in between a hope and an inalterable belief. She would probe the matter no further...at least, for right now.

While her thoughts were running riot, she had climbed the three flights of steps to the uppermost story of the house. She had not lied. She was going up to see Uncle Harold—but she had more to say to their great-uncle than a simple warning that the Bow Street Runner was on the premises.

"Come in, come in, child," said the old man, answering the door quite promptly when he heard her knock.

The garret room was lit by half a shilling's worth of candles, their soft lights glinting off the gilt frames, bright pictures, pinned medals, and mounted weaponry that covered every inch of the walls. Coming into this room, Eda always felt a little bit like Ali Baba entering the cave of the forty thieves—there was treasure everywhere, each piece with a story behind it.

Without being invited, Eda took a seat on the great, green-cushioned chair that sat beside the fireplace. Uncle Harold, who had been preparing to toast some bread and cheese over the fireplace, resumed his task with the utmost concentration. He usually took his meals in his room, at whatever hour he wished and of whatever food he wanted.

Eda watched while he brought the toast to the perfect state of brownness and happily accepted her share of the collation, using her handkerchief to hold the crisp bread and keep from burning her fingers.

"A tastier cheese than yesterday!" said Uncle Harold, taking great delight in the melted morsel atop his bread. "Wouldn't you agree?"

"Much nicer," said Eda, wiping a few crumbs from her lips. "And, about yesterday, Uncle Harold...." Thankfully, someone had already thought to inform Uncle Harold of the sad event at the bridge, and the only new piece of information Eda brought was the appearance of Mr. Hastings' bloodhound.

Uncle Harold tutted a little at the news. "Well, if he wants to know my whereabouts—though I shouldn't think it would matter—it's easy enough to tell him that I was—"

"Yes," interrupted Eda, "I know what you ought to tell him. But I was thinking, perhaps it might be better to keep that between ourselves. Perhaps, if you were to say that you were feeding your birds?"

Uncle Harold looked at Eda in surprise. "You're a deep one, my girl, and I'm certain you must have some reason?"

Eda shrugged and wiped off a pile of crumbs that had fallen onto her black skirt. "Well...Haro was all alone in the woods. And since that's the case, the less alibis, the better, don't you think?"

Their eyes met, and Uncle Harold's wrinkled face broke into a smile. "Aha!" He touched his finger to his nose in a knowing way. "You're thinking that we should all hold our hand of cards a little closer to the chest, so to speak, while he tries to find which one of us was dealt the knave?"

"Well, yes, in fact. Although I hope that the knave is none of us here at Woldwick—or, at least, none of us that we care about."

"A fine hope, my girl! And on that note, another piece of toast, I think." Uncle Harold buttered a piece of bread and placed it on the toasting fork.

19

JACOB PEVENSEY BEGAN TO draw, with large, swooping lines, in the small notebook he always carried. He was rather enjoying this afternoon's interviews. It was amusing to hear the staff whispering behind his back about the "Bow Street Runner" and then hushing to a scared silence as soon as he turned around, afraid that he had heard them use that offensive term.

Upon his arrival, he had gone through the side door into the kitchen like any traveling tradesman and introduced himself to Mrs. Alfred, the housekeeper. In most houses, the butler would be the person to apply to, but it had not taken more than a moment to ascertain that in this household the housekeeper ruled the roost. Before he had even met the earl, he had learned the names and relationships of all the inmates of the house and of most of the servants too.

A footman had taken him up to the drawing room where he had made the acquaintance of the family, or at least most of them. The earl had been younger than he had expected—and more polite too. In Pevensey's experience, the only thing more distressing to the nobility than a murder in the house was an investigation of who had committed it. But Lord Anglesford seemed willing to have him on the premises. Such cooperation could only mean one of two things—he was innocent...or he was guilty.

The younger brother had been less welcoming. He had neither the physique of a sportsman nor the style of a dandy. He seemed a bookish fellow, still a boy but on the verge of becoming a man. He looked quite capable of strangling a gnat in conversation, but not quite so capable of strangling an attractive female.

And then there was the girl—nay, the woman—with the dark blue eyes. A distant cousin and longstanding member of the family, according to the servants, a beauty through and through, with Irish blood in her if he was not mistaken. Though she'd been standing quite close to the younger brother, Pevensey sensed an even greater closeness between her and the older brother, the earl. Perhaps it was the way they'd exchanged a look when he'd entered...or the way they'd subsequently avoided each other's eyes while he was in the room. He wondered if there was a past—or current—interest between the two.

Whatever the case, that woman was too beautiful by far to be in the same house party as a man's fiancée. Especially if that fiancée were Arabella Hastings. Pevensey snorted down a laugh. He'd had occasion to meet Miss Hastings during his business dealings with her father. If anyone had painted him a picture of Woldwick's inmates a week ago, he would have predicted murder...although, somehow, he would have supposed Miss Hastings to be on the other side of the equation.

Upon leaving the earl's presence, Pevensey's visit with William Hastings had gone much as expected. "Pevensey!" the mill owner had bellowed, pulling him into the private sitting room attached to his chamber. "Thank God you've come!"

"It's all very sad, sir." Pevensey had fingered his hat brim, fully familiar with the necessary posture when talking to the bereaved. "I can only offer my sincere condolences."

"Yes, yes, thank you—but the important thing is to see him hang!"

Pevensey raised an eyebrow. "Who?" Apparently, Mr. Hastings had already solved the case without him.

"Anglesford, of course. He's the one who did it. Went out to jilt my daughter and ended up throttling her instead."

"Ah!" Pevensey pulled out his notebook and a pencil. "And you know this because?"

"Because he came and told me first."

"That he meant to strangle her?"

"No, you dolt, that he meant to jilt her."

"I see." Pevensey put away his notebook. "Why was your daughter outside by the pond? Was she meeting someone out there?"

"Meeting someone? What a ridiculous suggestion! Who would she know to meet with around here? No, she must have been taking a walk, and Anglesford came upon her and attacked her." The mill owner buried his face in his hands, but there was more rage than sorrow in the tight set of his knuckles.

"Never worry, sir," said Pevensey, patting the portly man's shoulder with trained sympathy. "If he's the one, he'll be brought to justice. You have my word on it."

After his interview with Mr. Hastings, Jacob Pevensey had returned to the servants' hall and asked Mrs. Alfred to assemble the servants. Now here he was, notebook and pencil in hand, poised to begin his interrogation.

As everyone from the butler down to the scullery maid assembled, a large woman with strings of hair escaping in every direction from her cap bustled toward him. It did not take more than a cursory glance at her sauce-stained apron for Pevensey to surmise that she worked in the kitchen. And, if her lack of timidity was any clue, she was most probably the empress of that domain.

"Oh, lud, sir!" the cook said, latching onto his sleeve. Her face was as red as the fire she slaved over, and Pevensey caught a strong whiff of garlic and scallions on her breath. "I'm so glad you've come. How can anyone do their work, says I, with a murderer on the loose? Dinner at five, they want. And a full breakfast in the morning. And Miss Swanycke, she says she'll come down here and strangle me herself if I don't send up the tea!"

"You poor soul," said Pevensey, trying to disengage himself as best he could. He refrained from asking whether Miss Swanycke was particularly prone to threatening strangulation—although, under the circumstances it seemed a pertinent question. "Tell me, what did you send up for breakfast yesterday, the day of the murder?"

The cook rattled off a list of bread, rolls, jam, marmalade, eggs, ham, bacon, sausages, tea, coffee, ale, and chocolate.

"Hmm, yes." Pevensey's pencil swooped across the paper. This cook really did deserve a portrait of her own. He penciled in the greasy tendrils of her hair coming out from her cap before beginning to sketch her ample figure. "And did they eat it up, the same as usual?"

"No, come to think of it, they did not! The platters came back almost full again. Although Master Torin did his bit to clear the sausages, I could tell—them's being his favorite."

"Aha!" The scritch-scratching continued, and Pevensey only paused it long enough to give the cook a sly wink. "Thank you, ma'am—you've been most helpful."

"Oh, lud, sir!" said the cook with a giggle that was becoming to neither her size nor her age.

Pevensey scratched his right sideburn with the blunt end of the pencil and squinted—an observer might suspect that he was trying to make out what he himself had just written. In reality, he was noting that he had not quite captured the cook's ears properly. He pursed his lips and snapped the book shut as Mrs. Alfred approached. "They're all here now," said the housekeeper, informing Pevensey that the servants had gathered, just as he had requested.

"Very good," replied Pevensey. He cleared his throat to address the multitude. "Good morning. I daresay you all know I'm here on unpleasant business." He began to pace in front of the line of curious faces, looking intently into each set of eyes as he passed by.

"So, then, is everyone in the house here save the family and their guests?"

"Yes—well, that is, no," said Mrs. Alfred. She looked around the room thoughtfully. "There's Garth, his lordship's valet, and Otto, Mr. Hastings' valet, and Miss Hastings' lady's maid...what was her name?"

"Mademoiselle Mathilde," said the first footman, his cheeks coloring slightly as he supplied the requisite information.

"Hmm, yes, Mademoiselle Mathilde," repeated Mrs. Alfred, with a dour expression that said she was not one to judge, but that in this case, she might have to make an exception.

She continued listing off the absentees for Pevensey's benefit. "Her ladyship has a maid as well—and I do not know if you would count Mrs. Rollo as a guest or...otherwise. She is—or was—a paid companion to Miss Hastings."

Jacob Pevensey cocked his head. Apparently, Mrs. Alfred did not consider Mrs. Rollo on the same level as a guest, and one might easily speculate that this was informed by the companion's treatment at the hands of the family who employed her.

"Whom would you like to see first, sir?"

"Mademoiselle Mathilde, if you please." It was a selfish choice since all the others had been summoned here from their duties solely for the purpose of being questioned. But it was also the sensible choice. If anyone could give Pevensey more insight into the character of the murdered woman, it would be her lady's maid. And if he were to ask the right questions of everyone else, he would need that insight first.

"I'll interview the rest of you all in good time." Pevensey gave a smile that caused the housemaids to blush and rethink any previous aversions to red-haired men. "If you would be so good, Mrs. Alfred...."

"Of course," said the housekeeper, a little put out that her assembly of the servants had all been for naught. But it did not take much more than a quick compliment of her efficiency for Pevensey to win her over. "Well then," she said, smoothing down the dark fabric of her skirt, "Henry can direct you to the upstairs parlor, and I will send Mademoiselle Mathilde word to meet you there."

Pevensey fell in behind the dark-haired first footman and ascended the back stairs with a wrinkle in his forehead. It was obvious that the lady's maid was French. And Frenchwomen, he had often found, were not as easily charmed as English housemaids.

Henry delivered Pevensey to the upstairs parlor without mishap, but he seemed reluctant to leave even though his mission had been accomplished. Pevensey knew better than to ascribe this lingering to his own presence. He had seen the blush the first footman gave when Miss Hastings' maid was mentioned.

Mademoiselle Mathilde was not there yet. Pevensey had not expected her to be. Even if Mrs. Alfred's message had already reached her, she would doubtless keep him waiting, as was the wont of lady's maids and Frenchwomen.

"Mademoiselle Mathilde's a tempting armful, eh?" Pevensey asked the footman bluntly.

The footman gaped. "Oh's, I couldn't say, sir."

"But I daresay she hasn't looked in your direction?"

There was that blush again. Pevensey mused to himself that if he ended up needing to know Mademoiselle Mathilde's whereabouts on the day of the murder, Henry might prove immensely helpful.

The door opened and in flounced a skeletally thin but good-looking woman, with dark brown curls and a sprigged muslin dress far too fine for someone of her station. "Ah, Mademoiselle Mathilde," said Pevensey. "A pleasure."

"The pleasure, I think, is all yours." She settled herself upon the sofa. The footman took the opportunity to glide out the open door.

"I have some questions to put to you about the morning of your mistress' murder."

"Mon dieu! Then ask them. I do not have all the time in the world to sit here and listen to you."

Pevensey smiled inwardly. A lady's maid without a lady to attend was clearly not as busy as this one claimed to be. After all, Miss Hastings' corpse hardly needed to be dressed for dinner.

Pevensey looked at the gown the maid was wearing. It did not quite fit around the shoulders and had clearly been made for someone else. Perhaps that was why she had so little time to talk to him—she needed to finish going through her late mistress' wardrobe and helping herself to articles of dress before Mr. Hastings overcame his grief enough to dismiss her from service.

"What time did Miss Hastings wake yesterday?"

The lady's maid threw up her hands. "Je ne sais pas. I am not one of these English butlers with a pocket watch always in hand."

"Surely, you must have some idea."

The edges of Mademoiselle Mathilde's nose curled in derision as she deliberately looked the other way. Pevensey pulled out his notebook, and his pencil began a rough sketch of Mademoiselle Mathilde's upturned nose. The brown-haired abigail was not so attractive with that ugly sneer on her face, but in Pevensey's opinion, she was far more interesting.

There. He had perfectly captured the lines of that little Gallic chin. He had succeeded in rendering his subject curious as well, wondering what he could possibly be writing about when she had offered him no information. It was impossible to continue her sneer forever, and when Mademoiselle Mathilde finally turned her head back to look at him, Pevensey gave her another opportunity.

"So, in consideration for the fact that you do not often consult a timepiece, would you say that Miss Hastings woke before sunrise or after sunrise?"

"After."

Pevensey wrinkled his nose and finished drawing the curls on the left side of her forehead. Sunrise at this time of year would be around eight o'clock.

"And after she awoke, did Miss Hastings go downstairs for breakfast?"

Mademoiselle Mathilde shrugged.

"Did you dress her in garments suitable to go downstairs for breakfast?"

"I suppose so."

That answer was far too vague. It was essential to know whether she had been wearing an indoor dress or an outdoor one. In other words, had she intended to walk out to the pond from the moment she awakened or did the idea come to her later?

"Let us be clear with each other, mademoiselle. What exactly did you dress her in? Was it the red pelisse that she was wearing when she was found dead in the pond?"

The maid hesitated. Could it be because she was about to tell him a lie? Or was it because, after all her prevarications, she was finally going to tell him the truth?

"*Oui*. In the red pelisse."

20

HARO THUMBED THROUGH THE latest issue of The Sporting Magazine for a minute, read a short article on how to keep one's hunters in fine fettle, and then listlessly tossed the magazine down on the end table. All morning they had been waiting for the Bow Street Runner to arrive, and now that he was here there was nothing but more waiting. If only the fellow would hurry up and ferret out the culprit. Although, unless it were some stranger from the woods who had done away with Arabella, Haro was not so sure he wanted to hear the results of Pevensey's inquiry.

Haro fidgeted in the armchair, jumped up, and paced. He wished that he took snuff so that he would have something to do with his hands. Blast this inactivity! He wanted to ride, to dig his heels into his favorite mount and send the beast bounding through the woods, to have the winter wind slicing at his face like a cutlass and the rhythm of hooves soothing his spirit. But he had given his word to Hastings—he could not leave the house until Pevensey had finished his investigation.

Ah well, if he could not ride, perhaps he could locate a companion, someone to shoot billiards with or play a game of chess. For the last week he had cared little about how the other inmates of the house were spending their time—except for Arabella, whom he had felt the burden to entertain and amuse. Now, all he could think about was how pleasant it would be to have some company. Torin was still sitting with their mother upstairs, and Eda had not come back to the drawing room. He certainly did not want to seek out William Hastings, and the servants were out of the question.

That left no one. Or rather, it left Philippe Bayeux, the architect. Haro cocked his head to the side. He hadn't caught a glimpse of the Frenchman since the incident. Supposedly, he was keeping to his room to spare the feelings of the family. Or maybe to spare his own feelings? Eda had said the fellow had a *tendre* for Arabella. If so, he was probably sitting in his room all Friday-faced and broken up. A slight twinge of guilt attacked Haro, insinuating that as Arabella's fiancé he ought to be more broken up about what had happened too.

Haro picked up the magazine again and rolled it into a child's telescope. He would go have a look at what Bayeux was up to, and if he could not distract the poor fellow from his grief, why then, at least the poor fellow could distract him from his anxious pacing. The telescope slipped out of his hands as he dropped it carelessly onto the sofa.

It took Haro a few minutes to locate which chamber Bayeux had been placed in. The housekeeper, sensing the confusion over whether the architect was a guest or an interloper, had assigned him a small bedroom somewhere between the family and the servants. Haro rapped on the door with polite knuckles. There was no response. He rapped on it again.

"*Oui*?" came a voice—whether grieving, harried, or irritated, Haro could not tell. "What do you want?"

"I say, Bayeux," replied Haro with as much cheer as he could muster. "I was hoping to coax you into an afternoon game of billiards."

There was a pause. "Non. Merci beaucoup, *mais non*."

Haro grimaced. The fellow sounded distraught. "Well, in all honesty, the billiards were just a pretext for pouring down a glass. Care to join me for some brandy in the billiards room?"

There was another pause, and then Philippe Bayeux swung open the door. His face was as haggard as a night watchman's at the end of his shift. But whatever the circumstances might be, it seemed he was a man who improved his own spirits by drinking other people's.

"Your lordship is a generous man," said the Frenchman. Haro was not entirely sure if it was a compliment.

"Terribly unfortunate you having to be detained here," said Haro, making small talk as he led the way down the corridor. Just after the words left his mouth, he realized how callous they sounded—as if he were bemoaning the dratted inconvenience of having his fiancée murdered.

Fortunately, Bayeux had receded into his shell of silence and seemed to take no notice of the earl's gaffe. They entered the billiards room and Haro, for the sake of appearances, set the billiard balls up on the table. "And now then," said Haro, throwing open the door of the liquor cabinet. "I'm for brandy. You?"

Bayeux walked over to the cabinet and took hold of the bottle of gin.

"Blue Ruin, eh?" said Haro with a whistle. He had a dim memory of his father indulging—and perhaps, overindulging—in it, which was probably why the bottle was in the house. It was not a selection he himself favored. Gin always tasted like eating an evergreen forest, and although he liked the scent of pines when riding through the woods, he did not fancy them blended up in a glass. "Well then, help yourself."

The architect had not waited for the invitation. And indeed, if the earl had not been present, it was likely that he would have ignored civilization's dictates and drunk directly from the bottle.

Haro sipped his brandy in silence. He had gone looking for Bayeux because he needed something to occupy his mind, but now, he realized that the kinder and more necessary thing would be to occupy Bayeux's. "It's been quite the cold spell we've been having this year."

Bayeux shivered. "Yes, very cold." The clear glass of the gin bottle showed that its store had already been significantly depleted.

Haro floundered in the wake of that response. His mother had taught him how to converse fluently with strangers, but every single one of the scripted pleasantries that he weighed upon his tongue felt like cutting capers at a funeral.

"I'm sorry," he blurted out.

The Frenchman set down his glass of gin and buried his head in his hands. "It is not your fault."

Haro sighed. At least there was one person who did not blame him for Arabella's death.

After Miss Hastings' maid had flounced her way out of the parlor, Pevensey wandered over to the window and stared out of it for a few moments, hands behind his back. The conversation with Mademoiselle Mathilde, despite her recalcitrance, had been very illuminating.

His thoughts were interrupted by a gentle clearing of the throat. It was Henry. "Mrs. Alfred sent me, sir, to see who should be sent up next."

Pevensey wrinkled his nose. He had not heard Henry's footsteps on the staircase, as by rights he should have, had the footman been coming up from the kitchen.

"It seems only fair that if I've seen the lady's maid, I ought to see the gentleman's manservant."

"Just as you say, sir," said Henry, and he stepped out of the room smartly to alert the Earl of Anglesford's valet.

Pevensey took up his pencil as soon as Garth entered, but he found himself far less interested in this sketch than he had been in the previous one. The valet's manner was stiff and guarded, and he weighed all his statements like a butcher might do before wrapping them in brown paper and presenting them to Pevensey.

"Now, see here," said Pevensey candidly, after he had learned that Haro had not acted in any way unusual on the morning in question and displayed no agitation whatsoever, "if you had seen his lordship throttle Miss Hastings and dump her body in the pond—with your own two eyes, mind you—would you tell me?"

The question did not penetrate Garth's reserve, but he at least acknowledged the merit of it. "No, sir, I would not."

"So I thought. I thank you for confirming that his lordship rose early and dressed to go downstairs. But since you cannot confirm anything further regarding his whereabouts, I think I have no further use for you."

Garth inclined his head and exited. His presence in the room was swiftly replaced with the ubiquitous Henry. "Who next, sir?"

"Why, you, Henry!" Pevensey shrugged. "Since you're here." He tucked his pencil behind his ear. "Tell me about the argument that took place between the earl and Mr. Hastings."

"I don't know about any argu—"

"Nonsense, Henry!" said Pevensey, with a dismissive wave of the hand. "You are evidently adept at listening through keyholes."

The footman colored. "I don't know what you mean, sir—"

"I daresay you hid in the linen closet there, yes, just outside the door as Mademoiselle Mathilde was leaving?"

The footman swallowed visibly.

"So, tell me, Henry. What exactly was said during the argument between the earl and Mr. Hastings?"

It was a guess, but it might prove profitable. Henry's discomfort was a telltale sign. Pevensey pulled out his notebook and began to sketch—a man in livery with an exaggeratedly long nose and an unmistakable proximity to a keyhole.

"You'll not mention anything to his lordship about this?" the footman blurted out. "Or to Mrs. Alfred?" Of the two, it seemed like Mrs. Alfred was the more formidable in his eyes.

Pevensey's eyes flicked upward with disdain. "I will mention whatever I please and whatever proves pertinent. Continue."

The footman sighed audibly and gave in to the inevitable. As he talked, his speech settled into the familiar patterns of his childhood rather than the proper diction he had learned to assume around his betters.

"I weren't meaning to eavesdrop,"—a time-honored introductory statement to such stories, thought Pevensey—"but I had brought up a Cornish pastie and some ale for Mr. Hastings, just like he'd asked for, and I was about to knock on the door, when I heard voices. They were too loud not to recognize and too angry to interrupt. 'Why then,' thought I, 'here's no time to be delivering a pastie. I'll wait right here 'til the gentlemen settle down a mite and then knock on the door proper-like.'"

"You may omit what was thought," said Pevensey, the scritch-scratching of his pencil making everything seem very official from the other's perspective. "Simply state what was said."

"Well, the first thing that I heard was Mr. Hastings calling his lordship some names that I'd be ashamed to use on my worst enemy,"—Pevensey doubted that the first footman had any enemies more daunting than an envious second footman—"and his lordship started to shout a little too. He called Mr. Hastings a bully and said he had a mind to end the engagement."

"Aha!" Pevensey wondered if this decision on the earl's part was premeditated or if he had been provoked into making it during the course of this conversation. "What then?"

"Mr. Hastings roared something at him about not being a gentleman. And then they quieted down. I waited a few minutes and knocked to deliver the pastie. His lordship was just leaving as I went in."

Pevensey reflected that the story confirmed what Hastings had told him. The earl had decided that morning to jilt the mill owner's daughter. But it still did not tell him why he was jilting her. And the answer to that question might be of crucial significance in this case, for even if the earl turned out to be innocent of Miss Hastings' death, Pevensey had a hunch that the relationship between the two was still the prime mover which had set the event in motion.

"One more question for you," said Pevensey, "before I go back to the servants' hall to interview the downstairs servants. Have you ever heard Lord Anglesford shout at anyone before, the way he shouted at Hastings?"

"No," said the footman, with a pause. "Come to think of it, I never have."

"Time for your nap," Eda said, as Uncle Harold's eyes began to droop.

"Nonsense, my dear!" said Uncle Harold, but before many more minutes passed, he was snoring away in the chair by the fire in the garret.

Eda took the time to brown another piece of toast for herself, munched on it thoughtfully, and then put another log on the fire to ensure that Uncle Harold stayed warm. She wandered aimlessly down the stairs from the attic.

At the door of the music room, she paused. She thought about playing some Mozart on the pianoforte but realized that those sunny scale passages cascading through the house would be too heartless, even for someone who had despised Arabella as much as she had. Her lips compressed into a firm line. In life, Arabella had threatened to destroy the spirit of Woldwick, and now, even in death, she was still casting a pall over the place.

Throughout the last week, Eda had never thought any further than how to get Arabella's claws out of Haro. She had not realized that those claws would leave marks, some of them so deep that perhaps they would never heal. But then, it all depended on the outcome of this investigation.

She descended the main staircase down to the morning room, pulled out her paper and began to sketch. It was a face she knew by heart she had sketched it so many times. But she had never sketched it like this before, lips slightly parted, eyes filled with intense longing...what was it he had been about to say, standing before the mantel in the drawing room?

Her head bowed low over the paper, and her black hair, half of it unpinned, fell forward over her shoulders, framing the whiteness of her long neck.

The door opened, and Jacob Pevensey sauntered in unannounced as if he were a houseguest or a member of the family. Eda sat up sharply, dropped her pencil, and turned over the paper to conceal the drawing. "How can I help you, sir?"

"Oh, please! Stay seated, miss," said the Bow Street Runner, in a tone that he had doubtless cultivated to soothe the nerves of gentlewomen. But Eda was not taken in. He had come to ask questions, and she must be careful what answers she gave. She knew the general impression led to suspicion of Haro, so whatever she said must cast doubt on the general impression.

"I've just come from interviewing the servants."

"All of them?" Eda's eyebrows raised. He had only been here a couple of hours. Either the man was incompetent at questioning or a very efficient investigator.

"The ones that mattered," said Pevensey smugly. Eda was reminded of how much she had always disliked red-haired men.

"Do I matter enough to be interviewed?"

"But of course! Is there even a question of that?"

Eda supposed that a serving maid would have blushed at that or simpered coyly. She would give him no such satisfaction. If he dared to try to kiss her hand, as it looked like he might, she would box his ears!

"What are you drawing?"

She placed her hands protectively over the reverse side of the paper. "Is this part of the interview?"

"Just a question from one artist to another."

Such familiarity was not to be borne! Eda looked at the Runner coldly. "My sketches are private."

"All except the one you gave as a gift to Miss Hastings?"

Eda's mouth fell open. "Who told you about that?"

"The second footman."

She forced her mouth to close. It had never occurred to her that the servants would take an interest in her rivalry with the mill owner's daughter. But now that she thought about it properly, it was only natural for them to gossip about it belowstairs.

"It was a picture of Monsieur Bayeux, the architect, wasn't it?"

It seemed that he already knew as much. "Yes."

"Now that is curious. Why would you give the young lady a picture of Monsieur Bayeux? Surely, it would be more usual to give a picture of your cousin, her fiancé, for her to treasure?"

She had thought that this freckle-faced investigator could not penetrate her defenses, but at the idea of giving Arabella a keepsake picture of Haro, every sense revolted!

"I thought," she said, swallowing hard, "that she would prefer the picture of Monsieur Bayeux, seeing as how they had been previously acquainted."

"Acquainted?" Pevensey's ears perked up. Apparently, this piece of information was not one that he had already learned from the servants. "How so?"

"Oh, you'll have to ask him," replied Eda breezily, having completely recovered her composure and preparing to lead the Runner down another path. "He had drawn up some plans for her father in the past, but I think there was more to it than that." She looked up at him through her dark eyelashes. "I'm sure you know what I mean."

Pevensey tapped his nose in a knowing manner. "Certainly, certainly. I'll discuss the matter with Monsieur Bayeux. And for now, I have just one more question to put to you, Miss Swanycke."

Eda pursed her lips. "Yes?"

"What were you doing yesterday morning when the sad event occurred?"

"Why, I suppose I was in my room, sketching."

"Alone?"

"Yes,"—she looked him directly in the eyes—"quite alone."

Pevensey shut the door to his garret room. Mrs. Alfred had done her best to find him a comfortable place to stay, but he was used to the awkwardness attending his position where he was not quite a servant and not quite a guest of the family.

The afternoon and evening had passed quickly for him, though rather more slowly, he imagined, for those waiting to be interrogated. He had spoken to most of the servants and learned some very curious things about the more genteel inmates of the house.

He flipped through his sketchbook. There was a picture of Miss Swanycke—or at least, the closest rendering he could make of Miss Swanycke—striking Miss Hastings across the face. The scullery maid, who was not overly fond of Miss Hastings, had taken great pleasure in describing the scene. She was not certain why the slap had happened, although she was absolutely certain it was for good reason. It seems that the mill owner's daughter had leaned in to whisper something just before the vengeful slap had been administered. Pevensey would give a pretty penny to have been a blue-bottle fly on the wall close enough to hear what words had antagonized the Irish captain's daughter.

He turned another page in the sketchbook. There was the second footman opening the door for a haughty young woman in a modish pelisse. Pevensey had added the hall clock into this picture, with the hour hand set at eight o'clock but the minute hand missing entirely. Apparently, Mademoiselle Mathilde was not the only servant who paid little heed to the time, for the second footman could only give him the roughest approximation of when he had opened the door to allow Miss Hastings egress from the house.

He turned the page again. Here was a horse being led out of a shadowy stable with a lantern casting its rays into the stable yard. The groom, even though he had no clock on him, had a sharp eye for his surroundings. The sun had just been peeping over the tree line when he had led out a saddled horse for Monsieur Bayeux to ride to the village...or, at least, the village was the destination he had claimed.

Pevensey pursed his lips and rubbed his chin with a pensive thumb and forefinger. This put Bayeux outside the house before Miss Hastings had stepped out the door, with easy opportunity to meet her at the icy bridge. According to Miss Swanycke, there had been something between the two of them, an attraction, at least on Bayeux's side—and seeing as how Miss Hastings had engaged herself to another man, the attraction had most probably not been reciprocated.

Unless, of course, they were star-crossed lovers, with Miss Hastings having been coerced into the betrothal by her pater familias. Pevensey snorted. That was a possibility that could not be dismissed. It was apparent to any close observer that the mill owner would have sacrificed the feelings of his offspring if there was any consequence to be gained by doing so.

Pevensey unbuttoned his waistcoat and loosened his cravat. He sat down on the green brocade coverlet that lay across the bed and began to remove his boots. William Hastings' valet and Lady Anglesford's lady's maid had provided little information that he did not already know, but the important players were still holding their cards.

He must not neglect interviewing the architect on the morrow, although he suspected that the most helpful indicators in that area of the field would come not from Bayeux himself but from the others he had not yet interviewed—the earl, his mother, his brother, and the downtrodden companion Mrs. Rollo.

21

"I SAY!" SAID TORIN, chewing a hearty mouthful of breakfast while voicing his complaint. "That fellow Pevensey never came and spoke to me yesterday. Nor mother either!" He was seated at the end of the table with Haro and Eda on either side. It was a family gathering to discuss the state of affairs, missing only Lady Anglesford who had chosen to take breakfast in her room.

"He avoided me as well," said Haro, his broad shoulders obscuring the entire back of the small chair. He tried to hide his own annoyance. It would be an unpleasant interview—he was sure of it—and he wanted nothing more than to have it over with.

Eda, warming her white hands on the sides of her teacup, gave an arch smile. "I am the favored one then, for he interviewed me just before teatime."

"Oh?" said Torin, a hint of jealousy in his tone. "And what did he ask you?"

"This and that," she replied mysteriously and took a sip of her tea. "He brought up that ridiculous sketch, and I put him on the trail of Monsieur Bayeux."

Haro flushed as Eda mentioned the sketch, remembering the whole awkward episode and the trouble it had brought.

"Well done!" said Torin. "And, as I've said before, it was probably Bayeux that did it."

"Now, now!" said Haro, coming to the architect's defense. "You don't know that." He could not help but feel a great deal of compassion for the man, alone with his sorrow and his bottle of Blue Ruin.

"Why are you defending him?" demanded Torin. "He's a complete stranger to all of us—shows up at the house without an invitation and starts planning to knock down walls and set up columns in the courtyard. Eda says he told her all about how he was 'in love' with your intended. That alone ought to make you suspicious of him. No doubt when she refused to reciprocate his advances, his temper got the better of him and he—"

"Enough!" said Haro, raising a hand to halt the conversation. "I believe Mr. Pevensey is the one in charge of gathering and sifting through the evidence. We'll let him decide who to cry rope on."

"All right, all right then," said Torin with a sniff. "But if that Runner deigns to speak with me today, I shan't give the Frenchman a glowing character reference." He wolfed down a few more bites of sausage. "Did you give him an alibi for your whereabouts, Eda?"

The black-haired woman set down her teacup with nonchalance. "No. I left things very vague. Told him I was all alone, sketching in my room or doing some such thing." She smiled provocatively at Haro.

The earl closed his eyes. Was she doing this purposely to vex him?

Torin tsked. "That was silly of you, Eda. But we can at least hope that he hasn't heard of your drawing room duel."

"Oh, yes. He most certainly has. It is much talked of downstairs."

Haro began to massage his own temples. Really this whole thing would be easier if he just locked Eda in her room for the duration of the investigation. That taradiddle about the twisted ankle might come in useful to explain why she must keep to her bed. He lifted his thumbs gently away from his temples.

"Headache?" Eda enquired. "Shall I ring for Cook to send up some chamomile?"

Haro opened his eyes. "I hardly think chamomile will be of sufficient strength to cope with the problems you keep creating."

"The problems I keep creating?" Her voice was indignant. "If I recall correctly, it was you who invited the Hastings here in the first place, and you who betrothed yourself to that trollop!"

Haro pushed his chair away from the table and stood up sternly. "Trollop? I don't recall Arabella being the one pushing her way into gentlemen's bedr—"

Torin cleared his throat loudly. There, standing in the frame of the open French door was the Bow Street Runner who had precipitated this conversation with his presence at Woldwick.

"Good morning, my lord!" Jacob Pevensey nodded to Haro and bowed with a flourish to them all. "If Mr. Torin Emison would be so obliging, I would greatly enjoy having a word with him this morning.

"Well, it's about time," said Torin, but he did not get up from his seat.

Eda, her face as pink as a carnation, looked down at her half-empty teacup.

Haro abandoned his chair altogether and walked over to the window to scrutinize the frozen fog that was billowing out of the trees. He stole a glance at Eda and saw that she was too mortified to speak. How had he let the conversation spiral into accusations of that kind?

The Runner was still standing there, smiling and staring.

Haro cut through the silence. "And will you be needing me anytime soon, Mr. Pevensey?"

"All in good time, my lord," said Pevensey smoothly. "I suppose you could say I like to save the best for last."

"I'm not sure what that's supposed to mean in this case," said Haro, trying his best not to stiffen at the remark. He looked over at his brother. "But since Torin refuses to relinquish his breakfast, then perhaps we'd best relinquish the room to you for his interrogation."

Walking over to Eda's chair, Haro slid it back to help her rise. Then, taking her arm, he led her out of the room, down the hallway, and into the library.

A fire was burning in the fireplace, casting a warm glow over the parquet floor. The backs of two high wingback chairs shielded them from some of the heat from the flames, but even so, it was markedly warmer in this room than it had been in the hallway.

The library door had no sooner closed than Eda raised her hand, ready to strike. But Haro had anticipated the motion and caught her wrist between his own fingers. Eda's left hand attempted another attack, but Haro caught that and pinioned it as well.

"How dare you!" she hissed. Her dark blue eyes blazed.

"May I remind you that you said the word trollop first!"

"Yes, well...not in reference to myself."

"It's not very charitable to speak ill of the dead."

"I never claimed charity as one of my better qualities."

Haro loosened his grip. "Oh, I wouldn't say that. You've been charitable enough not to cast my mistakes up in my face...until just a moment ago, and in front of that Bow Street Runner, to boot."

He dropped his hold on her wrists, but he still stood directly in front of her, his face no more than a hand's breadth from hers.

"Well, if it's any comfort,"—she put a small white hand on the lapel of his jacket—"I'm sure my little outburst only served to prove to him that I'm a jealous virago, capable of committing any crime to steal back the man she loves."

Haro held his breath and tried to keep his tone jovial. "Oh, so you're in love with me, are you?"

Eda's eyelids dropped demurely, and her hand slid off his lapel onto the white muslin of his shirt front. "It adds a pleasant touch to the story, don't you think?"

"A very pleasant touch indeed." Haro's heart was threatening to leap outside of his chest.

He reached out his right hand, ever so slowly and was just about to place it on the curve of her face when a loud sniff came from the recesses of one of the wingback chairs. With one swift, guilty motion, they both sprang apart.

Eda clapped her hand over her mouth and, motioning to Haro to follow her, tiptoed toward the door handle. The earl was no more than a step behind, and before half a minute had passed, they were back in the hallway on the other side of the library door. With tacit consent, they darted towards the main staircase and only stopped once they had put a flight of stairs between themselves and the mysterious eavesdropper in the wingback chair.

"Who was that?" demanded Eda, breathless, leaning on the banister. "William Hastings?"

"I don't think so," said Haro. "He would have been thundering away at us the moment we started talking.

"Philippe Bayeux then?"

"Maybe...." said Haro. He would not have expected the Frenchman to sniff like that.

"If Mr. Pevensey were not with your brother, I would almost say it was him. He seems to have a penchant for surprising us."

"Dashed annoying of him, don't you think?" said Haro lightly. This last interruption was more than annoying—it was downright infuriating.

"Now, now, Lord Anglesford." Eda took on a tone of mock reproof. "I must remind you to watch your language in front of a lady."

"Oh, is that what you are calling yourself now? I beg your pardon!" Haro grinned. He had forgotten how much he loved sparring with Eda; it sharpened his mind and magnified his mirth—and made the sentimental exchanges Arabella had been so fond of all the more cloying.

"Eda, dear, is that you?" said a thin voice from a nearby room. It was Lady Anglesford lying on the sofa in her sitting room with a bottle of hartshorn in hand. "Come sit with me a while, if you will. My nerves could use some company."

"Yes, of course, Aunt," Eda called out. She glided past Haro, stopping in the hallway for a short moment to send him one last look.

Haro sighed and held out a hand in supplication. "My nerves could use some company too."

Eda arched an eyebrow. "Nonsense. It's really quite good for you, you know."

"What's good for me?"

"The prospect of being hanged. It puts everything in such glorious perspective." She placed a hand on the door leading to Lady Anglesford's sitting room. "But in case you feel faint without me, I'm sure your valet can find you your own bottle of hartshorn."

"A poor substitute," said Haro gallantly, but she had already disappeared, and he was once again left to his own devices as he waited for Pevensey to interrogate the other members of the house.

"Of course, I will answer your question," said Torin smugly. "I breakfasted here in this very room with my mother, and then we spent the rest of the morning together in the drawing room."

Pevensey listened as he made a hurried sketch of the young man sitting at the table, empty breakfast plate in front of him. "And what exactly does a young man such as yourself do all morning in the drawing room?" He slid the barest hint of condescension into his question, as if to imply that Torin sat at embroidery with his mother or worked on his needlepoint.

"What is that supposed to mean?" Torin's tone turned belligerent. "A gentleman can enjoy his books, can he not?"

"Of course, of course," said Pevensey soothingly. He could see that this one was more prone to outbursts of temper than his elder brother seemed to be. "Was anyone else in the drawing room with you?"

"No."

"I see." The pencil scratched across the notebook as he finished his sketch. He clapped his book shut. "Were you fond of Miss Hastings?"

"Why the devil should I have been?"

"She was engaged to your brother—three weeks away from being your new sister." Pevensey was beginning to enjoy himself.

Torin snorted. "Not at the end, she wasn't. He called it off."

"Oh, but I thought he was only intending to call it off. Unless he actually did see her that morning and break the news to her?"

Pevensey watched Torin flounder. "Yes, you're right—only intending to call it off. Because, of course, he didn't see her that morning. Nobody in the house saw her before she wandered off alone and was attacked by some footpad."

"A footpad, was it?" said Pevensey. "Do you have much trouble with them in this part of the country?"

Torin hemmed and hawed a little. "I wouldn't know...you'd do better to ask the local constable, or Sir Robert, him being the magistrate."

"I see." Pevensey's face was blank. "Well, I think that will be all. I have several more interviews to do this morning. Do you know if Lady Anglesford is in her room? Would I be able to speak with her?"

Torin had been far from helpful during Pevensey's previous questions, and he could see that the young man regarded this last question as an even greater intrusion than the ones before.

"She is too frail to speak with visitors"—or at least visitors of Pevensey's ilk, Torin's tone implied. "I already told you she was with me all that morning, and I'm sure there's nothing she could tell you that someone else has not already said."

"I shall be very brief," said Pevensey smoothly. "She is an important person, and I would not like to leave her out of my report."

Torin glared. "Oh, very well, I will go speak with her and see if she can spare you five minutes." He rose from his chair and stomped over to the door.

"Thank you," said Pevensey to the back of Torin's slight shoulders. It was interesting, the hostility radiating from this young man. He wondered how much of it had been exhibited to Miss Hastings. The boy had clearly disliked her and was not old enough, or worldly enough, to conceal the fact.

Pevensey tapped his chin with the end of his pencil. He would not be surprised if Lady Anglesford confirmed her son's story. It was an alibi given by a severely prejudiced party, and Torin, ascending the stairs to warn his mother of the imminent interview, would have ample time to make sure she corroborated every detail of his story.

Eda was just leaving Lady Anglesford's sitting room when Torin popped his head in.

"How did things go with the investigator?" she asked.

Torin shrugged and gave a noncommittal grunt. The fellow had asked some extremely impertinent questions, but he felt that he had kept his wits about him through it all.

"That well?" said Eda with a grin. "Well, I suppose that you shall not be hanged for murder then."

As Eda disappeared into the hallway, Torin came over and put his hand on his mother's shoulder. "How are you feeling today?"

"I confess I'm a trifle overset at present," said Lady Anglesford. The large frills of her dressing gown made her look even more diminutive than usual. She put her hand on her bosom as if to still the palpitations of her heart. "It's this murder investigation," she said with a shudder as Torin took a seat beside her. "And do you know what Eda's just told me?" She lowered her voice. "She wasn't with a single soul when it all happened. I'm afraid that—"

"That the Runner will think it was her?"

"Yes, well...yes. She did slap Miss Hastings, and there was certainly ill feeling between them."

"You don't think she did it, do you?" asked Torin.

"My dear! Of course not!" There was a great deal of energy in Lady Anglesford's voice, and the question seemed to bring her out of her languor. "It's impossible for us to think such a thing. We know her. But the investigator doesn't know her, and he may be misled by the circumstances. I think it would be best to tell him she was with me that morning."

"But he's just asked me," said Torin, "and I told him you and I were together in the drawing room!"

Lady Anglesford patted his hand. "Leave it to me."

"Very well," said Torin, "but I think I'd better stay for this. If your story starts becoming too farfetched, he'll think we're all lying and arrest me for murder."

Lady Anglesford rang for the footman, and within a few moments, Henry was escorting Jacob Pevensey upstairs to the mistress of the house's sitting room. As their footsteps sounded in the hallway, Lady Anglesford pulled her lap rug up about her like an invalid, and Torin jumped to his feet and stood—arms crossed—behind the sofa where she was reclining.

"Thank you for agreeing to see me, Lady Anglesford," said Pevensey, after the footman had been dismissed with a nod. "I was hoping to speak with you alone...." He turned a questioning glance at Torin.

"My mother is not at all well," replied Torin, "and I will be here to support her while you ask your questions. Please, keep it brief."

Pevensey tried to hide his smile. This young man was contorting his face into such a serious expression. It would have been a far different matter if his brother, the broad-shouldered earl, had adopted this stance, but as it was, the youth was more amusing than imposing.

"As you wish, my lord," said Pevensey, purposely giving the young man a title that did not suit him.

He wondered which brother the late earl had most resembled, the blond giant or the dark philosopher. The younger brother had a temper that was always smoldering, while the current earl seemed far more placid—indeed, Harold Emison almost seemed content to let others direct the part he played in this life.

But at the same time, there was also the glimmer of something more, some force that had awoken within him and given tongue two days ago when he had thundered an unequivocal denial to William Hastings and broken off the engagement to his daughter.

Was it also a force strong enough and angry enough to extinguish a life that stood in the way of his desires? Of that, Jacob Pevensey was not yet sure.

Pevensey had brought his notebook with him when he went to interview Lady Anglesford, but the story the lady of the house told him took him so much by surprise that his mouth fell open and his sketchbook fell closed.

"Let me make certain I understand you," Pevensey had said. "You were in the drawing room with your younger son and with Miss Swanycke all morning?"

"Yes, that is what I said," replied Lady Anglesford, her pale blue eyes blinking innocently.

"And what was Miss Swanycke doing in the drawing room all this time?"

"Sketching," said Torin promptly. "That's what she's always doing."

Pevensey raked a hand through his bright red hair. He would have given half a crown to have had this conversation with Lady Anglesford unchaperoned.

"I am sorry, Mr. Emison"—he tried to maintain a smile—"but I don't remember you mentioning that Miss Swanycke was in the drawing room."

"I daresay it's because she was sitting over in the window seat and keeping quiet while I was on the sofa keeping Mama company." Torin smirked as if he had just said something extremely clever. Pevensey, on the other hand, thought that this attempt to bamboozle him was rather feeble.

"And did Miss Swanycke leave the drawing room at any time?"

"Not that I recall," said Lady Anglesford. "I believe she was with us when we heard the alarm raised and then learned the dreadful news."

Pevensey stared, not knowing whether to be amused or incensed. This dowager countess was serving him one bouncer after another. Why would she feel the need to lie to protect her ward? Was she suspicious that Eda had been involved in the murder?

"Since we are on the subject of Miss Swanycke, could you tell me what transpired between her and Miss Hastings after dinner on the evening before the tragedy?"

"Something transpired?"

"According to your servants, yes."

"I am not accustomed to listening to the tittle-tattle of servants—I can't think what on earth you could mean."

"Very well then," Pevensey said, deciding to take a different tack. He peeled off the mask of charm that had done such wonders with the downstairs staff. "I have just one further question for you. Have you any proof that would contradict the prevailing notion that your elder son quarreled with Miss Hastings at the pond and strangled her in a fit of rage?"

The countess gave an inarticulate squeak. She reached for her bottle of hartshorn. "You are offensive, sir! What further proof could you need other than his proven character and position as a gentleman and peer of the realm!"

"What further proof indeed?" echoed Pevensey with a smile.

Later, after Torin had barked at him to leave Lady Anglesford's sitting room, he had drawn the scene, the dowager countess sitting tensed on the sofa looking ready to cast aside her lap rug at any minute and hurl her bottle of hartshorn, like a gauntlet, at his face. As he sketched, a broad smile nearly split his freckled face in two. He'd wager that the story of the countess' invalid state was as accurate as the story about Eda Swanycke sketching away the morning while her rival plunged to the depths of an icy pond. And since the countess had made a point of lying, he would have to make a point of finding out why.

22

IT HAD BEEN TWO days since Arabella Hastings' death, and Eda had assumed that the shock and rage displayed by the victim's father would have dissipated by now into a quieter sort of grief. It was with great surprise, however, that she heard shouting and falling objects coming from behind the closed door of the room that had belonged to Arabella.

"What on earth is going on, Garth?" she asked Haro's valet, who had also heard the noise and had stopped polishing his lordship's Hessians to come out into the hallway and listen.

"It sounds as if Mr. Hastings is ringing a fine peal in there."

"Over whom? Is that a woman's voice?"

"Aye. That'll be Mademoiselle Mathilde, she who was lady's maid to Miss Hastings."

"Good lord! How on earth can he treat her so? I wonder if I should intervene."

"I suspect Mr. Hastings' outrage is not without reason," said Garth carefully. Apparently, he had eavesdropped for longer than Eda had and knew some of the particulars of the row.

"Has the lady's maid done something wrong?"

"Well—"

The screeching grew louder, and Eda, signaling to Garth to keep quiet, tiptoed over to the door and placed her ear against the panel.

"She meant for me to have them!" said the woman's voice. "It is a standard arrangement between a lady and her lady's maid."

"Rubbish!" shouted Hastings, and a few worse things besides. "You'll put everything you took back in the trunks, you thieving hussy."

"Mon dieu! I am not a thief!"

Garth had tiptoed over to the door also, and he and Eda looked at one another with raised eyebrows.

"Quiet! And as soon as you replace the items, I want you gone from this house!"

"What? Where will I go?"

"Why should I care?"

"I served your daughter well for these three years and more. Will you at least write me a good character?"

"Absolutely not! You're lucky I don't send for the village constable."

"Very well, *monsieur*," said the Frenchwoman, but not in a tone of defeat. "I will give you back the gifts *mademoiselle* made to me, but I warn you! I will keep none of your secrets any longer—neither yours nor hers."

"I hardly think any of those secrets matter any longer!" barked Hastings.

"We shall see!" the French maid spat back.

Garth took hold of Eda's arm and pulled her away from the door, a familiarity for which she soon forgave him as she heard the heavy thud of William Hastings' footsteps coming towards them. Any minute now and the door handle would turn and he would be upon them. The valet jerked his head towards a nearby linen closet that he had left ajar earlier while going about his duties. It did not take Eda more than an instant to act on his suggestion, and quickly and silently as a pair of cats, the two of them slipped into the small space afforded by the towels and tablecloths.

The chamber door opened with an angry rattle and shut again with a bang. Eda could well imagine William Hastings' red face as he stomped by their hiding place. She was no coward, as earlier events had amply proved, but she exhaled in mild relief that she would not have to encounter him.

Once the mill owner had disappeared, the strangeness of their situation dawned on Eda and the valet. As they started to extricate themselves from the linen closet, Garth let loose a volley of apologies.

"Thank you, Garth," said Eda primly, but with a twinkle in her eyes. "I wonder what his lordship would say if he saw us now?"

Garth grinned, smile lines rippling from his eyes all the way to his graying sideburns. "No wondering about it, miss. 'Tis certain he'd have my head."

After his perplexing interview with the countess, Pevensey determined that he would move outside the Emison family circle for the moment. He would have to press Miss Swanycke on the question of her whereabouts at some future point, and he had yet to hear the story of the eventful day from the earl's own mouth—but despite this, he decided to cast his net wider and interview some of the humbler actors in this tragedy. He could think of two, the architect and the female companion, that still merited his attention.

He had already heard much to interest him in the architect, and he secured the first footman's assistance in bringing Philippe Bayeux the message that his presence was desired.

The Frenchman, when he came into the drawing room, was sober, but from the way that he rubbed his head and squinted his eyes, it looked as if it had taken him a great deal of forbearance to be so. Pevensey's freckled face gave a disarming smile. "Jacob Pevensey, at your service—up from the magistrates' office in London to look into these sad events."

The architect only grunted.

"Could you enlighten me as to why you are here at Woldwick?"

"Could I sit down first?"

"Oh, I beg your pardon, of course!" Pevensey gestured to an armchair as if the spacious drawing room belonged to him. As Bayeux collapsed into the cushioned seat, Pevensey sat down circumspectly in the armchair opposite and crossed one leg over the other. "Are you here as a guest?"

Bayeux gave a short laugh—bitter and far too ugly for a man with such sculpted features. "A guest? Mais non. Are you?"

"Not of his lordship's, no," said Pevensey smoothly. "Someone else invited me. Perhaps someone else invited you as well?"

"Yes. The Hastings did. I'm an architect. I was to look at making some renovations to this...relic." He looked at the corniced ceiling with a sneer.

"And just to be specific," said Pevensey, unable to resist pulling out his sketchbook and beginning on the Frenchman's aquiline nose, "which of the Hastings invited you?"

There was a pause.

"Miss Hastings."

"Ah." Pevensey allowed that monosyllable to hover for a while in the air, pregnant with indeterminate meaning. "How did you become acquainted with Miss Hastings?"

"Through her father. I designed his home and some other projects that he had invested in."

"Did you ever encounter Miss Hastings in society?" Pevensey had started shading in Philippe Bayeux's dark eyebrows. They were perfectly shaped, like the rest of his face, but strangely inert. Pevensey had the impression that their lack of motion—no matter what Bayeux said—was due to a concerted effort on the Frenchman's part to eliminate all emotion from his face.

Bayeux shrugged. "I think I may have danced with her a few times at assemblies or balls."

"Ah." There was that monosyllable again. "And was there anything...roma ntic between the two of you?"

"Just what are you suggesting, *monsieur*?"

Pevensey dropped his pencil to the floor, on purpose, and bent down to retrieve it. Clearly, Miss Swanycke was correct—there had been some sort of attraction between the architect and the mill owner's daughter. Why else would he take such umbrage at the question? And yet, Bayeux was French, Pevensey reminded himself, and in his experience the French were able to take umbrage at even the most innocuous question or statement.

Pencil back in hand, Pevensey changed his tack. "And so, Miss Hastings invited you here to renovate the house?"

"I have already told you as much."

"And had you finished drawing up plans for these renovations?"

"Yes, I had. The whole face of the building was to be modernized and some of the interior as well. I had also investigated the availability of local stone so that the project might begin in the springtime." Bayeux seemed more animated now, interested in his work instead of irritable.

"And the morning of the sad event—I understand you left the house on horseback?"

"Yes, I went into the village to see the stonemason. There is a quarry near here, and he showed me the granite and limestone he could come by easily."

"At what time did you leave Woldwick?"

"Half past seven."

Pevensey noted that this time sorted well with the groom's remembrance of when Bayeux had departed. He also noted that Bayeux was the only person so far who seemed to have any cognizance of the clock on the day in question.

"How long did it take you to ride to the village?"

"Forty minutes."

Again, the architect showed no doubt. Pevensey wondered if the precision was due to his profession or to something else. "So that puts you at the stone mason's at ten past eight—"

"No. I went first to the tavern and had some breakfast."

"Which tavern?"

"The only one in existence in this grand metropolis. I don't recall the name."

"And after breakfasting, you saw the stonemason at...?"

"Nine o'clock."

"Had you an appointment?"

"Oui."

It was refreshing to hear someone chronicle his movements so exactly, but Pevensey was well-versed enough in the study of mankind to know that precision did not always equal veracity.

Waiting, waiting, still waiting—Haro looked at the time and realized that tea was still several hours off. He wondered if Eda was still sitting with his mother. He paced before the tall windows in the billiards room. How did he normally pass the time when in the country? He could not, for the life of him, remember.

Reading? He flipped through the pages of a book and then tossed it away just as quickly. No, that was Torin's province.

Drinking? He eyed the closed door of the liquor cabinet. No, he was of no mind to play the sot like that bosky Frenchman.

Filtering through the cherry wood paneling and the white wainscoting, he heard a few bars of music. Not Beethoven, not Mozart, he thought, but something far older—an intricate sinfonia in three parts written for the harpsichord a century ago.

Haro strode out of the billiards room and went to the music room, across the broad landing. He slipped through one of the double doors and stepped quietly into the room.

No sooner had the earl's soundless footsteps touched the parquet floor than the music halted on the leading tone of a scale passage.

"Haro, my boy?" asked the piano player, his back towards the intruder. He must have had ears like a rabbit's.

"Yes," said Haro, glimpsing the white hair of his great-uncle with a surge of disappointment. "I thought perhaps it was Eda on the pianoforte."

The old man played the final tone of the scale, then swung his legs around spryly and rose from the bench. "You don't know your music, lad, if you think Eda would play that." He gestured to the keys that had just been put through the sinfonia's paces. His eyes caught Haro's. "Either that, or you don't know your cousin."

"Oh?" Haro walked over to the instrument and ran a hand over the polished wood. "Enlighten me. What would Eda play?"

"This," said Uncle Haro. He sat down again and began to play a sarabande—slow, stately, and full of minor chords.

"Or this." He played something much faster, lighter, and brighter, one of Beethoven's more exuberant creations, but still with the same grandeur of the sarabande.

Haro began to smile. He could well imagine those chords coming from Eda's fingers. She had an innate understanding of depth, of dignity, of ceremony. But at the same time, she had a vivacity that would never sleep, a tempestuousness that would challenge and change whatever it came across. She would be the perfect queen but also the perfect consort.

"Did your Miss Hastings play?"

Haro's smile died on his lips. "I...don't know."

He did not want to think about Arabella. She had certainly never played while at Woldwick. He imagined that she knew enough about the pianoforte to pass herself off as accomplished. Her father's money had doubtless procured any necessary tutelage.

But he doubted that she had played music with her heart, the way Eda played it—or that she had drawn pictures as a quest for creating life, the way Eda did. For Eda, these things were not just accomplishments to be learned and paraded before admirers, but a part of herself.

The only time Haro had heard Arabella passionate about a subject was when discussing the architecture—or the revamping of the architecture—of Woldwick. On that cold day, walking back from the pond, she and Philippe Bayeux had gabbled on and on about the components of the building. Haro had been piqued then. Now he was simply perplexed.

"I beg pardon for disturbing your music, Uncle," said the earl. He stepped out of the music room into the hallway and closed the door.

If the architect had been able to strike that chord in her that brought the soul to life, it should have been his name in the banns beside hers, not Haro's. Eda had said the architect had a *tendre* for Arabella. Haro wondered if Arabella had returned the feeling. And if so, was the engagement as much of a burden for her as it had been for Haro? Would Arabella have been as relieved as he was if he had found her that morning alive and called off the match?

23

PEVENSEY WRINKLED HIS NOSE as he evaluated his sketch of Philippe Bayeux. All of the face was drawn in detail except for the eyes. Pevensey had always considered eyes to be windows into a subject's character. He had drawn Mademoiselle Mathilde's eyes sly and seductive with a definite air of snobbery about them. He had drawn Torin Emison's eyes as clever, but overly conceited in regard to his own worth, with the spark of idealism that young men possess who have never had to work for their bread. But Philippe Bayeux's eyes he had not drawn at all, for the Frenchman's character was, at best, enigmatic.

Pevensey gnawed on his lower lip and looked at the picture once more. He would have to go into the village and find bystanders to corroborate the Frenchman's story, but as it currently stood, it seemed that Bayeux would have had no opportunity to accost Miss Hastings by the pond and do her harm. If Pevensey had correctly pinpointed the time when Miss Hastings left the house, then Bayeux would have been safely entrenched in his tavern breakfast while Miss Hastings was meeting her unfortunate demise. Yet, be that as it may, Pevensey still did not feel confident enough to add Bayeux's eyes to the sketch—there was something the clock-conscious architect was concealing. Was it a past relationship with Arabella Hastings or was it something even more sinister?

Closing his book on the unfinished sketch, Pevensey wandered out of the drawing room into the hallway. The scullery maid, her arms full of kindling, was coming the other way, and her cheeks reddened at the sight of him. Pevensey gave her a wink as they passed by each other like ships in the harbor—more from habit than from any actual admiration—and her homely face colored completely. She ducked her head and hurried along, lingering at the end of the hallway long enough to send him a lovelorn glance.

"Ah, there you are, Pevensey!"

He turned around to see William Hastings bearing down on him from the other end of the hallway. "Good morning, Mr. Hastings." Pevensey managed a thin smile. He had hoped to avoid Arabella Hastings' father until he was reaching the end of his investigation. He should have known from past experience that William Hastings was not a man easily avoided.

"Nearly afternoon by now," grunted Hastings, "and the second day you've been here. Well?"

Pevensey raised an eyebrow, refusing to answer the question until Hastings elaborated on it.

"Do you have enough to hang him yet?"

"Regrettably, no," replied Pevensey. He used the word "regrettably" loosely, for nothing he had learned, as yet, had convinced him the earl needed to hang.

"What do you think I'm paying you for? To swap civil whiskers with the servants?"

"I think you're paying me to find the truth, sir," Pevensey's tone was careful, in a manner designed to lower William Hastings' hackles. "Which I will, all in due course. And speaking of truth, I've a couple of questions you might be able to help me with."

Hastings grunted, and Pevensey took that as leave to proceed. He pulled out his sketchbook and began with the most innocuous inquiry concerning the questions plaguing him.

"About what time in the morning would you say your altercation with the earl took place?"

"Shortly after eight o'clock. Why?"

The end of Pevensey's pencil began to waggle as it scribbled a clock face on the page. "I am still establishing the timeline of the morning in question and cross-checking it with all pertinent parties."

"Hmm."

Pevensey nearly grinned, thinking about how little William Hastings appreciated the methodical manner in which he was conducting the case. On the one hand, the man's insistence on haste was understandable, but on the other hand, it was clearly a hindrance to finding out the whole truth of the matter.

"And another question for you...." Pevensey's eyes left the sketchbook and came level with William Hastings' so that he could watch his reaction. "Did you invite Philippe Bayeux, the architect, up to Woldwick?"

"No!" Hastings initial response was emphatic, but it did not take more than a couple seconds before he started to pole his ship backwards through the treacherous waters. "Well, that is to say, yes, I did! He's worked for me before and I wanted to see what he would come up with for renovating this place." Hastings' jowls pulled back into a sneer. "But that's all in the past now—I won't be spending any of my blunt saving this gloomy disaster of a country house."

Pevensey continued to press. "So, Miss Hastings had no part in inviting the architect here?"

"No, certainly not."

"And this architect, Philippe Bayeux—was there a...romantic attachment between him and your daughter?"

"How dare you, sir!" The mill owner raised his voice, but to Pevensey, the outrage felt almost perfunctory—as if Hastings had been expecting that question.

"I regret seeming impertinent, sir, but as you know, my profession requires me to pursue every avenue of inquiry."

"Philippe Bayeux was nothing to my daughter. Nothing!"

It was not exactly a straightforward yes or no, but Pevensey forbore from pushing the point any further.

"I expect a full report from you tomorrow," said Hastings, jamming his thumbs into the pockets of the waistcoat encircling his upper half.

"As you wish," said Pevensey, sensing that he had just been dismissed. The disappearance of William Hastings down the hallway confirmed this suspicion.

Where to go now? Pevensey checked his pocket watch; it was still a few hours before tea. The door to the library, just across from him, was ajar. And from inside, he could hear the faint snoring of someone asleep.

Pevensey's profession did not require a good deal of tiptoeing about, but he had a slight build and a quiet step, and it was not too difficult to enter the library without waking its occupant.

Tiptoeing towards the sound of snoring, Pevensey rounded the set of wing-back chairs which had their backs to the door. Leaning back in one of them, with feet propped up on a cushioned footstool, was an undistinguished woman of indistinct age. Her iron gray hair and worn face placed her at fifty or sixty years of age, but something about her thick figure made her seem younger.

Pevensey searched his mind for who this might be—she was certainly not a member of the family. But then, would a servant make free of the library chairs as a place to nap away a wintry day? He remembered Mrs. Alfred's comments from a day ago. This must be the duenna who had accompanied Arabella Hastings, a Mrs. Rollo, if he remembered the name aright.

The strange flickering of the firelight on Mrs. Rollo's immobile figure appealed to him. He was not accustomed to drawing females in their sleep, but his sense of the picturesque outweighed his sense of propriety and he pulled out his sketchbook.

Either the suddenness of the movement or the slight rustling of the pages disturbed the subject of his intended portrait. Mrs. Rollo's eyelids sprang open. She saw immediately that she was being observed, but instead of making an outcry, she simply lowered her feet from the footstool, crossed her ankles, and folded her hands in her lap, waiting for whatever was to come next.

For a brief instant, Pevensey felt guilt and closed the cover of his sketchbook. He recovered quickly, however, and gave an encouraging smile. "I beg your pardon. I am Jacob Pevensey, attached to the magistrates' office in London. I stepped inside to look for a Mrs. Rollo...might you be she?"

"Yes."

This heavy monosyllable might have stopped a lesser man in his tracks, but Pevensey carried on effortlessly. "I have a few questions to put to you regarding the tragic events of two days ago. Would you mind if I sit down?"

Mrs. Rollo simply stared at him.

Pevensey slid into the other wingback chair without waiting for an answer that was not forthcoming, positioning it slightly as he sat down so that he could see the woman more clearly.

She had broad features beneath her gray hair, features too large to be called pretty and more becoming in a man than in a woman. Her shoulders were broad as well, ungainly, some might say, beneath the ill-fitting fabric of her gray dress.

"I understand you came to Woldwick with the Hastings family?"

"Yes."

"And what...position do you hold in that family?"

"I am, or rather, I was companion and chaperone to Miss Hastings."

Pevensey was delighted to hear Mrs. Rollo form her first full sentence. He had been afraid she would be no help to him at all.

"What were your duties?"

She shifted in her chair. "I accompanied Miss Hastings to social gatherings when her father was unable to attend."

"And...?"

"That is all."

"Ah," said Pevensey, a little surprised. It seemed a small task. "Did Miss Hastings confide in you?"

"Certainly not." Mrs. Rollo's hands twitched in her lap. Pevensey noted that they were almost as large as his own.

"How long had you been Miss Hastings' companion?"

"Three years."

"So, even before she was out in society?"

"Yes."

"Were you her governess?"

The woman smiled oddly. "In a manner of speaking."

"What manner of speaking would that be?" Pevensey strongly believed that murder investigations demanded forthright questions and forthright answers.

"I taught. Miss Hastings did not always learn."

"So, she was not a bright student."

"No, she was bright enough." Mrs. Rollo leaned forward, the broad features of her face filled with intensity. "But she refused to apply herself to anything that required discipline."

"Music and French, you mean?"

"Quite. Though she had other means of exercising her French besides my tutelage." Mrs. Rollo's voice took on a snide quality as if she were making a joke that only she would understand.

"Are you referring to Monsieur Bayeux?"

Mrs. Rollo stiffened. "No, why would I be?"

Pevensey ignored her denial and focused more on the dismay his own question had occasioned. "What was the relationship between Miss Hastings and Philippe Bayeux?"

Mrs. Rollo's thick knuckles laced themselves together. She made no reply.

"I have reason to believe that this matter has direct bearing on Miss Hastings' murder." It was an overstatement, of course, but first Mr. Hastings and now Mrs. Rollo had flimflammed him on this subject, making him more than a little suspicious.

"I am a poor spinster," she said at last. She would not meet his eye. "With Miss Hastings gone, I no longer have a place in this household. My only hopes for survival will be a small pension and good recommendation to find another position."

"So, Mr. Hastings has forbidden you to speak on this topic?"

She looked away into the depths of the flickering fire. This interview, it seemed, was finished.

24

After extricating herself from the linen closet and exchanging another conspiratorial look with Garth, Eda disappeared into her own bedroom to ponder what they had heard. Walking over to the bed, she turned around, leaned back, and let herself fall against the goose down coverlet with a satisfying thump. Her shape imprinted onto the bedclothes and sent a few stray feathers wafting into the air.

What secrets could the French maid have been speaking of? Were they secrets pertinent to the murder? Were they secrets that could save Haro? A tight knot grew inside her throat. She could barely swallow—or breathe—and she felt her air-hungry lungs begin to collapse in on themselves.

The whole time they had been engaged—no, not engaged, simply bound by an understanding—he had never kissed her any more romantically than a farewell kiss on the cheek. And in all that time, she had never felt the lack. But now, after the fires of desire had been blown hotter by the bellows of jealousy, she knew that she wanted nothing more than for his lips to meet hers.

He had almost kissed her today, but the murder of Arabella Hastings lay between them. It was a putrid fly in the heady perfume of requited love. As much as she desired his touch, she knew she could not kiss him until that impediment was gone.

How could it then be removed?

She flung her head back against the bed. Perhaps Mademoiselle Mathilde's secrets were the answer. Was there a hushed-up story in Arabella Hastings' past that would shed light on the identity of the strangler? Or did the secrets merely concern Arabella's father, nefarious business dealings he was keen to hide from the public eye?

She sat up suddenly. It was all well and good to let the mind wander, but it would be far more useful to Haro to ferret out the truth. She must go and find Mademoiselle Mathilde before she departed and wring from her the secrets of the Hastings household.

Pevensey did not often leave an interview feeling dissatisfied, but in the case of Mrs. Rollo, he felt extremely vexed that his store of essential information had not increased one jot during the course of their conversation. He stood outside the library door for one minute, and then another.

It had been impossible to press the Countess of Anglesford when she told him her taradiddles about her niece being present in the drawing room. Had he questioned her further, her rank and her delicate constitution would have made Pevensey seem a boor at best, or a scoundrel at worst. But the possibility of pressing Mrs. Rollo seemed a far more promising matter. She had neither rank nor connections. Who was to object if he applied a little force to the shell of this nut, just enough to crack it and get at the meat that lay inside?

Perhaps such sentiments were reprehensible, but Pevensey had to admit they were also responsible for his success in his chosen profession. The magistrates knew he would not rest until he had obtained the answers they needed.

Pevensey re-opened the door of the library and re-entered the sanctum of tastefully arranged books and dark mahogany panels. This time he made no effort to disguise his footsteps.

Mrs. Rollo was enjoying the same chair that he had left her in not three minutes since, her feet once more propped up like an ancient laborer's after a long day swinging his scythe in the field.

"Did you like Arabella Hastings?" Pevensey demanded, his opening assault far less politic, or polite, than his previous questions.

The Countess of Anglesford would have twittered in outrage—and reached for her hartshorn—but Mrs. Rollo's inscrutably set face became demonstrably less set and decidedly less inscrutable. "No, young man. I did not."

Pevensey breathed a sigh of inward exultation. The forthright approach had worked. She was opening up to him like a flower, albeit a very drab and unattractive one.

"Why is that?"

"She was lazy, sharp-tongued, untruthful, unkind, and irreligious."

Obviously, the old biddy had thought about this subject at some length.

"Did she have any good qualities?"

"She was content with seeming to have them...when on display for potential suitors."

"But she made no such pretense at home?"

"No, and certainly not for the benefit of the servants."

She said that last word bitterly. Pevensey knew that the life of a governess was a sad one—as gray as the faded dress Mrs. Rollo wore. She was not quite a member of the family and not quite a member of the hired help. Many governesses could at least take comfort in the joy of imparting knowledge, the affection of their students, or the respect of their employers—but for Mrs. Rollo, it seemed, none of these solaces were available. A debutante not interested in schoolroom instruction or societal guidance would undoubtedly treat her governess-turned-companion no better than a cook, a washerwoman, or a scullery maid. Mrs. Rollo was, to all the parties that mattered, a servant in the Hastings household, a servant disgruntled at the estimation of her own worth.

"Shortly before Miss Hastings' death"—Pevensey did not feel the need to use a euphemism in front of Mrs. Rollo—"there was an altercation between her and Miss Swanycke. I understand you were present for that."

"Yes."

"Did Miss Hastings say something to provoke Miss Swanycke into slapping her?"

"I imagine she must have," said Mrs. Rollo, her lips pulling back distastefully and revealing her large teeth. Pevensey was already imagining how often Miss

Hastings must have provoked this woman, and how often Mrs. Rollo must have wished she could repay her in the same coin that Miss Swanycke had displayed.

"But you did not hear the exchange between the two of them?"

She hesitated. Pevensey held his breath—she was on the cusp of answering him, he could sense it.

"It was only a whisper, but I did hear it. Miss Hastings was assuring Miss Swanycke that she could drop a word in the ear of one of her gentlemen friends and obtain a *carte blanche* and a snug hunting bungalow for her, if she would only vacate the premises and release the earl from the net she held him in."

Pevensey whistled in astonishment. No wonder the black-haired beauty had taken offense. "You seem to be an astute observer of your surroundings, Mrs. Rollo. In your observation of the family and household here at Woldwick, who would you say had the deepest resentment towards Miss Hastings?"

Her lip curled. "Other than myself, you mean?"

Pevensey raised an eyebrow. So, this broad-shouldered woman nursed a sense of humor as well as an implacable grievance. He looked down at the thick knuckles of her hands. When he first heard that the crime had involved strangling, he had assumed that the suspect would be a man, but could this woman—this bear of a woman—have been baited enough to react with a masculine strength?

She turned silent again, and Pevensey saw that she was refusing to speculate on others' resentments.

"Where were you on the morning of the murder?"

"Breaking my fast with Mrs. Alfred, the housekeeper."

"Thank you for being so forthcoming." This detail should be easy enough to verify, and if it were true, then Mrs. Rollo—large knuckles and all—was not the strangler he was looking for.

Haro was tired of sitting with himself. Eda was nowhere to be found. Torin insisted on burying his nose in Terrence, or Plautus, or some other tedious

Roman tome. And Haro had given his word not to leave the house, making a brisk gallop through the cold woods an enticing idea but utterly forbidden to him. He discarded the idea of going to sit with his mother, and—well, one could only handle so much of that pickled Frenchman, Bayeux.

The earl wandered into his father's study—his study now—leaving the door open behind him. Sitting at the desk still seemed as foreign as putting on another man's waistcoat. Haro remembered his father hunched in that chair, burning the candle far into the night at that desk during the few weeks of the year he was at his country home. His mother had always remarked how thorough her husband was with the accounting. Little did she know that his thoroughness was merely to conceal or mitigate the damage that a deck of cards had done to the Emison estate.

Haro sat down at the desk and opened the largest drawer. There was a locked wood case inside, the one that held his father's pistols. Haro opened another drawer and fished out the key that would open the lock. There they were, the two silver pistols he had always coveted when he was a boy. He fingered the filigreed hilt of the polished firearm. His father would ride out with the hounds on occasion, but he had never been one for dueling or target practice—and yet the pistol was as clean and bright as if it had been the late earl's most prized possession.

Haro fingered the trigger. He wondered what Edward Emison would have done if he had not lost his life to illness, if he had lived to face the financial ruin that now beset his family. Would he have taken the coward's way out—a bullet through the temple? Or would he have braved the storm with them, retrenched, reformed, and resided in genteel poverty in a house in Russell Square?

"Ahem! Pardon me!" A freckled face peeked in through the open door. "If you are intending to shoot yourself, you will take the time to leave a note, won't you?"

Haro looked up in surprise. "A note?"

"Of course! Saying that you strangled Miss Hastings. Everyone will assume that was the case, anyway, but it would make my job much easier if it were in writing."

Haro leaned back in his chair. He resisted the urge to point the pistol at the Bow Street Runner. "What the devil is that supposed to mean? You've made up your mind against me?"

"Certainly not, my lord. But you do admit things look suspicious, do you not? A pistol in hand, finger poised to shoot, alone and indoors in one's study—if those are not signs of a guilty conscience, I don't know what is!"

Haro stopped leaning back, and the legs of the chair swung forward with a thump. He let go of the pistol, placing it carefully on the desk. "Mr. Pevensey, nothing could be further from my mind than committing suicide. I am, in fact, very much looking forward to putting these false accusations to rest and living the long life that lies before me." He cleared his throat. "I hope that your interviews over the past two days have produced some information that warrants my optimism...?"

Pevensey said nothing to fill the space that Haro had left.

Haro frowned. His hands balled into fists, and he placed them on the desk in front of him. He hated to ask the question so directly, but after all, it was his family's reputation, his future with Eda, and his neck on the line. "Have you a suspect other than me?"

The corner of Pevensey's mouth turned up into a wry smile. "I wish I could oblige you with a yes, your lordship. I've found more than a few who had reason to wish Miss Hastings ill...but opportunity? Aye, there's the rub. I still have more questions to ask, but so far, the only person I can place at the bridge at the necessary time is you."

25

EDA HESITATED BRIEFLY BEFORE tapping on the door of the room that Mrs. Alfred said belonged to the French maid. She was not generally a shy person, but she did feel some slight discomfort at initiating a conversation with an unknown foreigner on a topic overheard from a linen closet.

The door opened. "Qu'est que c'est? Can I help you?" The disdainful curve of the Frenchwoman's thin eyebrows belied the sincerity of this last question.

"Oh, yes, hallo," said Eda. She had not meant to knock yet. Her nervous fingers must have brushed against the wood by accident. "May I talk to you? Now? Inside?" she blurted out. Other than to Lady Anglesford, she had always found it easier talking to men than women.

The Frenchwoman's eyes radiated confusion, but she did not protest Eda's unconventional entrance.

"I overheard you arguing with Mr. Hastings earlier."

Mademoiselle Mathilde's eyebrows arched superciliously, but she offered no comment.

Eda thanked the good Lord that she had turned down Lady Anglesford's offer for a French maid of her own.

"I think I heard you say that there were some secrets that Mr. Hastings would not want you to reveal—"

"I do not think you heard me correctly." The Frenchwoman's words were clipped.

"Oh, but I did!" said Eda, suddenly panicking that the maid meant to dismiss her. "What did you mean? Please tell me!" She did not know why this woman had the power to fluster her so.

Mademoiselle Mathilde's eyes narrowed. She looked Eda up and down. "You have money? Yes?"

Eda breathed in sharply. "Of course! Whatever you need." She winced as soon as she said it. Her worldly-wise captain of a father would have known better than to offer an unlimited sum to a mercenary lady's maid. "That is...I mean to say...I will pay you handsomely for any secrets that shed light on Miss Hastings' death. Is there anything you can tell me about her past that will help?"

"What sort of thing?"

Eda floundered, not sure what to suggest. "Secret admirers, clandestine meetings...."

Mademoiselle Mathilde laughed in a way that was not at all good-natured. "You want to know about affairs of the heart? I am sorry to disappoint you, but Mademoiselle Hastings was more circumspect than you give her credit for."

Eda's hopes fell.

The maid, however, sensed her chances of remuneration were receding and dredged up one item of scandalous import to dangle before her buyer's nose.

"I suppose I could tell you, though, that she was engaged to be married."

"To Har—Lord Anglesford, you mean?"

"Non. To someone else."

"Did he jilt her too?" asked Eda, a little too pleased at the prospect. The idea of more men than Haro having abandoned matrimony to Miss Hastings held a strange appeal for her.

Mademoiselle Mathilde turned her head away. "Zut alors! I don't remember."

Eda clenched her teeth in annoyance. She should have thought to bring some half-crowns with her tied up in a handkerchief, but as things were, it looked like Mademoiselle Mathilde would talk no more until her palm was filled with coin.

Pevensey pulled his muffler up around his ears. Egad! But it was cold in these parts! He had been hoping that a brisk walk around the exterior of the house would clear his head and give a new direction in which to turn his thoughts. But it seemed more likely that his toes would freeze than that his thoughts would crystallize.

Who were the principal suspects in this case? He had his hands in his pockets, and he was not about to take them out in order to pull out his sketchbook. He excused himself for the omission, reminding himself that he could make pictures in his mind's eye just as easily.

First, there was the Earl of Anglesford. As tempting as it was to put on Revolutionary spectacles and look at every aristocrat with a jaundiced eye, Pevensey had to admit that he liked the earl. He seemed fond of his family. A blundering idiot where women were concerned and a babe in the woods when it came to managing Mr. Hastings, but a decent chap, nonetheless. It would surprise Pevensey if the earl had had any hand in the murder. No, he was too difficult to provoke and chivalrous to a fault. Even if backed into a corner or taunted beyond endurance, was it possible that he could have lashed out by throttling a woman?

The earl's nature was in his favor, but circumstances were not. He was the only person—so far—that Pevensey could place with certainty near the pond during the fatal window of time when Miss Hastings must have met her demise. But was this enough to damn him?

The second suspect that materialized in Pevensey's mind was Philippe Bayeux, the enigmatic architect. There was no good explanation for his presence at Woldwick. The projected renovations seemed a thin excuse at best, and Pevensey was willing to lay money at poor odds that the man had arrived without any invitation whatsoever, not even one from Miss Hastings. Why the pretense on her part then? And on her father's, he had to wonder? What was Bayeux himself trying to achieve? More than one interview had hinted at a romantic entanglement between Bayeux and Miss Hastings—although those in a position to confirm the rumor absolutely refused to do so.

Was Bayeux the murderer he was looking for? It was clear that his character was a brooding and a moody one. Jealous that his amore was affianced to another man, had his passions gotten the better of him on the bridge? Pevensey exhaled and watched his breath freeze in front of his face. It was well known that Frenchmen were volatile, especially when it came to affairs of the heart. Pevensey could far easier imagine the architect's thumbs purpling Arabella's neck than he could the earl's.

And yet, was it even possible for Bayeux to have been present at the pond given the time Miss Hastings left the house? He stamped his feet, attempting to regain some of the feeling in them. There were times that must be verified—Bayeux's visit to the village inn for breakfast and his appointment with the stonemason following. An adjunct to the magistrates' office was supposed to be as impartial as the law itself, but Pevensey could not help but admit that it would give him far more satisfaction for the brooding Frenchman to swing for this crime than for the well-mannered Englishman.

Of course, these two were not the only suspects in the case. Pevensey was drawn inexorably back to his recent conversation in the library and to Mrs. Rollo's large, bony hands. That grim-faced governess had hated Arabella Hastings—he had no illusions that it could be otherwise—and her quiet hatred had not dissipated even at the death of its object. During his career at Bow Street, Pevensey had met no female stranglers, but experience taught him that crimes could always surprise one. The housekeeper Mrs. Alfred had hesitated when asked whether she had breakfasted with Mrs. Rollo on the fateful morning—hesitated and then affirmed it. Was the hesitation because she was about to tell an untruth or was it because she knew that the friendship between a lady's companion and a housekeeper was irregular?

And then there was Eda Swanycke, the earl's black-haired, voluptuous relative. Hers were not the hands of a strangler—Pevensey refused to allow a possibility that farfetched—but she was hiding something, and he very much wanted to know why. Was she casting red herrings into the trail on purpose? Was she striving to protect the person who had killed Arabella Hastings?

A movement in the trees caught Pevensey's eye. There, where the naked branches met the edge of the carriage drive, he saw a tall figure, clad in an old-fashioned frock coat. Pevensey squinted trying to make out who it was. The tallest man he had met at Woldwick had been the young earl himself. This fellow looked like he would top Lord Anglesford by a hand's breadth, and his gait, though not unsure, was that of a far older man.

"Hallo there!" called Pevensey, waving a hand in greeting.

"Oh? Hallo! And who might you be?" asked the elderly gentleman—for though his frock coat was worn, Pevensey had an inkling that he was a gentleman of aristocratic breeding.

"Jacob Pevensey, at your service, sir, attached to the London magistrates' office."

"Ah, yes! The fellow here to investigate things. How do you do?" The old man dug into his pockets and pulled out several chunks of dry bread. Rubbing them between his hands, he began tossing the dry crumbs onto the frozen ground.

Pevensey combed his mind for clues to the gentleman's identity. Was he a genteel tenant with a cottage on Emison land? Was he a neighbor out for a ramble and curious about events at Woldwick?

Without the aid of his sketchbook, he remembered that Mrs. Alfred, when itemizing the list of upstairs residents for Pevensey's benefit, had mentioned an eccentric great-uncle, brother to Lady Anglesford's father. Harold Harding, he was called. He shared a Christian name with the current earl, and their height, blond hair, and blue eyes were just three of the similarities to their appearances.

As Pevensey watched, the old man took a polite step away from the crumbs, and a party of wildfowl—those that had not left the woods for the winter—darted in to devour them. "Are you bound for the house?" he asked, with a nod towards Woldwick.

"Just come from it! I usually stay out with my birds all day, as long as I can keep my fingers warm enough to crumble up their bread."

"Then perhaps you could keep me company? I'm on my way to—"

"The lake," interrupted the old man. "Yes, I will accompany you." He reached into his pocket and threw a few more crumbs in parting to the congress of winged creatures who had assembled.

Pevensey sensed that this offer to keep him company was a rare thing on the old man's part. "Many thanks," he said, pulling the collar of his coat up around his freckled face and falling in step along the path that led away from the house and into the woods. He cast a surreptitious glance at his pocket watch—half past noon. The time it took to reach the pond would be an essential piece of information.

"Drat!" said Eda, rifling through the drawers of her writing desk. Her quarterly allowance had been completely spent, and there were no overlooked piles of pocket change to be found. Should she go to Lady Anglesford and ask for pin money? It would be a strange request, and she would certainly have to explain herself.

Torin! Perhaps he had some money left over from his allowance—although it was more than likely that he had squandered it on books when they were in London. Still, it would not hurt to ask him. Eda hurriedly stuffed the contents back in her drawers and, opening her bedroom door, darted into the hallway.

"Oh!" she said, stifling a screech as she nearly collided with a broad masculine chest. "Haro, what on earth are you doing?"

"As you can see from my raised forearm, I was just about to knock on your door."

"Whatever for?"

Haro opened his mouth, then shut it again.

"Never mind then," replied Eda. "I'm looking for Torin. Although I suppose you'll do just as well. Have you any money?"

"Money?" asked Haro, with a shake of his head. His face broke into a wry smile. "Isn't that the reason we're in this predicament in the first place?"

Eda wrinkled her nose but could not refrain from smiling back. "Just some pin money, I mean."

Haro reached into his pocket and fished out a guinea, holding it out between thumb and forefinger. Eda placed her hand below, waiting for him to drop it into her palm. But instead, he just held it there, the round coin suspended in the air. She reached up to take it from his fingers, but as she did, he took her hand in his and pulled her closer until they were standing face to face in the doorway.

"Pin money? Are you planning to buy a new hat?" Eda felt his breath brush against her face as he looked down at her. She had the distinct impression that he was hoping to kiss her.

"No, I'm planning to buy secrets." She forced herself to attend to the task at hand.

"Secrets?" Haro's blond eyebrows arched. "Whose?"

"Never you mind that." Eda knew instinctively that Haro's gentlemanly nature would revolt against her plan. No matter the outcome of the investigation, he would not think it proper for her to stick her nose into Arabella's past. But Eda also refused to let Haro's sensibilities trump her own good sense.

That kiss could wait.

"Thank you for the guinea," she said archly. "And now, if you'll excuse me...."

Before Haro could protest, she slipped from his grasp and darted out into the hallway. She must find her way back to Mademoiselle Mathilde for more questions.

26

"SHE WAS A FICKLE thing," the old man said, staring down into the ice. The freezing weather had fully repaired the cracks from Miss Hastings' unceremonious tumble of two days ago. "Pretty, clever—a little too clever. I thought she had made up her mind to start afresh, but in the end, she went back to him. It was her fickleness that was her undoing."

"Went back to him?" asked Pevensey. "Whom do you mean?" The walk to the pond—nearly thirty minutes of cold trudging along a winding trail that seemed to point north, south, east, and west—had been conducted in silence, but now, poised upon the fateful bridge, his companion had suddenly waxed garrulous.

"Perhaps she cared a little too much about the prestige of being a countess. Perhaps she really did have feelings for him."

"Are you speaking about Arabella Hastings?" It seemed to fit, but Pevensey sensed that the old man's mind was somewhere else besides the present, in the mists of remembrance and times past.

"Arabella Hastings?" Harold Harding spoke the name as if he had never heard it before. "No, no. Maria—the Countess of St. Petersburg."

"Ah. What happened to her?"

The old man sighed. "Murdered. I heard of it later. Murdered by the hands of jealousy."

"Not your hands, I hope?" said Pevensey brightly. This fellow's hands were certainly large enough to fit around a woman's neck.

The elderly Mr. Harding did not respond.

"Did Arabella Hastings remind you of the countess?"

"Haro's fiancée? Yes, a little. She had much of the same figure and color of hair. But Maria would never do such a cold-hearted deed."

"What deed do you mean?"

"Why, cut down the woods, of course! She loved the trees, Maria did. And the birds—" The old man gestured toward the small bird chirping expectantly from the rail of the bridge. "She could get that titmouse there to eat out of her hand."

"Were you the only one distressed by Miss Hastings' idea to level the forest?" Pevensey studied the wrinkles around Harold Harding's mouth. He wished it were not so cold so he could pull out his sketchbook and draw the changing lines of human skin.

"No, of course not! Torin, and Eda, and Edith were against it. And Haro would have been too, once he came to his senses." He paused and pursed his lips, as if remembering something unpleasant. "Is it true that you think my nephew, Haro, is the murderer?"

Whenever someone asked Pevensey what he thought about a case, he made a point of obscuring the direction in which his mind was leaning. "I think he's the only one who can, of a certainty, be placed at this bridge at the time of death."

The old man's lips compressed into a thin line and his face looked grave. "If money were to be supplied, might you reconsider your certainty?"

"I'm afraid not." Pevensey had been offered bribes often enough to no longer be offended by the overture. Perhaps his face looked susceptible to such persuasion. Perhaps some people assumed that everyone's integrity could be bought. Or perhaps it was a single, desperate attempt from a compassionate old man who did not want his great-nephew to hang.

"I'm surprised that there would be money available to supply," said Pevensey, finding an opening to prolong the conversation, "since the Emison estate is so encumbered at present."

"Ah, it's not Emison money," said the old man, a spark lighting his eyes. "I've seen my share of adventure in the world and amassed my own chest of coin. I daresay if Maria had stayed by my side, she'd have run through it by now, but after her, there was no one else to captivate me so." He smiled modestly at the circle of birds surrounding him. "I have enough money to buy the Emison estate thrice over."

Pevensey rubbed his nose. This fellow was full of fantastical tales. One hardly knew whether to believe them or to consider them proof of his advancing senility.

"And what does the family think of your vast fortune? Surely, if you are as rich as Croesus, you have considered helping the earl out of his financial predicament?"

"Oh, they don't believe me. They never have. I daresay they will when I'm gone."

Pevensey glanced from the battered brown boots to the worn frock coat to the lined face. Nothing about Harold Harding's appearance indicated that his claim was anything more than the delusions of an attic-dwelling octogenarian. But Pevensey was willing to keep an open mind. In his profession, he had seen the contents of many wills, and it was true, more often than not, that the deceased's relatives were surprised by those contents—either favorably or unfavorably, as the case might be.

But even if these claims to wealth were false, they were still an important clue to the larger case. An old man who walked his beloved woods oblivious to the realities of life was an old man who might confuse an opinionated young lady with an enemy to be dispatched. And though Harold Harding was not in the prime of his life, he was still large enough and strong enough to do away with a slender antagonist of the opposite sex.

"Where were you the morning of the murder?"

The old man blinked. "Out walking, of course."

Haro peered around the corner. He had not been able to resist trailing Eda after she had slipped away—"like a woodland faerie" would be the more poetic description; "like an eel" would be the more accurate one. What secrets was she trying to buy? She had been so coy about the whole thing that he almost suspected she had meant for him to follow her out the door and down the hallway.

He had expected her to take the main stairs down to the ground floor, but instead, she had opened up a small door in the wall and disappeared into the servants' corridor. Although Haro was a large man, he was also lithe—when the occasion demanded, he could tiptoe around a covert without flushing the pheasant. He followed Eda down the corridor, keeping to the shadows, and as he peered around the corner, he saw her knocking on a dark wood door—once, twice, thrice without success.

Unable to resist, he came out of the shadows and had the satisfaction of startling her. Her large eyes, blue as deep water, conveyed surprise so well. "Oh goodness, Haro!" She put a hand to her heart. "It's just you!"

"Yes, just me," he said wryly. "Whose room is this?"

"Well, if you must know, it's the French maid's room.

Haro was not aware that there was a French maid on the premises.

"You know, Ara—Miss Hastings' maid."

"Ah, I see. And she's the one you wanted the guinea for? The one with the secrets?"

Eda did not respond, but her eyes turned defiant.

"I don't like this, Eda. Arabella's dead. Why do you have to go prying into her secrets? Why are you trying to paint her blacker than she was? Are you so mean-spirited?" He knew that he was lecturing her, but he could not help it. "Come away. I don't want you talking to her maid."

"Well, her door's locked and she's not answering, so for all we know, she could be lying dead in there. The strangler's struck again!"

"And locked the door from the inside?"

"Or owns a set of keys to the whole house," Eda shot back. It was the closest she had ever come to accusing him of committing the crime.

Haro set his jaw. That face, which he had wanted to kiss so much just a few moments ago, was eminently un-kissable at present. "Strangely, I don't seem to have my set of keys with me, so perhaps we'd better call Mrs. Alfred."

The scullery maid was scurrying by at this exact instant, casting sidelong looks at these intruders in the servants' quarters. Haro halted her with a word and dispatched her on a mission to find the housekeeper. They stood there in cold silence for the few minutes that it took to retrieve Mrs. Alfred. Haro could see that Eda was biting her tongue.

"Can I help you, my lord?" asked Mrs. Alfred, a little flustered to see the earl and Miss Swanycke in this unexpected location.

"Yes, Mrs. Alfred," replied Haro, trying to set her mind at ease with a smile. "You can open this door, if you please."

The housekeeper took out her large iron key ring and thumbed through the keys until she came to the correct one. Haro watched Eda's face as Mrs. Alfred inserted the key in the door and turned the handle. She did not think Mademoiselle Mathilde knew secrets involving him, did she?

With the door unlocked, Mrs. Alfred hesitated. Perhaps she disliked invading the privacy of an innocent domestic. But Eda, apparently, had no such qualms. She stepped past the housekeeper to enter the room, and Haro was close behind. The bedclothes were in disarray, and the chair was askew against the wall. There were no personal possessions in sight. Mademoiselle Mathilde and everything she owned had disappeared.

It had not taken long after their exchange on the bridge for Harold Harding to disappear deeper into the woods. Pevensey watched him go, hoping the old fellow would be able to navigate the patches of ice on the path without mishap. He returned to Woldwick the circuitous way he had come, making the trip again in a little under half an hour. It was two o'clock now, and he could think of no better way to spend his afternoon than by riding into the village. He had a hired horse in the stables—Mr. Hastings had been generous with the funds he had sent, desiring Pevensey's presence faster than the post would have been able to bring him—and the beast could doubtless use some exercise.

Confirming the Frenchman's whereabouts was to be the main thrust of this expedition. He had already timed the distance from the village to Woldwick on his initial journey. It was a forty-minute ride at a decent pace. He imagined a more delicate rider would take an hour or so, but the Frenchman hardly qualified as delicate.

Upon reaching the village, Pevensey noted the bright arms of the Rose and Thistle. It was the main establishment in the village, the dispenser of ale and gossip, and the stop for posting carriages that travelers less advantaged than the Emisons and Hastings would employ.

"Good afternoon, sir!" said Pevensey to the round man whom he took, quite rightly, to be the innkeeper. "May I have a drink of your best?"

"But of course!" said the innkeeper, wiping his hands on his apron and reaching for an empty tankard on the shelf. His bald head glistened as brightly as the copper pans hanging above the shelf. "What brings you to these parts?"

Pevensey suspected—again, quite rightly—that the innkeeper was already quite familiar with his name and business. A murder on the local landowner's estate could hardly have escaped public notice. "Just here to enjoy the wintry weather," he responded with a twinkle in his eye.

The proprietor of the Rose and Thistle plopped down the tankard of ale with a bit of disappointment.

Pevensey took pity on him. "And to ask you some questions."

The innkeeper rubbed his hands together. "Oh, certainly! What can I help you with?"

"Do you remember a Frenchman coming in here two days ago?"

"Yes!" The innkeeper's eagerness was palpable. "He sat in the exact same seat you're in, Mr. Pevensey." Pevensey smiled inwardly. He had not given the innkeeper his name, but it was apparently already common currency in the village. "I served him a breakfast pastie, the ones my wife makes."

"And at what o'clock did this take place?"

The innkeeper scratched his bald head. "It was before the morning post, I remember."

"And the morning post comes at...?"

"Nine o'clock. And the afternoon post comes at half past three." The innkeeper glanced out the window. "It should be here soon now."

"How long was the Frenchman here?"

The innkeeper scratched his bald head. "Hard to say. It was busy here that morning. I don't rightly remember how long he sat, but I did serve him that pastie my wife makes."

"And I'm sure the pastie was delightful," said Pevensey obligingly. He reached into his breast pocket and pulled out his notebook. The aproned innkeeper was too splendid a specimen not to be sketched. "Did he say anything about his plans for the day?" He drew the crown of the bald head with one bold, curving sweep of the pencil.

The innkeeper pursed his lips. "Not to my recollection. I had the feeling that he was planning on taking the morning post to London, but I probably just assumed that since he breakfasted at the same time as all the travelers. He didn't take the post, did he?"

"No," said Pevensey, working quickly on the lines of the apron.

"Oh, hallo there!" said the innkeeper suddenly, walking over to the window. "It's Henry, up from the big house. And who's that he's got in the dogcart?" He gave a low whistle.

Intrigued, Pevensey set aside his sketchbook and came over to the window just in time to see Woldwick's first footman lifting down an elegantly dressed female from the front seat of the wagon.

27

At first glance, Pevensey thought the elegantly dressed female was Miss Swanycke, based on the dark hair under that modish hat. A more thorough inspection of the woman's figure, however, revealed that she was too thin and angular to be the Emisons' cousin. He was also certain that Miss Swanycke would have taken the carriage into the village—that, or ridden her own horse. So, who was this woman arriving in the Woldwick dogcart?

She was opening her purse and seemed to be offering something to her escort, but Henry, the footman, shook his head and then leaned down and planted a tentative kiss upon her cheek. In that instant, Pevensey knew. It was Mademoiselle Mathilde. There on the ground was her trunk, and there, in the distance, was the post that she was meaning to travel away in.

"Thank you for your time," he said, shaking the innkeeper's hand hurriedly, and leaving his tankard of ale on the counter, he dashed outside for one last conversation with the dead woman's maid.

Henry had already climbed back into the dogcart, but he looked askance at the red-haired Pevensey and seemed ready to climb down again, probably to shield Mademoiselle Mathilde from any impertinent questions. Pevensey waved him away authoritatively, and the footman set the wagon in motion back towards the house with many a glance behind.

"Who gave you permission to leave Woldwick?" asked Pevensey, planting himself in front of the French maid. It was very trying when the witnesses for a murder investigation refused to stay at the location of the crime. He thought that the earl and the other members of the family had understood the need to keep everyone on the premises. Was she departing of her own accord?

"Monsieur Hastings ordered me to leave." Mademoiselle Mathilde's voice was filled with loathing and disdain. She pulled her angular shoulders back, attempting to fill out the bodice of the elegant dress she wore which had clearly been sewn for another.

Pevensey frowned. This woman was a pivotal witness in the investigation. And ever since his first conversation with her, he had the distinct impression that she was suppressing information. He was not the official magistrate in this part of the country, however, and he hardly had the authority to command her to stay. He decided to take a gamble.

"How much money did William Hastings pay you to keep the engagement between Miss Hastings and Philippe Bayeux secret?"

Her eyes narrowed. "Why?"

"Do you have possession of any of the letters that passed between them?"

Her face turned sly. "Perhaps. Do they interest you?"

They did. Very much so. But Pevensey was not prepared to pay for them. "If I need them, I will let you know. You are bound for London?" He flashed a smile, trying to disarm her.

"Oui."

"Might I have your address there?"

She hesitated, probably calculating whether such a revelation might prove profitable or perilous. In the end her cupidity won out, and she divulged a direction near St. Paul's Cathedral where a cousin of hers resided. Pevensey noted it down in his mind, preferring to save the pages of his notebook for more artistic pursuits.

The post had arrived, and the stable boy was leading out a new team of horses to replace the spent ones. Pevensey expressed his gratitude for Mademoiselle Mathilde's cooperation by handing up her trunk and was honored by a brief nod of the head.

He stood outside in the cold as the post carriage rattled away. So, it was certain then that Bayeux and Miss Hastings had been affianced at some point. He must find out when and why the nuptials had been called off. Jealousy was a fertile ground that, in Pevensey's experience, could breed all manner of mischief.

"I thought you believed me," said Haro, quite loudly, leaning in towards Eda. If Eda had not known better, she would have thought he was half-sprung. But there was no scent of brandy on his breath, and the wild intensity in his eyes seemed to stem from emotion rather than alcohol.

"Whatever are you talking about?" asked Eda. The two had been able to keep up appearances in front of Mrs. Alfred, but once they had left the servants' corridor and returned to the drawing room, the daggers had been drawn afresh.

"Two days ago. When the murder was first discovered. You asked me in Arabella's sitting room whether I had done it. I thought you believed me."

"What a lot of fustian nonsense, Haro! Of course, I believe you. Do you honestly think that I think you killed Arabella?"

Haro paused. "Yes." His tone was softer now, gentle, pleading.

Eda looked into his eyes and saw fear there, and vulnerability. But what was he afraid of? The hangman's noose or her poor opinion? At this moment, it seemed like it was predominantly the latter.

"Or at least, that you are unsure." Haro, it seemed, was not willing to let the question lie. "Well? Are you?"

"Of course not!" Eda stamped her foot. "The only thing I've been trying to do through the whole of this dreadful episode is to clear your name! Why do you keep getting in the way of that?"

Haro paced over to the window and stared out into the frosty world below. "I don't know. I suppose it's because I am afraid that if I am proven innocent, then someone else must be proven guilty. Torin, Uncle Harold...you."

"That is preposterous. Listen!" She took his hand, firmly, as one takes a child's hand to stop him from running out into the street. "Are we such strangers to one another that the swirling circumstances could cause us to doubt one another's character? You know Torin. You know Uncle Harold. You know me—inside and out. We must believe in each other's innocence as fervently as we believe in our own. Is that not the essence of love? To bear all things, believe all things, hope all things, endure all things?"

Haro's grip tightened on her hand. "But if not one of us, then whom are you suggesting? One of the servants?"

"Nay, not at all. They have been with us for years, and we can vouch for their characters as well. But think! Whose character remains unproven?"

"I take it you mean the character of our visitors."

"Exactly!" Eda pried his fingers loose from hers and settled herself on the sofa. "What do we really know about William Hastings, Mrs. Rollo, or Philippe Bayeux?"

"Only enough to wish them at Jericho!" Instead of sitting across from her to continue their tête-à-tête, Haro sat down beside her, at very close proximity, and placed his long arm around her shoulders.

Eda gave him a quizzical look but allowed him this liberty. "As much as I detest William Hastings, I do think it rather unlikely that he would toss away his key to unlocking the peerage. And Mrs. Rollo—that woman has the most masculine hands I've ever seen on a female. But she's so downtrodden and pitiful. I can't stand the idea of her being a murderess."

"I have no opinion on her. Although if she were prepared to own the crime, I would not object to her hanging instead of me."

"But don't forget the architect—Philippe Bayeux!"

"Oh, him? I feel rather sorry for him—"

"Good heavens! Why?"

"Well, if he did have romantic feelings for Arabella, his misery must be as great as, or greater even than that of her father."

"Haro!" said Eda, pulling away from his presumptuous arm. "You are too full of the milk of human kindness!"

"I beg your pardon, Lady Macbeth! The next thing you'll be saying is that I should have caught the nearest way and done the deed myself—"

"No, I'm simply saying that it's a little too...sentimental to feel sorry for Bayeux. To my mind, he's the most likely candidate for the murder."

"But he loved her!"

"And she was planning to marry someone else."

Haro made a fist with one hand and twisted it against the open palm of his other hand. "Wouldn't it be more logical for him to attempt to kill me?"

"What does logic have to do with it?" asked Eda, shaking her head. She had wanted to murder Haro when he engaged himself to marry someone else. No doubt Bayeux had felt the same impulse. "You have clearly not read enough novels."

"Yes, I must admit it is difficult for me to measure Monsieur Bayeux's actions by the yardstick of Mrs. Radcliffe's heroes—"

"Oh, Haro! Eda! There you are!" The couple's tête-à-tête was interrupted by Lady Anglesford, who had conquered her nerves enough to descend from her boudoir to the drawing room.

"I have been thinking, Haro, and I was wondering if it might be best to alter your version of affairs so that Torin went with you to the pond."

Haro had risen to his feet as his mother entered the room and now stared at her blankly. "Alter my version of affairs?"

Eda sat upright on the couch, wondering if the strain of the last few days, or indeed, the last few months, had been too much for her guardian.

"Yes, my dear. You know, so that you will have someone to vouch for your innocence."

"Mother! The investigator already knows that I went there alone. And didn't you tell him that Torin was with you?"

"Yes, but I'm sure we could tell him that we remembered it wrong."

Haro stared at Eda openmouthed. She rose from the sofa herself and took Lady Anglesford's small hand in hers.

"But Aunt Edith, surely you must see that the inspector will only think you are covering up Haro's guilt. He will know that you are lying."

"And I don't need anyone covering up for me," said Haro, "since I had nothing to do with it." He enunciated the last five words very clearly.

"Yes, dear," said Lady Anglesford, smiling wanly. "But there's no harm in looking at it from the perspective of 'what if?' It could have been an accident, after all."

"I hardly think throttling somebody can be interpreted as an accident."

Lady Anglesford winced at the indelicacy of Haro's statement. "Very well, my dear. If you don't want me to, then I won't tell the man that Torin was with you. However, I did assure him that Eda was with me in the drawing room,"—she gave Eda's hand a motherly squeeze—"so that protects you at least." She turned towards the door to make her way back upstairs.

"But, I've already told the investigator that I was alone!" said Eda, to her aunt's retreating figure. "Aunt Edith, what have you done?"

Eda's cheeks reddened a little at the realization that she had already told Jacob Pevensey the same kind of lie for which she was rebuking her aunt. She had not been alone that morning—she was simply trying, in her own way, to light the same sort of smoke screen that Lady Anglesford was attempting.

She looked back at Haro. He shook his head as he watched his mother disappear, and his lips pulled back into an ironic smile. "So much for your eloquent speech on believing in one another. It seems like the woman who has known my character the longest is not at all sure that I didn't strangle Arabella."

"Accidentally, of course," said Eda, still able, despite her dismay, to see the humor in the situation.

"Of course," said Haro. She saw him eyeing her white throat. "I'm in the habit of wrapping my hands around attractive young females' throats whenever I'm given the opportunity. You don't mind, do you—?"

Eda let out a high-pitched noise somewhere in between a laugh and a scream. "Stop it, Haro!" she said, twisting away from him. She ran giggling to the door and stood there leaning against the cherry door frame, flushed and out of breath.

"But I thought you believed the best of me!"

"Of course," said Eda, smoothing down her black hair to make herself presentable, "and that is why I am going to look for Philippe Bayeux and ask him why he killed Arabella Hastings."

28

PEVENSEY WRINKLED HIS FRECKLED nose as the post rolled away into the frosty fog of the winter afternoon. He had just learned the most excellent motive for murder and discovered the perfect solution to the crime—and yet he was afraid that events would not allow it to hang together.

So far, Philippe Bayeux's timetable was all verifiable. He had ridden into the village and arrived for breakfast at the Rose and Thistle sometime after eight o'clock. If Haro Emison had discovered Arabella's body at the bridge just before nine o'clock, that left very little time for Bayeux to ride back to Woldwick and out to the pond.

Pevensey began to pace in front of the stable yard while the stable boy looked on with awe. Even if Bayeux had rode hell for leather back along the road, he would have needed to pick his way with care along the narrow and circuitous path to the pond. Could he have arrived at the pond, argued with Arabella, strangled her, and still returned to the village by nine o'clock? Impossible. Pevensey was certain of it.

He gave a disappointed whistle. Though he tried to maintain impartiality during a case, he could not deny that he liked the earl. There had been a humility about him that was appealing—that, and a courteousness that was utterly lacking in the Frenchman's demeanor. A pity then that events seemed to place Bayeux away from the crime when it occurred.

But was it established that Bayeux was present in the village at nine o'clock? Pevensey ceased his pacing. Bayeux had claimed that he had met with the stone mason for an appointment at nine, but that still needed to be verified. Pevensey looked up at the windows of the Rose and Thistle and saw the bald-headed innkeeper—and his wife—watching him. He gave a smile and a salute in their direction.

"Pardon me," he said, approaching the stable boy. "Could you point me in the direction of the stone mason's workshop?"

Struck speechless at this notice from such a celebrated personage, the stable boy could only stare openmouthed and point down the main street of the village. Pevensey said a thank you and walked, hands in pockets, down the thoroughfare until he came to the sign of a hammer and anvil.

Pevensey saw steam coming from behind the shop and took the liberty of rounding the corner. A brawny-armed man in a dirty leather apron was holding a pair of tongs, and clasped in their arms was a perfectly symmetrical horseshoe that he had just pulled from the cooling depths of the water barrel. "I'm looking for the stone mason."

The blacksmith grunted. "Och aye, 'at will be mah brither. He's in th' hoose yonder."

"Did he have a visitor two days ago? A Frenchman named Philippe Bayeux?"

The blacksmith used a thick forearm to wipe his brow and nodded.

"At what o'clock, do you remember?"

"In th' morn, sometime after th' post had gain by. Ye can ask him yerself about it. Thaur he is."

Pevensey saw that another leather-aproned man, nearly the copy of the blacksmith except moderately cleaner and slightly fairer, had emerged from the cottage and was coming toward the forge.

"Colin," said the blacksmith, raising his voice, "here's th' Runner come tae ask ye about th' Frenchman!"

"Och, what dae ye need tae ken?" asked Colin the stone mason.

"What time did he come see you two days ago?"

"Nine o'clock. I min' jist whit happened. He came in an' said, 'I'm haur for mah nine o'clock appointment.'"

"And did you check the time on your pocket watch?"

Colin rubbed his head as if he had never heard of such a contraption. "Nae."

"When did you make this appointment?"

"A few days afore. He'd bin haur askin' about limestone. Truth tae tell, it had slipped mah min' he was comin' again 'at day. I was daein' some carvin' an' he came upon me right in th' middle of it."

"But you're certain he was here at nine o'clock?"

"Och aye, I've already tauld ye as much." The stone mason yawned. "At first I thought mebbe his cuddie had throon another sheen, but nae, it was me he was haur tae see, nae mah brither Brendan."

"Oh?" Pevensey quickly deciphered the meaning of that statement, thanking the Almighty that he had been endowed with the gift of tongues. He turned back to the blacksmith named Brendan. "Had you shoed his horse before?"

"Aye, a few days since. He came in ridin' a Woldwick mare, an' she'd throon a sheen in th' woods, he said."

"Was it strange that he was asking you for a new one and not the Emisons' stable master?"

Brendan shrugged. "That's mair than I ken. Mebbe he was closer tae th' village when she threw it than he was tae th' stable."

This week-old detail about the horseshoe, though interesting, in no way mitigated the certainty that Bayeux had arrived at the inn on the crucial day at a little after eight and at the mason's at nine o'clock. "I see. Well, thank you for your time." Pevensey gave a short nod to both brothers and stepped back into the street.

He was so annoyed at the destruction of the case against Monsieur Philippe Bayeux that he did not even take out his sketchbook to record the picturesque scene of two brothers, almost alike enough to be twins, standing in front of a heated forge feet apart and arms akimbo, the perfect picture of industrious craftsmen in rural Britain.

Haro was glad to see that Eda had decided to vary her approach to confrontation. Instead of racing to Monsieur Bayeux's room and knocking on his door, she had taken a cue from Queen Esther and was waiting until suppertime to make her accusation. The first footman, Henry, was nowhere to be found, so she sent the second footman, George, with a message to the architect, extending him his hostess' best wishes and hopes that he would join them at the table that evening.

Since Lady Anglesford was indisposed, Miss Swanycke would be the hostess, and Haro grimaced just thinking of the conversational topics she had in store. As much as he would enjoy being cleared of suspicion, he could not countenance such rudeness to a guest. One might quibble that the Frenchman was in fact here without an invitation, but Haro took the position that since he had allowed him into the house, the invitation was implicit.

Eda descended the stairs for dinner dressed in a very becoming shade of midnight blue. It was still dark enough not to occasion comment in a house of mourning, but the color was a more vibrant setting than black for the white perfection of her shoulders and neck. Haro admired the square cut of the dress' neckline, just low enough to show the beginning swell of its wearer's bosom. It would be hard to be disapproving of anything she said while she was so attractively clad, but Haro steeled himself to the task. He was an earl, first and foremost. Hospitality must be upheld at all costs.

Mr. Hastings surprised them all by appearing punctually before the dinner gong had rung. He had not deigned to eat with them since the incident, and Haro noted that he had chosen a particularly unpropitious time to grace them with his presence. Mrs. Rollo was standing there as well, a silent black wraith committed to remaining in the background. On the ending tremor of the gong, Torin stepped into the circle, his cravat so loose and poorly tied that the knot barely held together.

Eda frowned. Haro could see her disappointment that Monsieur Bayeux was not present. She pursed her lips, as if trying to decide whether to wait a few more minutes.

"Time to go in," said Mr. Hastings gruffly, and he offered Eda his arm, not so much out of civility as out of concern for the laws of punctuality. Haro reflected that after the death of his only child, his pocket watch must be his greatest comfort...that and the thousands of pounds he made annually from his mill.

As host and earl, Haro should have by rights been leading Eda into the dining room himself—her white arm over his while he held her fingertips in his hand. He forced himself not to take umbrage at Hastings' usurpation of his position.

He gave Mrs. Rollo his arm, relieved that the architect had not made an appearance but still dubious about the prospects of having a meal in peace. Even with Eda unable to launch accusations against Philippe Bayeux, it was not at all unlikely that William Hastings would resume launching accusations at him.

The erstwhile absent Henry had now resumed his duties, and both of the footmen placed the dishes for the first remove on the table: vegetables, boiled beef, a roasted fowl, and a dish of something creamy but unidentifiable.

William Hastings grunted as he speared himself some meat and ladled the cream sauce onto his plate. "Enjoy your meal, Mrs. Rollo. This is the last one you'll be having at my expense."

"I beg your pardon?" said Mrs. Rollo.

"Arabella's dead," said Hastings crudely. "If I were considering keeping a paid companion around, I don't think it would be you. That French harpy's gone today, and you can go tomorrow."

Mrs. Rollo's face registered no emotion, but Eda set down her fork and wiped her lips with deliberateness. An angry blush suffused her cheeks.

"I'm not sure I would consider this meal to be 'at your expense,' sir," interjected Torin.

Hastings gave a sneer which acknowledged the merit of that claim. "It certainly would be far more palatable if it were, you gobble-cock."

Haro caught Torin's eye and willed him into silence. "Please have a care with your speech in front of the ladies." He spoke firmly but tried to keep any belligerence out of his voice, as was becoming for a host.

William Hastings was not so considerate of the duties of a guest. "I'll thank you to keep your warnings to yourself, Anglesford." He barked at the nearest footman to refill his glass with wine.

"Mr. Hastings," said Eda, staying seated but drawing herself up to her full height upon the chair, "I think it would be wise for y—"

"I beg your pardon for my tardiness," said a heavily accented voice from the door of the dining room. Philippe Bayeux had decided to join them for dinner.

Haro did not know whether to cheer in delight or quail in dismay. The Frenchman's entrance had certainly defused an awkward situation, but it had the potential to precipitate another if Eda continued with her plan. "Delighted you could join us!" he said with a good deal more heartiness than was warranted.

Torin grudgingly handed over the dish of roasted fowl, and the architect helped himself to a generous portion. Mrs. Rollo looked at the man curiously and then averted her eyes to stare down at her own plate.

"So good to see you, Monsieur Bayeux," said Eda in a silky voice. "I hope you have been able to amuse yourself here at Woldwick during our enforced confinement."

William Hastings, who had just stuffed a large forkful of the boiled beef in his mouth, looked up sharply. The color began to mount on his already florid face.

"*Merci, mademoiselle*," replied Bayeux. "I have some plans that I am drawing up for a house in London—though the client does not need them for some time. I am hoping that since my services are, I think, no longer needed here that I may return to London tomorrow?" He cast a glance at Haro and then at William Hastings.

"Oh, I don't think that would be possible," said Eda, answering for the both of them. "The investigation is not finished."

"I've already had my interview with the inspector," said Bayeux. His lips drew together into a tight line beneath his prominent nose. Haro reflected that if the man was indeed innocent, he would desire to leave the house for the sake of the unpleasant memories as well as to resume his work in the capital.

"Oh, yes?" Eda blotted her lips delicately. "And what exactly did you say to the inspector? Where were you on the morning of the incident?"

William Hastings harrumphed loudly. "I will not have my daughter's death discussed as dinner conversation!"

"Then you should have had the decency not to come to dinner two days after she died!" Eda sent a scathing look toward the man's full plate. "Out with it, Monsieur Bayeux! Where were you?"

Haro wondered what he would do if he were in Bayeux's position. He suspected that he would tell Eda to take her questions back to the sewing room where she belonged. But instead, the Frenchman shifted in his chair and recited an answer that seemed previously prepared. "I rode out to the village at half past seven. There, I had breakfast at the inn—what do you call it?—the Rose and the Thistle. Afterwards, I met with the stone mason near his brother's blacksmith shop at nine o'clock."

Eda, it seemed, had also noticed that the architect's words were a little too pat and to the purpose. "This alibi is very convincing, monsieur. Perhaps a little too convincing. I wonder if I were to check with Mr. Lublock down at the inn, what would he say?"

A throat cleared at the open door of the dining room. "He would say that Monsieur Bayeux was enjoying a delicious pastie prepared by Mrs. Lublock just after eight o'clock."

All eyes went to the door where Jacob Pevensey was standing, still in his frock coat and dirty riding boots. "I've examined this man's story, and it seems to be as he says. He was fully occupied during the hour in question."

Bayeux inclined his head to Pevensey, a gesture of wordless thanks. "Then may I depart?" He looked again at Haro and William Hastings. "I know these things are not talked of in le bon ton, but my livelihood must suffer if I cannot be about my work."

Haro was not sure whether to say him yea or nay, but it did not matter since the red-haired Runner once again took charge of the conversation. "I've spoken to the magistrate and the inquest is set for three days from now. It is necessary for you to stay until then."

"And me as well?" asked Mrs. Rollo suddenly, an unexpected query coming from an unexpected quarter.

"Yes, you as well," said Pevensey with firmness.

The duenna looked at William Hastings with a slight smile about her mouth that bordered on smugness. But it faded as quickly as it came, and her face relapsed into its downtrodden lines of inscrutability. Haro pitied her, not from any knowledge of her person but simply from a knowledge of the difficult position she was in. If Hastings did turn her out without a shilling, as seemed likely, Haro resolved that she could stay on with them at Woldwick until she secured another position—or until Woldwick was sold and they were *all* turned out of doors.

William Hastings rose from his chair and dropped his napkin onto the seat. "I hope, Mr. Pevensey, that you are coming to the conclusion of your investigation."

"Very close to that, sir. Very close."

"Excellent." He reached for his plate, still full of food, and carried it away to the door. "I thank you for your hospitality, my lord," he said with a sneer, "but I believe that I will be taking my meals in my room from now on until the inquest. Or perhaps I shall remove to the Rose and Thistle altogether, since from the sounds of it, the woman there is a far more competent cook than the one in your employ."

"As you wish," said Haro stiffly.

He glanced at Eda. She returned his gaze, a slight tremble in her lower lip. Pevensey's interruption, he knew very well, had not been at all what she wanted to hear. It occurred to Haro that, for the first time in the past two days, Eda was afraid of what lay ahead.

29

"HAVE EITHER OF YOU seen Uncle Harold?" asked Eda.

Torin and Haro were enjoying a quiet breakfast, the only sound in the dining room the chewing of sausage or the clinking of silverware against the plate.

Torin grunted a negative.

Haro looked up. "No, not since yesterday. Why?"

"I've just been up to the attic, and it looks as if his bed hasn't been slept in."

"Are you sure? Perhaps the maid's already been there to make it up."

Eda frowned. She was familiar with the routines of all the housemaids, and it was highly unlikely that they would straighten up the attic room before they had finished their other duties. After all, the old man was hardly likely to notice whether his bedclothes had been put to rights or not. Just to be sure, however, she summoned Henry who was in the front hall polishing candlesticks. "Please tell Mrs. Alfred I would like to see her."

"Oh, there you are, Mrs. Alfred," said Eda as the housekeeper entered and stood there, hands folded, expectant. "I was wondering, have the maids been upstairs to straighten up Mr. Harding's chambers yet?"

Mrs. Alfred adopted a defensive posture, as if her competency as a housekeeper was under scrutiny. "Not yet, Miss Swanycke. They are not shirking their duties though, and as soon as they are done with the other rooms, they will be upstairs."

Eda held up a white hand. "There's no need to make haste. I just wanted to make sure that no one's been upstairs yet to attend to his room."

"No, miss."

"Thank you."

As the housekeeper departed, Eda looked at the gentlemen meaningfully.

Torin took a swallow of coffee to clear the clog of sausages in his throat. "You're jumping to conclusions, Eda. Perhaps he made up his own bed himself before he went out."

Haro pushed away his plate and stood up. "When was the last time you made up your own bed, Torin? No, Eda's right. Something's amiss. I'll go out to the stables and ask if the groom has seen him this morning."

Eda pressed his hand in thanks. It was warm and sympathetic, but somehow, she still did not feel completely comforted.

Opening the door, Haro sighted Henry and sent him upstairs for his top boots and coat. He tapped his foot while waiting at the door. "This is the first time I've gone out of doors in three days."

Eda's lips parted. "Since...?"

"Yes."

Henry trotted down the stairs, boots in hand, and coat laid over his arm. Eda took a deep breath. The last time Haro had worn that coat, it had been covered with icy water from the pond, and in his arms had been the lifeless form of Arabella Hastings.

The icy air nipped at Haro's face as he darted over to the stables to investigate, and even with his greatcoat on, he felt chilled to the bone.

"No, m' lord. Can't say as I've seen him this morning," said Jimmy, the groom. He was spreading fresh straw around the horses' stalls. "And he usually comes by the stables on his way out. Likes to give the horses an apple."

"What about yesterday?"

"Aye, I seen him then. He was with that Runner fellow. They went down the path to the pond, I recollect."

"Thank you, Jimmy."

When he returned to the house, Haro saw that Eda's anxiety had increased sevenfold. "I had Henry and George search the house," she said. "He's nowhere to be found."

"You'd best tell them to put their coats on then," said Haro grimly. It was the second time this week they'd begun a search for a missing person, and the first search had not ended well.

Pevensey shook his head in disbelief. An hour ago, the Earl of Anglesford had asked him for particulars on where he had last seen Harold Harding. He had mentioned the bridge and their conversation yesterday. Now the servants—four of them with sturdy backs—were carrying in a long body in a shabby frock coat, a corpse as cold and rigid as a block of ice.

"Another murder!" shrieked the scullery maid, which set the housemaids to wailing about the woods being cursed. "Hush!" said Mrs. Alfred sternly, but with little effect.

"Ho there!" said William Hastings, emerging from his room to see the source of the ruckus. "What is this?"

"Bring him to my study," said the young earl, an ashen pallor overcoming his fair face. "And Jimmy," he said, taking the place of the groom who was holding the dead man's right leg, "ride for Dr. Stigand and tell him he's needed right away."

"Is he...?" Miss Swanycke, descending the stairs, did not finish her own question. The blue cast to the old man's lips and face had answered it before it was even uttered.

The younger brother, Torin, had entered the hall as well, and quietly taken the place of the second footman to support the left shoulder of his great-uncle.

Pevensey's eyes flicked from one face to another. As far as he could tell, every mouth was open in genuine shock and surprise. There were many faces missing however—Philippe Bayeux's, Mrs. Rollo's, Lady Anglesford's.

Pevensey followed the body into the study and watched as the men deposited it on the sofa. The doctor would give the final verdict, but from a cursory glance, there was no sign of strangulation or other hints of foul play. Perhaps the cold winter itself was the killer, though it had chosen an unfortunate and highly coincidental time to claim its quarry.

It took another three hours for Dr. Stigand to arrive. The groom had found him at the house of his most prestigious patient, Sir Robert Blount, and despite his gouty leg, the magistrate was not far behind the physician.

"What's this, Emison?" said Sir Robert, entering the hallway leaning heavily on his cane. "A second murder in your woods? 'Pon rep! There's something rotten in Denmark!"

"Not murder this time, I think," said Dr. Stigand, exiting the study after having examined the body. "Our dear Mr. Harding died of hypothermia from spending the night in the woods."

"But why would he do such a thing?" said Eda. Pevensey noticed the crack of emotion in her usually cultured voice. "Why would he not come back to the house when evening fell?"

Dr. Stigand cleared his throat. "I found some swelling around the left ankle that indicates it had been injured. Perhaps he sprained it and was unable to walk well enough to return to Woldwick before dark. He may have become disoriented in the woods—"

"Yes, that's it!" interrupted Sir Robert. "The pain was too much for him. The poor chap sat down on the icy ground and round about midnight or so, gave up the ghost."

"We seem to have reached the same conclusions," said Dr. Stigand with a faint smile. Pevensey wagered that the medical man was used to guiding the magistrate's diagnosis of affairs.

"There was a good deal of ice on the bridge and the path," Pevensey offered, genuinely sorry to see that this old man had come to harm.

The earl said nothing. Miss Swanycke had buried her head in his chest to cry while he wrapped one arm around her protectively.

"Torin," said the girl, lifting her tear-stained face enough to speak. "Go upstairs and tell Lady Anglesford."

Eda's mind was numb. She wished she could faint and be put to bed and wake up tomorrow to find that this was all a dream. But fainting seemed like a highly unnecessary piece of theatrics, a ploy to draw attention to oneself used by the likes of Arabella Hastings.

Uncle Harold dead? Uncle Harold gone? For as long as she could remember, Uncle Harold had been there, always ready with an adventure to share, a story to tell, or a piece of buttered toast. Without Uncle Harold, she was bobbing about in stormy seas. The only thing anchoring her now was Haro's arm, pulling her tightly against his chest.

"Come, let's sit down," said Haro, taking her hand and leading her into the drawing room. They sat together, side by side on the sofa, and she laid her head against his shoulder without a care for who should see them.

"What now?" asked Eda. "What do we do, Haro?"

He lifted her hand to his lips and kissed it. "Thank God for his life and pray for his soul, I suppose." He sighed. "I believe he deposited a will with our own solicitor, Mr. Godwin. I will write him a letter and find out who is the executor—not that there will be much to distribute, but he has mementos that I know will be dear to you, to me, and to Torin. We'll have him buried in the woods—give him six feet of earth or however much more he is taller than other men. And there he shall lie, among the birds and the squirrels and the trees that he loved so well. He would be happy not to leave Woldwick, I think, and when the rest of us must go, there he shall stay in perpetuity."

It was beautifully said, and Eda had nothing to add. She lifted a hand to wipe one of her tear-stained cheeks and in the midst of this moment was overtaken by the mundane. "Your cravat—I've ruined it." Its damp and crumpled folds bore witness to the truth of her statement.

Haro looked down at the piece of fabric with a wry smile. "I think that, under the circumstances, Garth will be forgiving."

From the open door of the drawing room they could hear raised voices in the hallway. "Seemed like the fellow had gone all soft upstairs," said a crude voice which could only belong to William Hastings.

Eda saw Haro grit his teeth.

"Now what do you mean?" asked Sir Robert. "A little eccentric, I daresay, but won't we all be when we're eighty years old?" The magistrate was determined to stand up for a county man over and above a mill owner from the city.

William Hastings grunted a reply that was inaudible from the drawing room. Haro let out a deep breath.

Eda looked up at him, admiring the firm chin above the soggy cravat. In that instant she realized that there was no one with whom she would rather experience sorrow than Harold Emison. And if even a death could be braved with him beside her, what would the loss of a house and a fortune matter?

Her mind flew to Lady Anglesford, alone in her chambers. "Your mother," she said suddenly. "She'll be beside herself. We should go to her."

"You're quite right," said Haro, drawing her hand to his lips again. He stirred on the sofa just as a pair of footsteps entered the drawing room.

Henry cleared his throat. "You're wanted in the hall, my lord. The magistrate wishes to speak with you."

Despite Eda's concern for Lady Anglesford, it was two or three hours before they were able to go to her and offer some solace. Dr. Stigand had given his opinion of accidental death induced by hypothermia, but despite the absence of foul play, Sir Robert informed Haro that, as magistrate, he must needs see the place where the body was found. Perhaps he felt such a pilgrimage necessary to make up for the missed excitement of three days ago.

Haro wanted nothing more than the opportunity to grieve in peace, but he did his duty as head of the family and lord of the manor, leading the stocky magistrate out into the woods. Eda insisted on coming too, holding onto Haro's arm as they stepped over frozen underbrush and ice-coated earth. Sir Robert groaned aloud every few paces, reminding them all of the torture he was enduring from his gouty leg.

The leafless forest was a homogenous wilderness, and it took Haro and Jimmy some time to work their way back to the place where the body had been discovered. When they finally located the spot, the magistrate wished to stand near it a while for a moment of silence.

"Very sad business, my boy," said Sir Robert, clapping Haro on the shoulder. "Very sad, indeed." He lowered his voice. "And the other business...how is this Bow Street Runner getting on? I've had to entrust the investigation to him, you know, being so incapacitated with this dashed leg."

Haro took a breath, not certain how to best answer this sort of question, and, in the interim, Eda interjected her own assessment. "More's the pity, for he's bungling it badly, Sir Robert. He seems convinced that Haro's the only possible suspect simply because Haro had the misfortune to find the body."

"Tut, tut! That is unfortunate," said Sir Robert. He had known the earl since Haro was a child, and his own son Stephen was of a similar age. "I'll have to speak to the fellow about the wisdom of casting a wider net. Poachers, I should think. Has he considered that?"

Haro shrugged. "He holds his cards close to his chest. I suspect he's considered a great many things."

"Hmm. Well then," said Sir Robert, quite finished with viewing the scene of the accident. He smacked his cane on the ground and turned around sharply. "Let's return to the house, shall we?" He followed up that question with a howl of pain. The cane, it seemed, had landed on his gouty foot.

"Please, allow me!" said Haro, bending over nearly sideways on his right to allow the shorter man to lean on his shoulder. At a nod from the earl, Jimmy came to support Sir Robert on the other side, and so between them, they were able to return him to the house in a far shorter time than it had taken them to find the scene of Uncle Harold's demise.

"Ah, doctor," winced the magistrate as they passed through the grand old columns to enter the front door of Woldwick. "I'm afraid I will need you to attend on me once again."

"But of course," said Dr. Stigand, fully aware of his importance to his most prestigious patient. "There is nothing left for me to do here. Shall we return in your carriage?"

"Indeed," said Sir Robert. "Go on, then, my boy." He gestured Haro away as he sat down on the hall bench to rest. "Your groom can alert my coachman that we are ready, and we shall be on our way. Where has that Pevensey fellow gotten to? A pity—I wanted to speak to him again."

30

AFTER BIDDING FAREWELL TO the doctor and the magistrate, Haro and Eda climbed the stairs to look for Lady Anglesford. She had never shown an especial fondness for the old man, but to have the last of her family gone—it would be a blow.

The door to Lady Anglesford's sitting room was open, and Eda and Haro would have gone inside had not a surprisingly cheerful voice interrupted them.

"Ah, my dears, there you are!"

"Mama! What are you doing?" asked Haro, seeing her come out of the door that led to the attic stairs. It was a steep flight of steps, not one that Eda would have expected Lady Anglesford's nerves to enjoy.

"I've been going through Uncle Harold's things, searching for some clue to this senseless tragedy. I found this." Lady Anglesford held out a folded letter.

Haro took it and unfolded it while Eda peered around his shoulder. The ink seemed very new, as if the letter had been freshly written in the last day or two. It was certainly not a memento from the long-ago days of Uncle Harold's adventures.

My dear family,

If you are reading this letter, it means I am no more. It is only right that you should know what transpired three days ago. I encountered Miss Hastings at the pond. She said some things that angered me. I attacked her in rage and her body fell from the bridge. I am sorry for what I have done and hope that you can all forgive me for a momentary lapse in judgment.

God bless you all.

Harold Harding

Eda gasped. Haro's eyes widened as he finished reading the letter out loud. "You say you found this in his room, Mama?"

"Yes, on the seat of his favorite armchair," said Lady Anglesford.

"And what are you going to do with it?"

"Why, give it to that Bow Street Runner, of course. No, rather, to Sir Robert. He is the proper person to see it. Has he gone yet?"

"We've just said farewell to him," said Eda, "but his carriage may not have come to the door yet."

"I shall have Henry go see," said Lady Anglesford, taking the letter back into her hand and darting down the stairs with unexpected agility.

A frown began to gather on Haro's face like storm clouds on the distant horizon. "This is all very peculiar. Why would he write 'three days ago'? It would have to have been two days ago, if it were written on the day he disappeared. And what an insipid way to write a letter! I hardly think Uncle Harold would have made his last confession thus."

Eda swallowed. She had noticed the same discrepancies as Haro had, but she had also gotten a hold of something that he did not yet seem to grasp—if Harold Harding was deemed the killer of Arabella Hastings, then Harold Emison would be acquitted of the deed.

"You were in his rooms this morning," continued Haro. "Did you see the letter there? On the armchair, like Mama says?"

Eda pursed her lips. She had not only been in his rooms this morning but also on the morning in question. The story of him throttling Arabella was undoubtedly a fake, as was the letter. But she could hardly fault Lady Anglesford for trying to save her son at the expense of her uncle's reputation. "Oh, I can't remember," she said pettishly. "I was looking for Uncle Harold, not a sheet of paper."

"Do you think it was Mama that forged it, or someone else? The handwriting seems feminine to me—"

"Why don't we leave it to Sir Robert to decide whether the letter was forged? After all, the evidence is supposed to be presented to the magistrate, not to you."

Haro glared at her. "Did you write that letter?"

"No." That, at least, was true. If she had written the letter, it would have been a far more convincing cheat.

"Hmm...well, come on, then. Let us see if Mama managed to catch Sir Robert before he left."

Pevensey pulled out his sketchbook. It was the only possible recourse when witnessing a scene such as this.

Lady Anglesford, who had apparently overcome the indisposition that kept her bound to her chambers, had flown down the stairs like a canary and sent the footman out the front door to halt the carriage that had just begun to roll away.

"My dear Lady Anglesford, what is it?" Dr. Stigand had returned to the house to reconnoiter in place of Sir Robert, who wanted nothing more than to prop his foot up on the cushions of the coach. Pevensey wondered if these country doctors always feared the worst when receiving such an urgent recall—the gamekeeper accidentally discharging a loaded gun, the cook's hand slipping when cutting the shallots.

"A letter!" Lady Anglesford had declared, clutching her heart in a fit of histrionics. "You must read it. Sir Robert must read it!"

And so the suffering magistrate had been unearthed from the carriage and helped into the house once again. Pevensey was now enjoying the prospect of Sir Robert, seated in the drawing room, his leg propped up on the decorative pillows that matched the sofa, reading and re-reading the sheet of paper Lady Anglesford had handed him.

"Dash it all!" he said, forgetting Lady Anglesford's feminine presence in his excitement. "It's a confession!"

"So it would appear," said Dr. Stigand, taking his own look at the note. His enthusiasm was slightly more moderated, and when Pevensey had a chance to look at the letter, he understood why. One did not have to be familiar with the late Harold Harding's writing to recognize that this was indeed a forgery. Pevensey made no comment, however, deciding to wait for Sir Robert to give his verdict.

"He was an odd old fellow, very odd, I always said. Always walking the woods at strange times of day and saying peculiar things. I'd like to say this comes as something of a surprise, but no, I had qualms about him in the past. I am so sorry, Lady Anglesford. You were right to bring this letter to me."

Pevensey grimaced. It was such a handy solution to the problem of Arabella Hastings' death. He wondered if the rest of the villagers would see it that way as well and exonerate the young earl at the expense of a man who was now safe from the punishment of the law.

Dr. Stigand said nothing to stem the tide of Sir Robert's conclusions. Here was one example, at least, of village nepotism papering over the truth.

"What's this? What's this?" demanded William Hastings, having correctly guessed from all the uproar in the hallway that something was afoot.

"It is a celebration, good sir!" proclaimed Sir Robert. He tried to stand using his cane but then winced and sat back down. "We have found the culprit in the death of your daughter."

It was Pevensey's turn to wince. Hopefully no one would think he was included in the "we" statement which Sir Robert had just issued. His sketch of Sir Robert's face was coming along nicely, a perfect blend of benevolence and pomposity.

The magistrate eagerly explained the exciting news of Harold Harding's confession.

William Hastings reached out a preemptory hand for the letter. "Give it here!" His greedy eyes raked it up and down, but in the end, his own conclusions were identical to Sir Robert's. "So! It was that raving lunatic that did it—God rot his bones!"

"Now, now, Mr. Hastings!" said Dr. Stigand, clearing his throat to remind all the gentlemen that Lady Anglesford was still in the room.

"I beg your pardon, my lady," said the mill owner grudgingly. He shoved his thumbs into the pockets of his wide waistcoat. "Although I daresay you're glad to be rid of the batty blighter too. It could have been you, Lady Anglesford, on that bridge when the old fellow lost his mind. Who knows?"

Lady Anglesford gave a wan smile. "I do see your point, Mr. Hastings, but you would do well to remember that Mr. Harding was, in fact, my uncle. However much I might deplore certain actions, I do still mourn his untimely death."

William Hastings snorted, as if the dual emotions Lady Anglesford claimed were utterly incompatible. "Well, I'm sorry the man's dead too. But only because I wanted to see someone hang for this. And now it looks as if justice will be cheated by frostbite, eh, Pevensey?"

"That depends on one's viewpoint, I think," said Pevensey, closing his book on the finished sketch. "But from the Almighty's perspective, justice is never ever cheated. It's merely delayed a while."

"Hmm, quite." William Hastings yawned dismissively. "At any rate, it looks as if your services are no longer needed."

"So it would appear," said Pevensey dryly.

Like the magistrate and the doctor, he had hoped that the young earl would be cleared of the crime—but not at the expense of all evidence, all logic, and all common sense.

It was too late to ride into the village that day and catch the afternoon post. Mr. Hastings had paid for Pevensey to switch horses several times on the way up to Woldwick, but no such largesse would be forthcoming for the return journey. No, Pevensey would have to travel inside the posting carriage, or if unlucky, outside of it.

He went down to the kitchen to say his farewells to the staff and was rewarded by some blushes from the cook, a ham dinner, and his own cake. He resigned himself to a quiet evening of packing up his meager luggage and completing some of the unfinished pieces in his sketchbook. He hated to leave a job half-done...although that was what he was doing now, there was no denying it.

He still had no alternative theory to offer as to the murderer's identity, and that was what made contesting the letter so impossible. Previous experience, however, had taught him that illumination often came when the clouds of confusion were the darkest. That was what made things doubly frustrating, to call off the chase now when the quarry was just on the other side of the hill.

Pevensey's opportunity to finish his sketches in quiet, however, was cut short by the arrival of two unexpected guests throughout the course of the evening.

The first was none other than Harold Emison, the Earl of Anglesford. Pevensey opened the door to find the earl's fair face looming several inches above his own. "My lord," said Pevensey with a bow. "What can I do for you?"

"Do you mind if I come in?" said the earl, smiling awkwardly. "There's something I want to talk to you about."

"Of course," said Pevensey, infusing his voice with cordiality. He had assumed his investigation was checkmated, but here was the tiniest of possibilities that his king could wriggle out of the trap. He gestured to the earl to sit down, and since the small room only provided one chair, sat down himself on the bed.

"It's that blasted letter," said the earl.

"I thought that might be it."

"Yes, well, it's a forgery, I think. No, more than that—I know it is."

"Of course, it is."

"Oh, so you already know?" The earl seemed taken aback. "Well, then can we have it removed from circulation, before Uncle Harold's name is tarnished forever?"

Pevensey clicked his tongue against the roof of his mouth. "Perhaps. Perhaps not. You see, my lord, you and I know that it is a forgery, but Sir Robert...well, he thinks otherwise. And is quite happy to do so." He decided to turn the conversation in a more profitable direction. “Whom do you think forged the letter?”

“My mother.”

“Ah.”

“She means well, of course.”

“Mothers always do. In this case, she wrote it to protect...?”

“Me.”

“And you are coming to me to reveal the truth of the matter because you—”

“—have no need of protection. I am innocent. I would swear as much on Holy Writ. And I dislike having my uncle’s name made into a byword simply on the chance that I might be wrongfully accused.”

Up until this moment, Pevensey had strongly wished to believe in the young earl’s innocence. But now, he had no further doubts. When a guilty man successfully weathers a murder investigation, he does not strive to reopen the case by discrediting the evidence pointing to someone else.

But without the countenance of the local magistrate, there was nothing Pevensey could do to continue the investigation. “You’re asking for help in the wrong quarter, my lord. It’s Sir Robert’s door you need to be knocking on, not mine.”

Pevensey’s second visitor arrived no more than ten minutes after his first had departed. Once again, Pevensey bowed. “Your servant, Miss Swanycke.”

“Thank you. I know this is unusual, but...may I come in?”

“If you think it wise. Perhaps we might leave the door ajar?”

She nodded.

“Thank you,” replied Pevensey with exaggerated seriousness. “A man can’t be too careful of his reputation.”

At that, she laughed, as he had hoped she would, a merry laugh that rang out like sleigh bells throughout the cold room.

“Please, do take the chair.”

"Ever the gentleman, I see."

She sat down with alacrity, and, instead of sitting on the bed, Pevensey took the liberty of putting one hand in his waistcoat pocket while leaning against the wall with his other arm. He expected her to come straight to the point—she seemed that kind of woman—and she did not disappoint.

"I assume you know that letter is a forgery?"

"Yes. Thank you for the compliment to my intelligence."

"You're welcome," replied Miss Swanycke. Her white skin, smooth and polished like alabaster, appealed to him. Pevensey regretted that he would probably never encounter her out of mourning and dressed in something softer than rigorous black.

"But there is something else you wish to tell me, isn't there?"

"Yes. I've agonized over this decision all day. At first, I thought it better to keep quiet, for Haro's sake, I mean—"

Pevensey nodded sympathetically.

"—but I could not still my conscience. Uncle Harold was not a murderer! Such an idea is not only inconceivable but also impossible. I know that you may hesitate to believe me, but I must tell you that I was in his company all morning on the day in question. I had just come downstairs from visiting him in the attic when Haro came rushing back into the house with orders for the servants to drag the pond."

Pevensey allowed an incredulous look to steal over his freckled face. "Miss Swanycke, when I interviewed you regarding your whereabouts, you told me, most emphatically, that you were alone that morning."

"Yes, well—"

"And when I interviewed Lady Anglesford, she was most emphatic that you were with her and Mr. Torin Emison."

"I know, but—"

"And now you propose a third story, that you were in fact ensconced with your great-uncle in the attic. Just what do you claim to have been doing up there?"

She blushed. "Eating toast. I know you won't believe me, but—"

"On the contrary. I do believe you. I have never heard someone fabricate a story that involved eating toast. Ergo, you must be telling the truth."

She looked askance at him. He could tell that she was measuring him, trying to determine if he was mocking her. "You see then that Uncle Harold could in no way have committed this crime?"

"I do see that...although I must admit that I ascertained as much from the outset."

"Then why did you not say as much to Sir Robert? You let him believe that the letter was genuine!"

Pevensey arched an eyebrow. "I could ask the same question to you, Miss Swanycke."

She paused, acknowledging the validity of his counter. "I had not decided yet what I meant to do. But now I have—and it is not right for Uncle Harold to be blamed for someone else's depravity. Please, Mr. Pevensey, you must contest that letter and search some more until you find the real murderer."

Pevensey pushed away from the wall and folded his arms. "I should like to oblige, Miss Swanycke, but unfortunately, I've been dismissed from the case, and I return to London tomorrow aboard the morning post."

31

PEVENSEY ROSE WHILE IT was still dark, and daybreak saw him saddling his hired mount to ride into the village.

"Is it true what they're saying downstairs," Jimmy, the stable hand, asked, "that it were Mr. Harding who done it?"

"It is indeed true that they're saying that downstairs," replied Pevensey brightly, and Jimmy, who was busy hitching a rough-coated mare to the dogcart seemed not to notice the avoidance.

As Pevensey walked his horse out onto the paving stones and swung himself into the saddle, he saw that Jimmy was loading a trunk into the dogcart while Mrs. Rollo stood by. Apparently, Mr. Hastings had succeeded in throwing her out on her ear now that the investigation had ended. By the looks of things, she was intending to take the same morning post that Pevensey was heading towards. He was not enthused by the prospect. One does not like to be forced into a social setting with people whom one has interrogated in an official capacity.

Once in the village, Pevensey rode straight to the Rose and Thistle.

"What can I get ye?" asked the innkeeper, smiling broadly to see Pevensey once again gracing his establishment.

"Might I have one of Mrs. Lublock's pasties? I have it on good authority that they are of superior quality."

"But of course!" The balding man beamed at Pevensey.

"Ah, it is Mr. Pevensey!" said a genial voice. Pevensey turned around to see Dr. Stigand seated at a table and already occupied with a pastie of his own. "London-bound, I take it?"

"Aye, no more to do in these parts," said Pevensey with a grin. The doctor motioned to the empty chair, and Pevensey took a seat. He wondered if Stigand would mention the egregious letter, but small talk about the weather and the village began to pass between them, and the doctor seemed happy to tiptoe around sleeping dogs.

"You look like you enjoy a brisk walk often enough," said Pevensey, nodding toward the doctor's ruddy countenance and rugged physique.

"I certainly do. It keeps my own health up to walk to my patients' homes. Although, I must admit, it gets cold these winter months to take it on foot."

"So, you go on horse then to places that lie farther out, like Woldwick?"

"Oh, occasionally, but I've walked to Woldwick more times than I could count. We country folk get used to the fresh air."

Pevensey gave a laugh at the friendly gibe. He was the first to admit that he was a Londoner through and through. "That's a long way on foot!"

"By the road, yes, but if you go through the woods, it can be done in less than an hour."

Pevensey put down his pastie and stared. This small talk had suddenly ceased to be small. "Through the woods, you say? How do you mean?"

"Just to the west of the blacksmith shop. That stand of birch is sparse and the ground is level. It's easy enough to come through to the pond, and from there, there's a good path to the house. A little circuitous, but well-marked and level. Why, one could even ride a horse through there easily enough, especially during times when the foliage is absent from the trees."

Pevensey stared. "Dr. Stigand...." His voice dropped to a hollow whisper. He reached into his pocket and pulled out the hallowed sketchbook. Very few hands besides his own had touched its pages. "Would you be so kind as to draw me a map? To scale, if you can."

"Oh, but of course," said the doctor. He took the pencil Pevensey proffered and set to work, seeming to sense the urgency radiating from his breakfast companion.

In one corner of the page he drew a clump of houses to represent the village. At the bottom of the page he drew a large rectangle with a roof—Woldwick. On the right, a thick line—the road—made a wide arc from the village to the manor house. Pevensey did not recollect the road having this much bend to it, but the curve was so gradual, he probably had not noticed it.

The pond, on the other hand, was situated in the center of the page. While the line connecting the pond to Woldwick was as squiggly as could be, a crow, if it were so inclined, could fly a straight line from the village to the pond to the manor house.

The scales, which had gradually been peeling away, now fell from Pevensey's eyes. Two things, the curvature of the main road and the circuitous nature of the pond path, had caused him to grossly overestimate the distance between the pond and the village. Dr. Stigand's map made everything clear: a man who had a horse and knew his way about might get from the blacksmith's shop to the pond in fifteen minutes or less.

"The post's a comin'!" came a shout from the door of the inn. It was the stable boy, performing one of his favorite duties, that of town crier.

Pevensey tensed in his chair.

The doctor looked at him questioningly.

Would Pevensey still need a seat on the post? That is what he had told the stable boy this morning when he handed him the reins of his horse. But so much had changed since then. There was a possibility, a slim possibility, that he could now make a case against someone other than the Earl of Anglesford.

"Dr. Stigand," he said, "if I were able to provide conclusive evidence that a different individual is responsible for Miss Hastings' death, would you support me to Sir Robert in claiming that the Mr. Harding confession is a forgery?"

The doctor sighed and leaned back in his chair. "Aye, I would. But only if the evidence is conclusive. Better to have the thing done with, one way or the other, than to have a cloud hanging over the county."

Pevensey shook the doctor's hand. It was a peculiar and myopic view of justice, but one that he had encountered often enough in his profession. He wondered, also, if the doctor's support would depend on whether his conclusive evidence pointed at the "right" person.

He looked out the window and saw that Jimmy had arrived with the dogcart and was helping Mrs. Rollo out. He stood up and scanned the yard to see if any of the other inmates of Woldwick were intending on taking the post this morning. But he only saw a pink-cheeked woman—probably a farmer's wife—and a young man in a dark coat—possibly a teacher—climb on board.

The horses stamped a little as they waited in the cold, the breath from their nostrils shooting into the air like plumes of smoke. The driver shouted for the stable boy to come over, and they began a heated discussion.

Waving a hand in good-bye to the doctor, Pevensey stepped out onto the porch. The driver looked up. "Are you the gent wantin' a ride to London this mornin'? 'E says I need t'wait for you."

Pevensey took a breath, the morning air cold and sharp on his lungs. "Thank you, my good man, but I think I'll be staying here a little longer."

The driver slapped his thigh and let out an unseemly epithet. "Second time this week," he snarled at the boy. "My 'orses have better things to do than stand outside in th' cold." He pulled hard on the reins and sent the post carriage out of the stable yard with a jolt.

Pevensey watched as the stable boy went back to his domain, hanging his head and kicking at a pile of straw in front of the stable door. He followed him. "What's your name, lad?"

The boy looked up. "Tom."

"Well, Tom, thank you for looking out for me by asking the post to wait, and I'm very sorry that I've made the driver angry with you. I didn't realize until just now that there's more to this murder investigation than I had thought. I'm staying a little longer—can you keep that just between us?"

The boy's eyes shone. "Yes, sir."

"Perhaps you can help me with something. What did the driver mean by 'the second time this week'?"

"Oh." Tom frowned. "He's angry 'cause the same thing happened earlier this week. I asked him to hold the post for a gent and then the gent never showed."

"How many days ago?"

"Three...four, maybe."

"And this was the morning post?"

"Aye."

Pevensey nearly held his breath. "And the fellow...was he French?"

"How'd you know, sir?"

Pevensey grabbed the boy and hugged him. "Thank you, my lad!"

"Y-you're welcome?" said Tom, obviously flummoxed by this strange behavior.

"My horse, if you please," said Pevensey releasing him. "I think it's time I head back to Woldwick."

32

"WHAT IS THIS I hear?" demanded Philippe Bayeux.

Haro looked up from his desk where he was composing a letter to Sir Robert. In the past, he had found the architect moody but unfailingly polite, but this morning neither the customary "my lord" nor even common courtesy were present in his address.

"I confess you have me at a loss. What is it that you hear?"

"That your uncle confessed to murdering her."

Haro put down his pen, careful to keep the ink from dribbling out onto his letter. There was a wild look in the architect's eyes. Haro reflected that for a man who loved a woman learning the name of her murderer would be like hearing of her death all over again.

"Allegedly, yes. Did you also hear that my great-uncle is dead?" Haro glanced over to the empty sofa where they had placed Uncle Harold's body temporarily before they had removed it to a spare room where it could be washed and dressed and await the delivery of a coffin.

"Yes, your valet told me as much." The man sounded relieved. "I assume I'm no longer needed here then—no need to wait until the inquest. I've missed the morning post already, but I'll take the afternoon one and be gone."

"Ah," replied Haro, not knowing how else to respond. He was not satisfied that the confession was genuine, and he was appealing to Sir Robert to reconsider his opinion of it. The trouble was wording the letter in such a way that it did not accuse his own mother of falsehood....

"What will you do back in London?"

"Resume my life," replied the Frenchman curtly. "Isn't that what one does?"

Haro sensed an implied rebuke, as if he should have spent more time mourning the death of his erstwhile fiancée before resuming his life, but he could not tell if the rebuke originated in the Frenchman's words or in his own mind.

"Will you leave your address with me?" Haro searched for a slip of paper to write it down.

The Frenchman hesitated. "Pourquoi?"

"In case the investigator or the magistrate needs any further information from you."

The other frowned. "I can think of nothing they would need."

"Oh, but I can!" said a voice from the door of the study. Both men turned to see Jacob Pevensey divesting himself of his greatcoat in preparation for a long conversation.

"Mr. Pevensey!" said Haro with a grateful smile. "I thought you were leaving for London."

"I thought so as well," replied the slight, red-haired man, "but then I realized I had unfinished business here."

Philippe Bayeux glanced from the earl to the investigator and walked quietly to the door of the room. "I will not disturb you gentlemen—"

"No, please stay!" said Pevensey heartily. "Please, I insist." He motioned toward the sofa. Haro noted that it was not so much an invitation as a command. The architect held out for a moment, standing stiffly, but finally acquiesced and sat down on the edge of the sofa.

There was a small wooden chair flanking the bookcase near the doorway, and Pevensey took it, positioned it between the door and the desk, and sat down. The three men formed a triangle, each of them easily able to see the others' faces, but neither Haro nor Bayeux would be able to leave the room unless they pushed past the investigator.

Pevensey rubbed his hands together. Haro thought he looked positively enthusiastic about what was to come. "Have you informed Monsieur Bayeux of the true nature of Mr. Harding's confession?"

"No," said Haro. "He has only just learned of the confession's existence."

"Ah," said Pevensey. He turned to the architect. "A forgery. Easily proven to be so, both by the content and the penmanship. But not, I think, forged by you."

"Mon dieu! Why would it be?"

Haro watched as Pevensey leaned back in his chair and crossed one foot over the other. What was the Runner going to say next? Haro could see that Bayeux was in suspense as well—one of his knees was bouncing erratically, and he was sitting so close to the edge of the sofa he looked ready to tumble off it.

"Tell me, Monsieur Bayeux, what is the quickest way to get from the pond to the village?"

"Je ne sais pas. I am not from this place."

"My lord?"

"Through the woods," Haro replied. "I went that way often when I was a boy."

"And how long do you think it would take for a man on horseback to make his way from the woods to the blacksmith shop?"

Haro shrugged nonchalantly, but his hands gripped the edge of his writing desk. "A quarter of an hour. Why?" Dear God in heaven, were Eda's suspicions proving correct? Had Jacob Pevensey found a chink in Bayeux's armored alibi?

Pevensey fixed his eyes on the Frenchman. "You, monsieur, were at the stone mason's shop at nine o'clock, yes?"

"I have told you as much."

"Which is just about the time that Lord Anglesford discovered the broken ice beside the pond. Fifteen minutes earlier, and you could have been at that pond yourself, talking with Miss Hastings, arguing with her, putting your hands about her throat—"

The Frenchman leaped up from the sofa. "How dare you!"

Pevensey stood as well, his body taut. Bayeux was several inches taller than the Runner, but Haro wagered that the smaller man could hold his own if it came to barring the door and preventing the Frenchman from flight. He half rose from his own chair at the desk, ready to intervene if Pevensey should need assistance.

Bayeux's nostrils flared. "Why should I do such a thing? Kill her and I lose my job renovating this relic." He waved a scornful hand at the Baroque moldings in Haro's study.

"Why?" echoed Pevensey. "Because she was not just your employer. She was your lover and had jilted you for him." He gestured toward the desk where Haro stood poised.

The Frenchman snorted. "Non! She did not jilt me. Her father broke off the engagement—that pig! I was the son of a French aristocrat. At first, I was good enough for his daughter. But then, as his fortune increased, he began to think he could do better. France was in turmoil; my title meant nothing. He wanted an English lord for his daughter, a viscount or a duke. But to bag an earl? Eh bien, the gods were smiling on him."

Haro loosened his cravat. This whole exchange was playing out before him like the scene from a tragic opera. He did not particularly like the role assigned to him either—the earl that had been bagged!

"So, you are saying Miss Hastings did not care for Lord Anglesford?"

"I did not think so. Why else would I have come all this way but to persuade her to defy her father's wishes?"

Haro eased himself back into his chair. He remembered the day Philippe Bayeux had appeared. It had been strange that neither Arabella nor William Hastings had mentioned his imminent arrival, and indeed, they both had seemed startled by it, and sought to explain the reason for it almost as an afterthought. No doubt they worried that Bayeux would make unpleasant revelations if they turned him away from the house and so had been forced to create a reason for it to ensure his silence.

Pevensey pressed on. "But she would not be persuaded, would she? You pressed her to call off the engagement, to run away with you, and all to no avail. You pretended to be drafting plans to remodel this house, but in reality, you were wandering the woods pining for her, watching her falling in love with him"—a finger pointed in Haro's direction once again—"and feeling the brick house of all your hopes crumble about you."

The Frenchman's mouth compressed into a thin line.

"You had given up in despair, and four days ago, you were prepared to forget your heart and take the post back to London."

Haro's own heart began to beat a little faster. Part of him wanted Pevensey to rush ahead to the end, but part of him wanted to linger on each piece of the story, climbing the mountain of evidence one slow step at a time until, reaching the summit, the whole would be revealed.

"But then, on the morning of your departure, you penned one last despondent note, begging her to meet you at the pond to say farewell. You rode into town, breakfasted at the inn a little after eight o'clock, told the stable boy you would be leaving on the morning post, and then set off to take a shortcut through the woods behind the blacksmith's shop."

"A shortcut? How would I know of such a thing? I am not native to this county."

"Ah, but you had stumbled upon it earlier in the week, when your borrowed horse threw a shoe in the woods and you walked it a quarter mile to the blacksmith's to have it reshod."

"So, it was you spying on us!" Haro said. "I saw someone walking in the woods, leading a lame horse, but it was too far away to see your face."

The Frenchman glowered in his direction then turned back to Pevensey. "A pleasant fiction, but one you will never, ever be able to prove."

"You talked with her on the bridge, perhaps even made one last appeal for her to run away with you. She refused—haughtily, I imagine. You became angry. She taunted you. You could not control yourself—"

"An utter falsehood!" Bayeux ground his teeth together. There was a storm building behind those chiseled cheekbones. Haro glanced at the lines of Bayeux's coat, trying to ascertain whether the fellow was carrying a pistol.

"We all know what happened next," said Pevensey, his eyebrows arching superciliously. "Perhaps you did not mean to kill her...just to make her stop talking, stop saying those things you did not wish to hear. When you realized what you had done—that she was no longer breathing—you shoved her away from you. And over the railing she toppled, down through the ice below."

An inarticulate cry came from Bayeux, and his hands balled into fists. No, he was not carrying a pistol, Haro decided, or he would have pulled it out at this moment.

"You panicked. You had just killed a woman. One might get away with such a thing in France with your 'Vive la Revolution!', but here in England such things are investigated, frowned upon, and punished.

"You are a foreigner. You had a checkered, albeit concealed, past with Miss Hastings. You would be suspected right away. You ran from the bridge, leaped onto your horse, and rode through the trees like a madman, stopping just briefly to compose yourself before you reached the blacksmith's shop on the outskirts of the village.

"You had planned to leave that morning on the post, but there was no guarantee that you could disappear into the warrens of London before your misdeed caught up with you. Besides, as you looked at your pocket watch, you saw that nine o'clock had come and gone, and so had the post.

"You had to create for yourself an incontrovertible alibi, an event that placed you somewhere else at the time of the murder. You remembered an appointment you had made with the stone mason, an appointment that you had decided to forgo when you packed to leave the county. But now you needed this appointment—needed it like old Boney needs his Josephine.

"You found the blacksmith and his brother. You told him several times that it was nine o'clock so that the time would stick like tar in his mind. And when you had wasted enough time looking at samples of stone, you swallowed down your gorge and headed back to Woldwick, prepared to feign shock and surprise when you learned of Miss Hastings' disappearance or demise."

Bayeux rose to his feet. "What proof do you have?" His hoarse voice was admitting nothing, but every drop of sweat on his face was a telltale confession.

Pevensey paused. "I think you are aware that the maid, Mademoiselle Mathilde, was both a letter-keeper and a secret-keeper. A blackmailer too, but that is beside the point." He pulled a sheet of paper out of the pocket of his coat. "The letter that you sent to Miss Hastings on the fateful day—"

Before the Runner could finish his statement, the architect had leaped upon him, seizing his wrist and snatching at the incriminating paper. Pevensey struggled manfully, but the Frenchman had the advantage of him in size. A fire was blazing in the grate on the wall opposite. Haro had no doubt in his mind what Bayeux was intending to do with the letter once he seized it.

He reached into the drawer of the desk that had belonged to his father and thanked God that he had omitted to lock the case which held the loaded pair of pistols.

Eda came out of Lady Anglesford's room and glanced down the stairs. The Bow Street Runner had left at dawn for London—or at least that was what Mrs. Alfred had told her. But not ten minutes ago, she had been looking out an upstairs window and had seen a man ride up with an unmistakable pile of bright red hair on the top of his head. She had excused herself from attending her aunt as quickly as she could and advanced to the top of the stairs to survey the situation. No one was in the entrance hall below, but as she darted down the stairs, she could see that the door to the study was ajar. Filtering out into the hall came the sound of men's voices raised in altercation.

Torin, who had popped out of the adjacent library, converged upon Eda just as she reached the bottom of the stairs. "I say, there's some sort of row going on in Father's study." A series of thumps now resounded through the entrance hall, as if something—or someone—was being thrown against the wall.

The cousins looked at each other conspiratorially, and then in tacit agreement, stepped forward to place their ears against the crack. They were just in time to hear the words, "Stop, Monsieur Bayeux, or I shoot!" followed by the earsplitting crack of a gunshot.

33

Pevensey winced at Lord Anglesford's words. When one's limbs are entangled with an opponent's, the threat of a gun being fired at close quarters is not an attractive proposition.

A bullet exploded from the dueling pistol. Pevensey winced again, just in time to feel the architect jerk away from him and go slack. A stream of blood began to pour out of Bayeux's left shoulder and gurgle down his dark coat. Lord Anglesford, it appeared, was not only an innocent man, but also a man with a cool head, a good eye, and a level hand.

The door to the study flew open, and there were Miss Swanycke and the earl's younger brother. "Haro! Are you all right?" demanded the black-haired beauty, her face even whiter than its normal fair complexion.

"Yes," replied Lord Anglesford, coming around the side of his desk to examine the Frenchman who had fallen to the floor, "but I suspect Monsieur Bayeux is not. Torin, send Jimmy for Dr. Stigand."

"And for Sir Robert," added Pevensey. It was time to contest that forged letter and present the magistrate with the case against the real murderer.

"I'll go myself," said Torin, disappearing to accomplish the task at hand. Miss Swanycke disappeared as well, and Pevensey could hear her giving orders to the servants in the hallway and allaying fears about the gunshot they had all heard.

Bayeux began to moan, and Pevensey shook his head. Clearly, the man was unused to physical pain. Pevensey had been shot in nearly the same place once—and still managed to overpower his assailant and bring him to justice.

The disputed piece of paper, now crumpled and torn, was still in Pevensey's hands. He folded it carefully and returned it to his pocket.

"Once upon a time, she really loved me," said the architect, gritting his teeth against the pain. He tried to prop himself up on the elbow opposite his wounded shoulder. He looked up at the earl defiantly. "C'est vrai!"

The earl's face clouded with some emotion. Guilt? But over what, Pevensey wondered—over injuring Bayeux's shoulder or injuring Bayeux's heart?

Miss Swanycke reappeared with a bowl of warm water and some cloths and walked slowly towards the wounded man.

"But she would not admit it," the Frenchman groaned. "'I was naïve,' she said, 'and you were quick to take advantage.' It was like hearing her father's rant all over again."

Miss Swanycke knelt on the floor beside the Frenchman and motioned for the earl to ease the architect's shoulder out of the coat that was covering the wound. The scene was perfectly framed by the fireplace in the background, and Pevensey pulled out his sketchbook to record it.

"I daresay you think me a fortune hunter too," Bayeux panted savagely, a comment more directed to Miss Swanycke than to the two men.

"No," she said softly. "I think you something worse—a murderer. But also, a murderer who needs his shoulder dressed. Come, hold still and let me tend to this."

Pevensey looked up from his sketchbook with increased admiration for Miss Swanycke. She had heard none of the evidence he had presented, but she had apprehended the essential point as soon as she entered the room.

He wondered if she might prove useful now in more than just leech craft. Bayeux's attempts to seize the letter from Pevensey's hand was an indication of guilt, but the case against him would be easier if they could draw out a confession while he was still in this mood to dwell on the past.

Miss Swanycke seemed to know what was needed and pressed on. "How does it feel—to know that you have killed the woman you loved?" She pulled the bloodied white muslin shirt away from his skin and pressed a cloth on the oozing wound.

The architect did not answer, but Miss Swanycke was relentless. "If you had waited half an hour, Haro might have come upon her first. He would have jilted her, you know—ended the engagement for good. You would have come upon a very different woman on that bridge, a woman ready to throw herself on your bosom instead of heap your head with scorn."

The Frenchman pulled away from her ministrations with a fierce cry. "Mon dieu! Do you have to remind me of that? Is it not the very thought that has been dancing through my dreams and turning them into nightmares?

"She told me that she was going to be the toast of London! 'A countess,' she said, with an earl at her beck and call. 'A life with you would be misery,' she said. 'What can you possibly have to offer me?'"

Pevensey caught Miss Swanycke's eye and nodded. It was enough.

After Eda had bandaged the wound as best she could, Haro called in the footmen and had them carefully relocate Monsieur Bayeux to the drawing room. There the footmen stood guard over him, waiting for Dr. Stigand and Sir Robert to make their appearance.

The other three stood silently in Haro's study for a moment. "A clean shot," said the Bow Street Runner approvingly, and Haro smiled at the praise. He was surprised himself at how quickly his hand had grasped the pistol and how easily his mind had made the decision to shoot.

"I did not want him to destroy that letter since it was the only tangible piece of proof against him."

The investigator smiled. "This letter?" He pulled the folded piece of paper out of his pocket and handed it to Haro.

Haro unfolded it and found the paper as white as eggshell inside. "But...what does this mean? Does Mademoiselle Mathilde really have a letter from Bayeux to Miss Hastings?"

"Oh, I'm certain she has one or two of them in her possession...as William Hastings and his pocketbook know all too well. But not, I think, the one from the morning of the murder. That one Miss Hastings must have burned upon receipt."

"So, you—"

"—assumed the existence of the letter and pretended possession of it for Monsieur Bayeux's benefit. His readiness to believe me confirmed that I was right to do so."

Eda let out a squeal and clapped her hands in delight.

Haro laughed. "Well done, Mr. Pevensey! Well done!"

"Thank you, my lord," said the red-haired man with a bow and a smile of his own.

"I know Mr. Hastings has already recompensed your travel expenses and paid your fee, but I wish I could reward you for your time spent here and your unwavering commitment to discovering the truth. Alas,"—Haro held out a pair of empty hands—"the Emison estate is on the verge of dissolution."

"I quite understand, my lord," said Pevensey, and Haro could feel a true warmth in those words. "It has been a pleasure to meet you, despite the unpleasant circumstances, and should your lordship ever need my services again, send your card to the office at Bow Street."

Haro hoped fervently that such an occasion would never arise, but he thanked the man anyway.

"It occurs to me that there may be a few shillings in the Harding estate to help recompense you, Mr. Pevensey." He took a few steps over to his desk, crumpled up the outdated letter to Sir Robert, and taking a new sheet of paper, scribbled a few quick lines. "My father was the executor of Great-Uncle Harold's will, and I believe I inherit that duty." He folded the paper, melted a bit of wax on it, and stamped it with his seal. "I hardly expect there will be much—after all, Uncle Harold lived in an attic off the generosity of others for the last twenty years—but perhaps there are a few pounds left to the family that we could bestow on you."

He wrote a direction on the letter and handed it to Pevensey. "Since you're London-bound, would you deliver this letter to Mr. Godwin, our solicitor?"

"Certainly," said Mr. Pevensey, taking the letter.

Haro offered him his hand as well, and he shook it with feeling.

Pevensey then offered his hand to Eda—a bold gesture, thought Haro—but she gave him her own hand gladly, and he brought it halfway to his lips before letting it go again. "Your servant, Miss Swanycke."

He looked at Haro with a twinkle in his eyes. "I take it you'll not be looking for another heiress to replace Miss Hastings?"

"I think I've learned my lesson on that score," said Haro. He cast a sidelong glance at Eda, and her mouth curved up into a soft smile. There was a conversation waiting to be had there, one that he hoped would be ending with a kiss. If only Sir Robert would come quickly so he could finish the unpleasant side of this business.

As he departed, Jacob Pevensey crossed paths with Sir Robert in the paved carriage drive, and by the time Sir Robert approached the front door, he was already fully apprised of the new state of affairs. Torin, who had ridden back in the carriage with him, helped him up the steps, and the excitement of the moment seemed to ameliorate the usual pain from his gout.

"'Pon rep!" he said, pumping Haro's hand and congratulating him on the fine shooting. "I always did say those French are up to no good! That confession from your uncle was very suspect I thought, very suspect indeed. It doesn't surprise me at all to think that Frenchman planted it in his room. It had some curious turns of phrase in it, I think, that could only have been written by a foreigner."

Haro hemmed at that but did not contradict the notion outright. He had no wish to bring his mother into the conversation, or the fact that her maternal instincts apparently outweighed her concern for veracity.

William Hastings, who had been closeted in his room all morning, emerged to inform his host that he would be departing for the Rose and Thistle and unlikely to return to Woldwick in this lifetime.

"That Pevensey's a good man," said Sir Robert, congratulating Hastings on the latest discovery.

"Eh?" asked Hastings, painfully oblivious to the news.

"You haven't heard?" Sir Robert bellowed with delight. As was human nature, he loved to be the bearer of new tidings. "It was that French fellow all along! He made an appointment to meet your daughter at the bridge, and...well, you know what happened after that."

The color in William Hastings' face slowly drained into the purple veins bulging on his neck. "Bayeux? Bayeux! I should have known." The entrance hall began to explode with epithets. "Fiend seize it! Where is he?"

His eyes darted to the drawing room door, but Haro intervened, unwilling for a third death to take place at Woldwick in one sennight. "I'm sorry, but it's impossible for you to see him now. Sir Robert has not yet interviewed him."

"Now see here!" Hastings thundered, trying to push past the earl.

"Please, Mr. Hastings," said Haro, catching his arm. "Please! Let the law take its course." Hastings tried to pull away, but Haro refused to let go of him. They struggled silently.

Then, suddenly, all the strength seemed to disappear from the mill owner, like water which has run out through the hole at the bottom of a bucket. Haro felt the man about to collapse and put his other hand out to steady him. "It's over, sir. Take heart—it's over." He helped the man to a seat on the bench. And though he could not swear to it, he thought he saw the mill owner's eyes glistening with a thimble's worth of unshed tears.

Sir Robert questioned the accused with the footmen still present as guards. The loss of blood had weakened Bayeux enough to accept the inevitable, and he made a full confession. Henry and George later regaled the downstairs servants with all the lurid details, and Eda overheard many whispered conversations among the housemaids with phrases such as "secret trysts" and "lovers in every sense of the word." No wonder William Hastings had been so eager to keep his daughter's past relationship a secret!

Dr. Stigand arrived soon after the interrogation, bringing with him the village constable who would take the prisoner into custody. He unbandaged the wound, cleaned it, and extracted the bullet, complimenting Eda on the good work she had done to stop the flow of blood. "Although I think you deserve more compliments," said Eda to Haro, "for drawing the blood in the first place!"

She could tell that he appreciated the praise, and the look he gave her was both tender and ardent. She felt heat rise to the top of her cheekbones. Yesterday, the murder of Arabella Hastings had been the only thing to stand between them. Today there was nothing, absolutely nothing, and all she needed to do was to wait for him to declare himself.

William Hastings departed for the Rose and Thistle as he had earlier announced, although without the feelings of high dudgeon that had reverberated from him earlier that week. Eda noted that he made his farewells with a tone approaching politeness, and that even though relations with him could not be called cordial, she would no longer consider him an implacable enemy of the Emison family—which was just as well, since rumor had it that the importance of manufacturers was on the rise in England. He was still determined to stay in the village until the inquest, but there was little doubt that Philippe Bayeux would be arraigned for murder, given the evidence that Pevensey had compiled against him.

Lady Anglesford was so overjoyed by the news that she discarded her dressing gown in favor of a black day dress and gave Cook instructions to make a celebratory dinner. The resulting feast was something at which not even William Hastings would have turned up his nose—had he not already vacated the house for the easier procurement of Mrs. Lublock's pasties.

Lady Anglesford's eyes glistened with tears as she looked around the table at her two sons and her ward. "Three weeks ago," she said, "the worst that I imagined could befall us was to give up our town house, to give up Woldwick, and let a place in Russell Square." She took Torin and Haro's hands and squeezed them gently. "My dears, how foolish I was. What does all this matter"—she nodded at the jellied eels, the crab soufflé, the servants, the tall ceilings of the dining room—"compared to the more important matters, that you are all safe and well and free to live a long life with love and happiness?"

She sighed, perhaps remembering that there was one member of the family whose life had been cut short two months ago. "Let us go to the music room as we used to. And Eda, you must play the pianoforte, some of the songs that Edward loved."

Eda swallowed. She had been hoping to slip away to the library after dinner—and hoping that Haro would slip away as well and join her there. "But of course, Aunt Edith," she replied, forcing a smile onto her lips. She sent a sideways glance at Haro and saw his eyebrows narrow into a good-natured frown at his mother's plan for entertainment.

She chose Mozart. It was what the late Lord Anglesford had liked best. But the lilting melodies and delicate scales were a strange contrast with the black crepe that Lady Anglesford wore and her own dark dress. Torin yawned repeatedly, but Lady Anglesford paid him no heed. Eda could barely keep her mind on the music, stumbling far more often than her virtuosity warranted but not enough to dim Lady Anglesford's enthusiastic applause.

She glanced at Haro, who usually enjoyed her music, but saw that even his attention was wavering. The flickering light of a score of candles only brought out the shadows on his face all the more. She saw that he was bone-weary after the events of the last week but too well bred to retire.

She trilled the chords of the last cadenza and then dropped her hands into her lap with a smile. "That is all for tonight, I think." Rising gracefully from the piano stool, she walked over to Lady Anglesford to plant a kiss on her cheek. "I am for bed, Aunt Edith. Good night."

"Good night, my dear," said Lady Anglesford, pressing her hand. "Enjoy your rest."

Eda slipped out of the music room and down the passage to seek the disappointing normalcy of her own chambers. She had never liked waiting for her birthday sweets as a child—until one had seen the colored icing with one's own eyes, there was always the fear that someone had forgotten and there would be no cake after all. She breathed in deeply. Why should she doubt? Had he given her any reason to question his affections?

She thought back to the day when he had reneged on his promise to drive with her in Hyde Park. And she, foolish she, had retreated behind her wounded pride and let him do so. She had fancied herself in love with him at the beginning of the season and fancied herself out of love with him again when he deserted her for Arabella. It had taken the cat-clawed taunts of that cold-hearted minx to make her realize that the flames of love were not dead, but still glowing, as red and hot as embers in the hearth. And instead of surrendering Haro, she had made up her mind to fight for him, in spite of his betrothal to another, in spite of the suspicions of murder, in spite of the whispering doubts her traitorous mind entertained.

A footstep sounded in the passageway behind her, and she spun around. It was the earl following her.

"Oh, it's you." Her heart skipped first one, then two, then three beats of its regular rhythm.

"Yes." Haro's face was serious.

Eda waited expectantly, feeling small as she tilted up her chin to look into Haro's eyes.

"Miss Swanycke," he said formally. "Might I have the pleasure of an interview with you tomorrow morning at ten o'clock in my study?"

"An...interview?" Eda could barely refrain from laughing. Was this not Haro whom she had known from childhood?

"If you would be so kind," said Haro, his slight smile also acknowledging the ridiculousness of the situation.

"Of course, my lord," said Eda, matching formality with formality and dropping a curtsy. "I would be delighted."

"Thank you," said Haro, taking her hand and putting it to his lips. "Until tomorrow then."

"'Til tomorrow," replied Eda, following him with her eyes as he retreated down the passageway.

34

HARO BARELY SLEPT THAT night, on the heels of a whole week of insomnia. But whereas the previous nights had been spent in apprehension, this night was spent in anticipation...mostly. He had treated Eda abominably, that he knew, but he also sensed that she was ready to forgive him and that she still—dare he think it?—loved him. He tossed fitfully amidst a storm of bedclothes, heaving a bolster pillow overboard and longing for the daylight.

He recalled the night she had invaded his chambers, clad only in her white nightgown. That was an unmistakable sign of romantic interest, was it not? Although, perhaps it was simply a calculated move to get him into Arabella's black books.

He sighed. But surely, the unfailing constancy and support she had displayed throughout the murder investigation was proof enough of her feelings? Or perhaps it merely meant that although he had killed any hopes of love, she still held him in brotherly affection.

He left off pretending to sleep at dawn and, knowing that Garth was an early riser, summoned him to dress him.

"And will you be wanting your usual waistcoat, m'lord?"

Haro hesitated. "Which would you advise?"

"If I might be so bold, m'lord, this one is Miss Swanycke's favorite." He reached into the wardrobe and held up a waistcoat made of dark blue brocade. Haro's eyes widened at Garth's prescience. Did the whole household know that he was having an interview with Eda this morning, an interview upon which hung the whole of his future hopes?

"And I believe it is dark enough, m'lord, to not be wholly unsuitable for mourning wear."

"Ah, yes. Mourning," said Haro thoughtfully, extending his arms for Garth to slip the waistcoat onto him. That was another fly in the ointment. Was it even proper for a man mourning his father—and his great-uncle and his fiancée—to propose marriage? If Eda did agree to marry him, the wedding would certainly have to be delayed until his mother was out of blacks.

"Well, Garth, how do I look?" Haro asked after a cravat, a coat, and top boots had completed the ensemble.

A smile split the wiry old man's face all the way up to his graying sideburns. "I am certain that no young lady could fail to find you distinguished, virile, and handsome."

"No higher compliment," said Haro with a grin, and he headed downstairs to break his fast before the most important interview of his life.

"You're looking dapper," said Torin with a mouth full of sausage. He had been heard to voice upon occasion that the absence of the fairer sex allowed, or even necessitated, the absence of table manners.

"Thank you," said Haro, toying with the eggs on his plate.

"Whatever for?" Torin eyed the elaborate knot of Haro's cravat with suspicion. Apparently, the news of the earl's morning plans had not traveled as far as his younger brother.

Haro sent a quelling stare, but Torin refused to be quelled.

"It's a reasonable question. I don't recollect hearing that guests are descending on us today. In fact, out of the guests from our last house party, one is dead, one is in the gaol, and one has removed himself to the comforts of the village inn. So, the question remains—whatever for?"

"I have an important meeting this morning."

"With Sir Robert? I would not have suspected an Oriental, or a Gordian Knot, or whatever it is you call that, to impress him."

"No, not with Sir Robert." Haro pushed his half-eaten breakfast away and rose from the table.

"Well then, I see you're determined to be cryptic. Go on then. I shan't encourage your vanity with more questions." Torin opened the heavy tome that lay on the table beside his plate, and stuffing another forkful of sausage into his mouth, devoted himself to his reading.

Haro strode into his study and looked at his pocket watch. Still nearly two hours until ten o'clock. He picked up the account ledger that lay on the desk. It was his responsibility now, but he had not steeled himself to look through it since his father's demise. Mr. Godwin's news had been too final, too devastating to think that any economies or shrewder management would alter affairs. But still...he had time on his hands, and it would keep his mind from worrying if he could see who had wages owing and how the estate was being run.

A half hour passed, and then another as Haro fished his pocket watch out of his waistcoat at regular intervals. She was a punctual person, although in this case, she might intentionally keep him waiting.

There was only a quarter of an hour left....

A knock sounded on the door. Haro straightened at the desk, prepared to rise. But an unexpected figure filled the doorframe—it was Henry, the first footman. "Beg your pardon, my lord, but there is a special courier here to see you."

"A courier?"

"Yes, my lord. Come straight up from London this morning."

"Very good," said Haro, puzzled at what this could portend. "Send him in."

And within seconds, the courier had entered, still in his mud-spattered coat and boots, to hand Haro a letter, the direction of which looked to have been written in considerable haste.

Eda paused on the staircase. She had been waiting all morning for ten o'clock to come. It was near enough now, although she would doubtless appear over-eager, and she was on her way to visit Haro's study for the desired interview. But instead of a closed door, she saw a muddy and rough-shaven man exiting the study. Who could it be?

She wrinkled her nose and waited a bit, watching the footman show the fellow out the front door.

"Who is that, Henry?"

"Special courier, miss, for his lordship."

"Ah," she said, and waited a little longer. Whatever the man had been carrying would be something of an urgent nature. Haro would want to open it immediately.

It occurred to her that it was very well-mannered of her to wait, especially when the butterflies in her stomach were all straining their wings to propel her in through that door...into, what she hoped, were Haro's waiting arms.

The clock in the entrance hall chimed ten. She rapped her knuckles on the study door and went inside.

Haro was sitting silently in the horsehair-stuffed leather chair behind the desk. His furrowed brow looked over the sheet of paper in his right hand.

"Good morning!" she said brightly, for it was a good morning—she was willing it to be so, no matter what news that letter contained.

"Eda." His face put on a smile, but the element of delight was missing from his tone. He rose to his feet. "I had intended to speak to you on one subject, but it appears that a more urgent matter must occupy our conversation. Please,"—he gestured to the sofa near the fireplace—"take a seat."

He abandoned his chair at the desk to sit closer to her, bringing the piece of paper with him, and once they were both comfortably installed, he cleared his throat ominously. "I have here a letter from Mr. Godwin, our solicitor. It appears that Mr. Pevensey lost no time in calling on him yesterday evening after he had returned to the metropolis and acquainted him, most thoroughly, with the events of the past week."

Eda squirmed. Why must letters from solicitors always contain unfortunate news?

"Mr. Godwin writes that I am indeed the executor of Harold Harding's will, in the place of my late father. It is imperative, he says, that I journey to London immediately to receive a full copy of the will. In most cases, he would not forward on information about a will's contents prior to the executor's reading of the will, but in this case, knowing our family's 'delicate financial situation,' as he terms it, he will be so bold as to name the primary bequests and beneficiaries of the will in this letter."

Haro paused and looked over at Eda.

"You seem somber," she said. "There must be something unpleasant in the bequests."

"No, not at all," said Haro. His face relaxed momentarily but then tensed again as he continued. "Mr. Godwin first reveals the amount of money bound up in Harold Harding's estate...."

Haro named a sum.

Eda gave a shriek.

It was four times the fortune that the late Edward Emison had gambled away.

"Oh, Haro! He always told us that he had stored up treasures on his travels. Did you ever think—"

"Not in the least! I assumed he had collected a few trinkets here and there—mementos from St. Petersburg, artifacts from Egypt. But a fortune of this magnitude? How could we have ever guessed? He wore the same frock coat for twenty years, and I daresay he spent more money on food for his birds than he spent on himself!"

"Does Mr. Godwin say who...?"

Haro nodded and read aloud. "As you are the chief executor of the will, I feel it only right to inform you that the entirety of this fortune is bequeathed to Harold Harding's great-niece, Edith Swanycke."

Eda gasped. "To me?"

"Well, we have not seen the official copy of the will yet, but I find it unlikely that Mr. Godwin would be telling us taradiddles."

Eda did not know whether to laugh or cry. "So, this means, I'm...I'm..."

"...an heiress. Yes. And one of the richest heiresses in England."

At that, she truly did burst into tears. In all her time as Lady Emison's ward, she had been treated as a daughter; she had never suffered want and never been made to feel as if she were a poor relation. But the knowledge of her true circumstances had always lingered in the back of her mind, and with the loss of the Emisons' own fortune, that reality had become increasingly unsettling.

And now, what was this that Haro was telling her? That she was wealthy? And, even more importantly, that she was independent and secure?

She wiped the tears from her cheeks with the palm of her hand. "I don't know what to say—Uncle Harold was a rascal to gammon us all these years. I must tell your mother!" And with that, she leaped to her feet to leave the room.

As her hand touched the doorknob, Eda froze. She looked back. "Haro, what was the other subject...the matter about which you wished to speak to me initially?"

Haro, who had also risen when Eda left her seat, tossed the letter from Mr. Godwin onto the desk. "Oh, that...I think it is better saved for another time, or perhaps not mentioned at all."

Eda's heart fell into her stomach. All the excitement from her newfound inheritance melted like a piece of ice. Her fingers retreated from the handle of the door, and she walked back to face the earl. "Harold Emison, I insist on knowing what you intended to say to me before this letter made its appearance. Out with it, my lord, for I will not be denied."

Haro took a deep breath. His emotions over the last fifteen minutes had run the gamut from eager expectation to shocked amazement to stoic acceptance. How could he possibly, in his straitened circumstances, make Eda Swanycke an offer of marriage just moments after she had been discovered to be one of the richest heiresses in England? He had played the fortune hunter once, and it was not to his credit. How could he ever prove, either to Eda or to the watching world, that his motives in this case were honorable?

"You owe me an answer," said Eda, those full red lips of hers tantalizing him to no end. He could still see the traces of tears on her face, and how badly he wanted to take his thumb and wipe them away from her cheeks.

"I am sorry," said Haro slowly. "But I cannot in good conscience broach the subject that I had previously intended to."

Her eyes glinted with irritation, and Haro had a suspicion that she was suppressing the urge to slap him. "Is this because of the money? It is, isn't it?"

"Yes, of course it is. It changes everyth—"

"I don't see how!"

"Because you haven't had time to look at it properly. How can I, as your guardian now that Father's gone, propose such an unequal alliance, the advantage of which would be all on my own side? It would be wrong of me."

"So, you were going to make me an offer?"

Everything else he had said seemed to be lost on her.

"Of course, I was. You knew I was going to make you an offer. But the point is, that I'm not going to do so anymore."

"But that is ridiculous!" She stamped one of her little feet on the floor, taking a step closer to him so they were less than an arm's length apart.

"I agree. But there it is." If he took her face in his hands, he could point those full lips into the air and meet them with his own.

"Haro?"

He paused. "Yes?"

"Why is it that whenever you're just about to kiss me, we always get into some frightful row?"

It was all the invitation he needed. He reached one long arm around her waist and brought her near. His lips descended on hers, gently at first, then hungrily, pulling her even closer as she responded in kind. How had he never kissed her before? And what madness had inspired him to think any other woman's kisses could compare to this?

He broke away, finally, to take a breath, and discovered that his idealistic scruples had shrunk as surely as the distance between them. "As your guardian, I would insist that you merely set me an allowance."

Eda's dark blue eyes twinkled. "You shall have your pin money quarterly."

"But you must retain full control of the principal."

"You shall not touch a penny of it except on my death."

"And I must be assured that you are obeying your heart in this matter."

"Yes, of course—although I will say that my chief impulsion would be the title you possess. We are well-matched, my fortune hunter, for I have always aspired to be a countess."

Haro laughed. "Then, in that case, Edith Swanycke, will you marry me?"

"I will," she said and stood up on her tiptoes to claim another kiss.

Finis

Author's Note

One day, while reading William of Malmesbury's account of the Norman Conquest, I paused at the part where Duke William promises his daughter to Harold Godwinson in exchange for the kingship of England. A strange thought occurred to me—what if this story was transported across the centuries as the inspiration for a Regency romance? The Middle Ages and the British Regency have always been my two main periods of historical interest. Could I combine the iron-willed characters of the Conquest narrative with the fairy-tale world of a Georgette Heyer novel?

In the historical tales of the Norman Conquest, the death of the childless monarch Edward the Confessor produces a crisis of succession. Harold Godwinson and Duke William of Normandy both claim the crown, and Harold, with the support of the English lords takes the throne.

William objects to this, asserting that a few years prior, on a trip to Normandy, Harold had promised the crown to him! The medieval chronicles vary on whether such a trip and such a promise actually did occur. William of Malmesbury acknowledges both but also says: "Harold, once crowned, did not spare a thought for the agreement between himself and William, declaring himself released from his oath because William's daughter, to whom he had been betrothed, had died...."

As Duke William prepares an invasion fleet to take the crown by force, Harold makes his own preparations to defend England. He is obliged to put aside his concubine Edith Swan-Neck in order to make a more expedient political alliance. He is also obliged to defend England from another claimant, Harald Hardrada. A giant of a man from Norway, Hardrada invades shortly before William does, dying at the Battle of Stamford Bridge and receiving "six feet of English ground, or perhaps more seeing that he is taller than most men."

The Norman fleet lands at Pevensey, and Duke William's army advances to the field at Hastings. When Harold's tired English troops arrive, they make a valiant stand but lose the day. Harold perishes in the battle, pierced through the eye by an arrow (a detail considered apocryphal by many historians). His body is later identified by Edith Swan-Neck and given Christian burial.

For many students of history, the results of this battle are dismaying. William the Conqueror is frequently seen as an oppressive monarch who rode roughshod over the persons and property of the defeated English. But despite any personal distaste for William, it is impossible to deny his organizational genius (his census in the Domesday Book was an astonishing feat for that day) and the impact his invasion would have on the history of England.

This novel of romantic suspense does not purport to be an accurate retelling of the Norman Conquest—the fact that William Hastings does not gain the estate of the Earl of Anglesford is proof enough of that. It is simply a light-hearted recasting of the characters from the Conquest period in the world of the British Regency.

If you have enjoyed Jacob Pevensey's investigation and are inspired to read more of the *Pevensey Mysteries*, keep reading for a preview chapter of *The Duke's Last Hunt*.

Cheers,

—ROSANNE E. LORTZ

THE DUKE'S LAST HUNT

(PEVENSEY MYSTERIES #2)

ELIZA STARED INTENTLY OUT the window, ignoring the argument taking place across from her in the carriage.

"But my dear," said Lady Malcolm. "How can you possibly desire our daughter to ally herself with an irreligious man? How could she ever trust his prudence, his honesty, or his morals?"

"Upon my word, Margaret!" said Sir Arthur with a glare of annoyance. "It's not as if the man is a confirmed libertine. So what if he does miss a Sunday service or two? And I'm not asking her to accept his offer right away. I'm simply asking her—and you—to keep an open mind on the matter."

Lady Malcolm sniffed. Eliza recognized it as the sniff of longsuffering, somewhere in between the sniff of bearing one another's burdens and the sniff of embracing one's calling to living martyrdom.

"Come now, Eliza," said Sir Arthur. "What have you to say on the matter?" He drummed his fingers on his knee.

Eliza opened her mouth and then shut it again. She had landed in the middle of her parents' quarrels before and knew better than to do so again—although, in this case, she could hardly help but be in the middle of it. It was her future they were considering, her marriage to Rufus Rowland, the Duke of Brockenhurst.

"Well?" It had been a long carriage ride. It was a warm August day, but the dust from the road did not permit them to open the carriage windows. Sir Arthur's patience was wearing as thin as the auburn hair receding from his high forehead.

"I feel..." Eliza hesitated. "I feel that I hardly know the man, Papa." She glanced over to her mother and gained some courage. "I've stood up with him at a few balls over the course of the season, and I spent one half hour of awkward conversation with him at Almack's. But it was a complete surprise to me when you said he'd called and asked permission to pay me his addresses."

"And a complete surprise to me that you would say yes so readily!" interjected Lady Malcolm, fixing her husband with a steely glare. Her own hair was far darker than Eliza's reddish-brown curls, but they shared the same deep green eyes.

"And why shouldn't I say yes?" Sir Arthur blustered. He had never been one to hesitate when a bird was in the hand, or in the bush, or in the tree, or over the hill. "He's a duke, Margaret! And it's not as if it's Eliza's first s—"

He caught himself abruptly, and an uncomfortable silence settled over the closed compartment. No, thought Eliza bitterly, it was not her first season. It was the end of her third—and still no matrimonial prospects on the horizon other than this sudden and perplexing interest shown by the Duke of Brockenhurst.

"In any case," said Sir Arthur, "he's called upon us in Grosvenor Square—"

"Twice," said Lady Malcolm, acidly.

"—and you'll have time to better your acquaintance during our stay at Harrowhaven, time to be certain before you make your decision."

Eliza felt a new wave of warm air turn her cheeks pink. "Are you so sure, Papa, that he will even...ask?" How mortifying it would be to go to all this trouble to visit his country estate and then discover that the duke's intentions were not serious. She pulled out her fan and tried to drive away the heat.

"Of course, he will! The man's smitten!" Sir Arthur's voice was much too loud for the smallness of the carriage. "And who wouldn't be?" He gave his daughter an encouraging smile.

Plenty of men, Eliza thought, unable to manage a smile in return. Every man who had danced with her during her first and second seasons—danced with her once and never approached again after a taste of her shy conversation. She moved her fan faster and began to breathe more quickly.

Lady Malcolm emitted another principled sniff.

Eliza laid down the fan. She would stay calm. She must stay calm. She touched the glass of the windowpane, once more feigning preoccupation with the scenery. They had entered a colonnade of tall oak trees lining the roadway, their full branches creating a screen that filtered the rays of the summer sun.

"Almost there now," said Sir Arthur.

Eliza was not sure whether to be glad or begin to cry.

The carriage drive leading up to the house was interminable. The avenue of oaks, planted a hundred or more years ago by one of the Rowland ancestors, stretched out in a straight line far into the distance, paralleling the road on either side. The house, at first just a pinprick of stone amidst a sea of green, grew steadily larger until Eliza could make out the square towers and tall windows. Behind the house, the measured planting of oak trees gave way to the more natural growth of forest, wild and unrestrained.

"Prime place for hunting," Sir Arthur noted approvingly.

"I believe the duke mentioned he is fond of hunting," said Eliza, swallowing hard. The house was larger than she had expected. Would she know anyone else at the house party? Probably not. It was not as if the duke and she traveled in the same circles.

"More than fond of it!" said Sir Arthur. "He's devoted to it!"

It was an unfortunate choice of words. Lady Malcolm uttered a tight-lipped comment about idolatry, and Eliza felt her ribs constrict even further.

On the edge of the forest, they saw a small country church, its whitewashed stone a pleasant contrast with the green. "At least there will be somewhere for us to worship our Lord tomorrow," said Lady Malcolm grimly.

"Of course, there will be!" retorted Sir Arthur. "They're not all heathens in Sussex, Margaret!"

The post chaise rounded one half of the circular drive to pull up at the door of the house. The wheels came to a stop. In the rear, Sir Arthur's valet hopped down from the seat on the back of the carriage, covered with a yellow cloud of dust from the journey. In the front, the coachman handed down Frances Ollerton, Lady Malcolm's lady's maid, who had been mounted precariously in the box beside him. It would have been pleasanter for all concerned to have taken two coaches down to Harrowhaven, but then, reflected Eliza, they could not have gone to the expense of renting a second one. This journey was costing her father enough money as it was.

The carriage door opened, but instead of the driver waiting to hand her down, Eliza discovered two perfectly matched men in immaculate livery ready to perform the task.

"Thank you," Eliza said, giving the nearest footman a faint smile. She was rewarded by a look of surprise.

"You're welcome, miss," the footman said tentatively and then faded away into the background behind the wheel of the post chaise.

They walked up the steps and in through the marble columns flanking the front door. Eliza's lower lip dropped a little as they came into an entrance hall that seemed half the size of their entire London townhouse.

A welcoming committee had formed; however, a cursory glance showed that the greeters were composed entirely of domestics. Eliza, who had been dreading a conversation with the Duke of Brockenhurst, found herself disappointed that he was not at hand to welcome them. And neither was his mother, the dowager duchess.

The butler came forward with a bow and introduced himself as, "Hayward, at your service." He beckoned for two more footmen to assist with unloading the carriage. Then he introduced the housekeeper, Mrs. Forsythe, and assured them that she would attend to their every need.

Mrs. Forsythe briskly escorted the Malcolms out of the entrance hall, through the saloon, and over to the great oak stairway that led up to the next floor of the house. All the while, she kept them apprised of the history of the rooms they were passing through and asked questions about their own needs and comfort. "I see your valet and one lady's maid have arrived. Will Miss Malcolm's lady's maid be coming in another carriage?"

Eliza flushed pink. Her mother saved her from the embarrassment of responding.

"My maid attends to Miss Malcolm's hair and gowns as well as my own."

"I see," said Mrs. Forsythe, in a tone that was both polite and unreadable.

Eliza supposed it would be unheard of for the dowager duchess to share a lady's maid with her daughter, Lady Adele. She sighed. Here was one small incentive to entertaining the duke's suit—as mistress of this house she would be able to have her own lady's maid at last.

"When will the family be expecting us to join them?" Lady Malcolm asked.

Mrs. Forsythe hesitated, the first pause that Eliza had noticed in the housekeeper's effortless industry. "I will let her grace, the duchess, know that you are here. Tea will be served in the drawing room in one hour."

"Thank you," said Lady Malcolm.

Eliza echoed the thanks, but her thoughts were more filled with apprehension than gratitude. What did the housekeeper's hesitation mean? Was the dowager duchess even planning to receive them?

She wished she had been introduced to the duchess prior to this visit. How strange to be staying in someone's house that one had never even met! But it was not the duchess' house anymore, she reminded herself—it was the Duke of Brockenhurst's. And with him she was acquainted—or as acquainted as a few dances and morning calls could make them.

The curving stairs paused on a magnificent landing, the walls decorated by a plethora of portraits in gilt frames. The portrait of the current Duke of Brockenhurst was situated most prominently. Eliza lingered in front of it. She had always found portraits to be a fascinating study. Those done by the best painters—such as the ones the Rowland family could afford—revealed a glimpse of something far deeper than the flat physiognomy of the subject.

Rufus' eyes—could she call him Rufus in her mind? It was so strange to think of being that intimate with him!—were the first thing she noticed about the picture: bright, glittering, alive. She had never seen them that animated in person—certainly not on the dance floor or over the glass of punch they had shared at Almack's. No, there was one time she had witnessed that excitement—when he had waxed eloquent about the merits of the hunt and the delights of the forest adjoining Harrowhaven.

She smiled wryly to see that the artist had toned down the brightness of the duke's red hair. In the picture, it was more of an auburn color, the same shade as her own, not the shocking, brilliant red it was in real life. Perhaps the duke was not fond of his coloring—or perhaps his mother was not, since it was probably she who had commissioned the portrait.

Mrs. Forsythe had paused in her ascent of the stairs, noticing Eliza's interest in the portrait. Eliza's eyes flicked over the wall hurriedly. She did not want to keep the others waiting, but her curiosity had gotten the better of her.

There was another painting, placed higher and more out of the way than the duke's, which looked like it had been done by the same artist at much the same time. The subject was darker, with brown hair and a more even complexion. He had the same broad shoulders as the duke, but his brows were more heavy-set, his smile more serious. There was a steadiness about this one, especially in the eyes.

The housekeeper walked back over to where Eliza was standing and, following her eye, gazed up at the same picture. Eliza sensed a hint of approval in her eye and gained the courage to ask a question. "Please, Mrs. Forsythe, who is this one?"

"That would be his grace's brother, Lord Henry Rowland."

Henry Rowland tiptoed into the cavernous library with care. It was as he suspected—the only person wasting a hot summer's day in the library at White's was his friend Stephen Blount. Light-footed as a cat, he glided over to the wingback chair where his friend sat, and without warning, threw down a silver case on the ebony table nearby. "What do you think of this?"

Stephen Blount jumped in his chair as if he had sat on a pin. "Might give a fellow warning! I thought you'd gone to the races."

"No, I went to the stationer's." Henry sent a meaningful glance at the case he had dropped. He needed to show this to someone—it might as well be Stephen.

Setting down his newspaper, Stephen dutifully extracted a small white card from the silver case. He adjusted his spectacles to read aloud.

HENRY ROWLAND, DUKE OF BROCKENHURST
HARROWHAVEN, SUSSEX

Stephen started again. The card slipped from his fingers, clipping the edge of the ebony table before fluttering to the floor. "I say, Henry! What's this supposed to mean?" He rubbed a knuckle against a left sideburn that was so thin as to be scarcely there. "Duke? You? I didn't know your brother was so eager to abdicate the position...."

Henry smiled devilishly, flexing his broad shoulders with enjoyment. "I'm riding out to the old house to visit Mother tomorrow. I thought I'd leave one on the tray for him to remind him that I'm still alive. He's having a house party, I hear. Strange—he didn't think to invite me!"

Stephen took off his spectacles and shifted uncomfortably.

"Oh, you know about that, do you?" Henry's dark eyebrows fell into a frown.

"Well, I...I...yes, dash it all, Henry! He invited me to come down for the week."

"And you said yes, I take it?"

Stephen's tentative smile was confirmation enough.

"Not on account of Rufus' merit, I hope?" Henry already knew the answer to that question. "Don't tell me you're still dangling after that headstrong sister of mine!"

Stephen rose from his chair, a wounded look on his face. "I'm sorry if that offends you, but yes, I am still dangling after her, as you call it. And she has given me some reason to hope that my suit will not be in vain. I understand that you may see our situations as somewhat unequal—"

"Good Lord, man," said Henry, clapping him on the shoulder. Why was it always the gentry who were so old-fashioned about these things? "I've no worries on that score. I was thinking more of your own domestic happiness." He cleared his throat. "Adele's a willful woman, Stephen...."

Willful? He was putting the matter far more politely than it deserved.

Stephen colored. "I'm not such a milksop as all that!"

Henry raised both eyebrows. It took all his willpower to refrain from argument. "Well, good then! You'll be there when I leave my card at the door. I shan't stay long enough for him to throw me out. You can tell me how Rufus takes it."

"If I know your family's butler, he'll throw the thing in the rubbish heap and not even give it to him."

"Hmm." It seemed that Stephen did know their butler. Henry wouldn't put it past Hayward to hide the card knowing the tempest it would create. "Who else is going to be at this house party?"

"Walter Turold, of course."

Henry growled in annoyance. There was no point in hiding how he felt about Walter in front of Stephen. There was a time that Henry and Walter had been as close as a stand of silver birch trees, but that time was long since gone.

"And...Rufus didn't say who else, although I gathered that there were to be ladies in the party, for he told Adel—I mean, Lady Adele that he was bringing some pleasant company for her."

"Perhaps he meant that you were the pleasant company."

Stephen blushed. "I hardly think—"

"No, quite right. I hardly think so either." Henry gave another devilish smile as he snatched up the loose card from the floor and the silver case from the table. "Well, whoever these ladies are, I shall be eager to discover it. My brother's not usually one for inviting respectable females to his house parties."

"Perhaps he's turned over a new leaf."

Henry's mouth fell open, and all his willpower disappeared like water through a broken dam. "Stephen, you're a babe in the woods. An utter milksop! It's good I'm coming after all, I think. And perhaps I'd better stay at the house instead of simply stopping by to see Mother. Between Rufus and Adele, you wouldn't stand a chance!"

Henry strode into the Blue Boar and called for Ned Hornsby to give him a pint of his finest. He had left early to reach the village by noontime and was thirsty enough to drink a whole hogshead himself.

"Back in the country, eh, Lord Henry?" said Ned with a grin that was nearly lost in the big brown beard which hid his neck and came down over his shirt collar. He pulled down a tankard from the shelf and shined the outside with his apron.

"For the time being," said Henry, returning the grin. Ned was much of an age with him and, before he had taken over proprietorship of the Blue Boar, had always been ready to come along for a hunt, a wager, or a bout of boxing.

"You staying at the big house?" Ned gathered up a tray of dirty dishes from the counter. "Or will you be needing a room here?"

Henry might have stiffened if any of the other villagers had asked that question, but Ned was too old a friend to bristle at—and besides, the whole village knew the Rowland brothers were on bad terms. "That's yet to be determined. Do you have a room for me if I should need it?"

Ned gave a laugh that shook his great brown beard. "That depends. You's not the only one waiting on the duke's pleasure." He jerked his head toward the table by the window.

Henry's eyes followed Ned's until he saw a dark-haired gentleman sitting alone—a slender man with a light-colored coat in the pink of fashion, eating his luncheon and squinting at the counter. "Hello, Hal!" he said abruptly once his presence had been discovered.

"Robert!" said Henry in a tone of surprise that was not precisely good-natured. How many times had he told his half-brother to leave off calling him Hal? "What the devil are you doing here?"

"Here to visit Mother, of course." The dark-haired man lifted his monocle and adjusted it to get a better look at Henry.

"And to apply to Rufus for some money while you're at it?"

"Well, yes, there is that too." The man let the monocle drop. "There's this fellow in London with a locomotive machine...."

Henry turned away. He did not care to hear about another of Robert's foolish speculations. As the son of the duchess' first marriage to an untitled landowner, Robert Curtis had always ranked below his brothers in consequence and—now that Rufus has come into his own—in fortune. Ten years Henry's senior, Robert never ceased importuning Rufus for money, both to support his highbrow style of living and to finance a perpetual string of unwise investments.

"Perhaps we can ride up to the house together," Robert said brightly. He stood up, his willowy frame contrasting sharply with his brother's sturdy physique. Then he put on his beaver and headed for the door of the tavern.

"Aren't you forgetting something?" said Henry, looking pointedly at his half-brother's empty plate.

"Oh." Robert's fingers fished around in his waistcoat pocket but came up empty. "Ned, might I trouble you to—?"

"Put it on your account? Of course, Mr. Curtis." Ned's brown beard split into a half smile. One did not have to know him well to see that it was forced.

"Thank you," said Robert. He gave Henry a shrug and stepped out onto the porch. The door swung shut behind him.

Henry's dark eyebrows beetled into a frown. He picked up the empty dish from the table and carried it over to the counter. The innkeeper reached for it with a look of confusion on his face, probably able to count on one hand the times an aristocrat had cleared a table in the inn.

"Ned," said Henry firmly. "You've been tavern-keeping long enough to know that what I'm about to say is true. Always insist the customer pays before leaving. You'll never get on in life if you keep letting fellows like that shoot the crow." He pulled a guinea out of his own pocket and slapped it on the counter. "Hopefully this will settle whatever he has owing."

Ned took the coin and put it in the moneybox under the counter. "Funny thing, your lordship, but seems like someone might offer you the same advice. How are you supposed to get on in life? I shouldn't think you'd be having guineas to spare for paying others' reckonings, what with—"

"Never mind that," said Henry curtly. "I don't want it talked of."

"What you want said and what the village wants to bandy words about ain't exactly the same thing now, is it, Lord Henry?" Ned waggled his eyebrows as he spoke, and Henry could hardly keep from laughing in spite of himself.

"'Tain't right, Master Henry. 'Tain't right." Ned slid an arm over the counter to wipe off the crumbs. "And there ain't a single one of my regular customers but would rather that you were still in charge up at the big house."

Henry snorted. "An unlikely eventuality. No, I'm simply here to visit Mother and then back to London. I'll stop back in tonight for a room if I find I'm less than welcome. And now for that pint, if you please. You'll find that I'm good for it." He placed another coin on the rough wooden counter.

Eliza took some water from the wash basin and splashed it over her face. It had been warm in the carriage, and this room at Harrowhaven, with the sun beating down on the tall windows, was not much cooler. She could not unlace her traveling dress herself, so she waited patiently, fanning herself when the air grew too close, until Ollerton would be done with her mother and come attend her.

The minutes ticked by. Eliza walked over to one of the three windows that overlooked the circular drive. Riding up the paved driveway was a thin man in a light-colored coat. Her breath caught a moment. Was it the duke? No, she chided herself, he was much too slender. Rufus Rowland's shoulders would nearly double this fellow's. The man rode up to the stables near the right side of the house and disappeared inside.

She looked over to the door to her chamber. Ollerton still had not come. She wondered if she should try to dress her hair herself. It was not the first time Ollerton had forgotten her, and she did not want to be late for tea.

She was about to move away from the window when she spotted another rider coming up the drive. This one rode straight up to the door, dismounting by the front steps and casting the reins of his horse to a footman with an imperious fling. Eliza began to breathe a little faster. The shoulders were right, the air was right—this must be him, the master of the house. She could not see his hair or his face—from this vantage point, his beaver concealed them both—but she knew it was Rufus.

She looked at the door again. Her hand ran over her gray traveling dress; she could feel the dust, but the color concealed it. There was a small looking glass on the bureau. Her auburn curls were pinned more loosely than she liked, but they were not in complete disarray.

A daring thought came to her. What if she were to go downstairs—by herself—and greet the duke as he came into the house? A tremor of trepidation almost extinguished the idea as soon as it had formed, but the spark refused to die.

She would be brave. She would go downstairs. And perhaps the look in the duke's eyes, when he saw her so unexpectedly, would tell her whether he truly had an interest in her...or whether this whole trip was a waste of time and expense.

Eliza opened the bedroom door and peered down the hallway. The appearance of a footman carrying candlesticks or an encounter with a maid bearing linens would have halted her in her tracks. But no one was in the corridor, not a soul. She tiptoed down the floral rug until she came to the stairs. Her hand glided over the polished banister as she descended. She glanced up at the portrait wall over the landing to shore up her courage.

As the staircase led into the saloon, she heard voices. She leaned breathlessly against a column close to a bright floral arrangement and listened to the conversation in the entrance hall.

"Good afternoon, Hayward. If I might trouble you to place my card on the silver salver for my brother."

"Your...card, Lord Henry?" The butler sounded perplexed.

"If you would be so kind."

There was a pause. Eliza's heart fell. It was not the duke after all, but his brother. She could not see him from where she stood in the adjoining room, but she could imagine that dark, serious face from the portrait gallery conversing with the immaculate butler.

"Lord Henry, I regret that I cannot—"

"Oh, do be a good fellow, Hayward."

"No, Master Henry."

There was another pause. Eliza thought it very strange that a servant would speak so to a son of a house. But then, it was no stranger than a man wanting to leave his calling card for his own brother.

"Very well then. I'll hand it to him myself. Is my mother at home?"

"In the drawing room, sir, waiting for tea to be served."

Before Eliza had time to wonder where exactly the drawing room was located, the duke's brother strode into the saloon. She froze like a deer trapped behind a thicket, staring at him intently with her green eyes.

"And who might you be?" he demanded, looking Eliza up and down as if she were some sort of trespasser.

Eliza's face flushed as pink as a summer sunset. "Miss Elizabeth Malcolm," she said. "I'm afraid I've not had the pleasure of making your acquaintance either, Mr....?"

He ignored her and continued on with his own line of questioning. "And what are you doing here?"

Eliza lifted her chin and folded her hands in front of her to stop them from shaking. "My parents and I are guests of the duke."

"The duke!" His dark eyes narrowed. "Whatever for?"

His rudeness was unlike anything she had ever experienced. Part of her wanted to slap him. Part of her wanted to run away and cry. She was certain that the latter outcome would occur if she were not rescued soon.

"I could not say, sir. As the duke's guest, though, I suppose I have as much right to be here as you—"

"More right, I should think," said another voice coming in from the opposite door of the saloon.

Eliza and the dark-haired man turned sharply to see Rufus Rowland, the Duke of Brockenhurst saunter into the room. He was in his shirtsleeves and vest, having divested himself of his jacket on this warm August day. His wavy red hair was wet from exertion, and his buckskins were caked with dust.

"Enchanted to see you again, Miss Malcolm." Rufus walked across the room, took Eliza's hand in his, and lightly kissed it.

He turned to his brother. "And you, dear Henry—not quite so enchanted."

"Likewise, my dear Rufus." Lord Henry glanced from Eliza to Rufus and then back again.

Eliza was struck by the contrast in manners between the two gentlemen. Her hand still tingled from the brush of Rufus' lips. Her spirit still smarted from the incivility of Lord Henry's words.

"You're not staying?" said Rufus. It was more of an assertion than a question.

"Would you rather I didn't?"

Eliza felt the younger Rowland's eyes dart toward her again.

"Whatever you like, brother," Rufus said dismissively. He turned his attention back to Eliza. "As you can see, I've been shooting. I'm mortified to say that I had exceedingly poor luck. Only two braces of pheasants. But now that you're here, perhaps my luck will improve."

He pressed another kiss on her hand. Eliza's eyes grew big. He had never been this familiar when calling on them in Grosvenor Square. Perhaps he really did mean to court her.

"I must change into something more presentable," said the duke, mopping his hair away from his face with a large hand.

Eliza looked down at her own dusty traveling dress, wondering, with a tinge of panic, how soon tea was.

"But I imagine my mother is eager to see you, so let's not keep her waiting." The duke's eyes glittered. "You can make yourself useful, Henry, and take Miss Malcolm to the drawing room."

Lord Henry gave no answer, watching as his brother disappeared toward the staircase.

Eliza took a deep breath and stared at the floor.

"Well then, shall we?"

She looked up. Lord Henry was offering her his arm. She took it and they walked back through the entrance hall toward the double doors that led into the drawing room, Lord Henry maintaining an aloof silence and Eliza summoning

Printed in Poland
by Amazon Fulfillment
Poland Sp. z o.o., Wrocław

42732126R00168

Also by Rosanne E. Lortz

Pevensey Mysteries

To Wed an Heiress

The Duke's Last Hunt

A Duel for Christmas

Allen Abbey Romances

The Gentleman in the Ash Tree

The Lady in the Moneylender's Parlour

The Vicar and the Village Scandal (coming 2023)

Historical Fiction

I Serve: A Novel of the Black Prince

up the whole of her courage to face a room full of people she did not know on the arm of a man she did not much like.

The Duke's Last Hunt (Pevensey Mysteries #2) is available in print and ebook formats on Amazon.